Summer in Good Hope

Also by Cynthia Rutledge / Cindy Kirk

Summer *in* Good Hope

CINDY KIRK

Published by Montlake Romance, Seattle

www.apub.com

Amazon, the Amazon logo, and Montlake Romance are trademarks of Amazon.com, Inc., or its affiliates.

ISBN-13: 9781503934641
ISBN-10: 1503934640

Cover design by Jason Blackburn

Printed in the United States of America

To Wendy.
You've grown into an amazing woman. I'm so proud to
have you as my daughter and friend!

Chapter One

Primrose Bloom Delaney stood at the edge of the dance floor, a smile frozen on her lips. Her sisters, heck, even her widowed father, were all out there laughing and having the time of their lives. Ami, her oldest sister, was somewhere in the center of the revelry with her new husband, Beck.

Only she stood alone.

As if the mere thought of her beautiful sister and handsome brother-in-law conjured them up, the two came into view as lines formed for the Electric Slide.

Ami moved into position, her green eyes sparkling with a joy that was evident from clear across the ballroom. Her golden brown hair was pulled back in loose curls, leaving a few face-framing tendrils. The relaxed, romantic hairstyle had been the perfect choice for her sister.

Dreamy. Down-to-earth. Nurturing. Those words were often used to describe her sister. After their mother died six years ago, Ami had become the keeper of the traditions in the Bloom family.

Her sister had taken on so much responsibility at such a young age. As Ami's thirtieth birthday had neared, Prim had wondered if the husband and children her sister had always wanted would be denied her. Then Beckett Cross had walked into her life, and their lives had both been changed when they'd fallen in love.

Now, Ami and Beck would begin building a life together. Until this moment Prim hadn't realized how much it meant to know she'd be here to share her sister's happiness. Not just on holidays and an occasional long weekend, but day in and day out.

As the newlyweds grapevined to the right under the large white tent, Beck tossed his jacket to his brother. His dark eyes never left his wife. His chocolate-brown hair appeared rumpled, as if her sister had recently run her fingers through it. Sometime during the evening he'd ditched his tie.

Prim's heart gave a lurch. While the sight of Ami steeped in such happiness filled her with gladness, it made her own loss more pronounced. A lump was attempting to form in the back of her throat when her sister Fin appeared out of nowhere, grabbed Prim's hand, and pulled her onto the dance floor.

"I haven't done the Slide in years," Prim protested.

"It's like riding a bike." Fin leaned close. "Or having sex."

Prim laughed. Fin's penchant for saying just what she thought was part of her charm. She was Ami's doppelgänger, except *down-to-earth* and *dreamy* would never be used to describe Delphinium Bloom. *Vibrant.* Yes. *Charismatic.* Definitely. *Irreverent.* Most of the time.

The subtle blond strands in Fin's hair caught the light as she moved to the seductive beat. Years in Los Angeles had given Fin a big-city polish, while Ami was small town to the core.

"You haven't left the dance floor since the band started playing," Prim remarked as she and her sister rocked forward in perfect synchronicity.

From the time she'd been old enough to bat those long eyelashes, Fin had attracted more than her share of masculine attention. Tonight, Prim thought she looked especially beautiful in a form-fitting satin dress of deep gold. The elegant yet surprisingly sexy style suited her sister.

"This is the most important party of our sister's life, Prim." Fin flashed a beguiling smile at Clay Chapin, the new high school principal, who stood at the edge of the mahogany dance floor. "Which means no sidelines for me. Or for you."

The vibrant smile appeared to have worked its familiar magic. The song had barely ended when Clay claimed Fin's next dance.

As Prim stepped off the hardwood, she caught sight of Marigold dancing with Anders Cross, the younger brother who bore a striking resemblance to his older sibling.

It appeared all the Bloom sisters were making fun a priority. The bride stood next to her husband less than ten yards away visiting with his parents, who'd made the trip from Georgia for the wedding. The classy woman with her hair in a chignon was now Ami's mother-in-law.

Mother-in-law. Prim cringed, thinking of her own. Even before her wedding, Prim had known Deb was going to be trouble. The woman hadn't disappointed.

The lights from the paper lanterns suspended overhead added a romantic glow, and when Beck's arm slipped around Ami's waist, she relaxed against him. He smiled and brushed his lips against her hair. The sweet gestures spoke volumes about the trust and love that existed between the newlyweds.

Certainly her eldest sister had never looked as joyful as she did beside the man who was now her husband. It hadn't taken long for the attorney-turned-café-owner to capture Ami's heart when he'd moved to Good Hope last summer.

When Ami's eyes met hers, Prim's smile came easily, though she was puzzled by her sister's subtle thumbs-up.

"Hey, Prim."

She swiveled at the sound of the familiar baritone and found herself face-to-face with Max Brody. Like Beck, he'd deep-sixed the jacket and tie. Prim couldn't help but notice how broad his shoulders were beneath his white dress shirt. She forced her eyes back up to his. Just when had the tall, geeky kid who'd been her math buddy turned into a blond Adonis?

When Max stepped even closer, Prim realized the flowers in the room might as well close up shop. No way could they compete with his delectable scent. The combination of soap and shampoo and an indefinable *something* brought a tightening to her lower abdomen.

"They're a good match, him and Ami."

"She found a kindred spirit in Beck." Prim hesitated, then continued, knowing if anyone would understand the emotions filling her heart to near bursting, it would be Max. Max had always understood her. "He completes her as a person . . . and she completes him. I know that sounds corny—"

"Not corny at all."

Prim met those brilliant blue eyes. Emboldened by the understanding she saw there, she continued, "You know how practical and down-to-earth Ami is . . ."

Max nodded, totally focused on her.

Something in that intense gaze had her insides jittering. She willed herself to settle down.

Focusing on a bouquet of hydrangeas, roses, and peonies for a moment gave Prim the time she needed to organize her scrambled thoughts.

What had she been about to say? Oh, yes, now she remembered. "When we were getting dressed for the wedding, Ami confided she was grateful Mom had read us fairy tales as kids and promised one day we would each find our prince. She said she'd begun to lose hope. Then she met Beck."

Remembering how emotion had thickened her sister's voice, Prim felt tears sting the backs of her eyes. "She said Beck was her prince, her soul mate, and he'd definitely been worth the wait."

What would it be like, Prim wondered, *to love someone with such intensity?* She'd loved her husband, but over time it had become clear that she wasn't his soul mate . . . and he wasn't hers.

"Though calling Beckett Cross a *prince* sticks in my craw," Max shook his head, a smile teasing the corners of his mouth, "I agree he and Ami are a perfect match. I'm sure they'll be very happy."

Though Max had kept his tone light, sincerity shone in his beautiful blue eyes.

Prim's heart kicked into doing the samba—or was it the rumba?—against her ribs at his nearness. She moistened her lips, resisting the almost overwhelming urge to lean into him as she'd seen her sister do with Beck only moments earlier.

"Champagne?"

Prim reared back, feeling like a kid caught dipping into a cookie jar.

The college-age server wore tailored black pants, a crisp white shirt, and a polite expression. He held out a silver tray filled with a dozen crystal flutes.

"I'd love some."

Before she could reach for a glass, Max confiscated two from the tray and handed one to her. As his knuckles brushed her fingers, she felt a jolt.

Static electricity, Prim told herself. Still, as he watched her watching him, she felt oddly out of breath.

A corner of his mouth curled upward. With their gazes locked and loaded, they toasted Ami and Beck. As the champagne bubbles tickled her throat, Prim began to finally relax.

"How are you holding up?" Max's penetrating gaze bored into hers.

Her smile faded. She shifted her attention to the band, idly recognizing the sax player as a high school classmate. She took another sip of champagne and wondered why she was hesitating. There was no need to lie to Max or pretend all was well. He knew her too well, or at least he once had.

Prim kept her tone conversational. "I had one bad moment. Just before I walked down the aisle, I couldn't stop thinking that if he hadn't died, Rory would have been a groomsman. He'd have been standing there at the front of the church, waiting for me."

Max placed a hand on her arm. When she shifted her attention back to him, his expression was soft with sympathy.

"I knew when I married Rory that because of his cystic fibrosis our life together would be cut short." Prim tightened her grip on the glass of champagne until it felt as if the crystal stem would break in two.

Though Rory had appeared strong and healthy on their wedding day, they both had known he likely wouldn't see his fortieth birthday. But she *had* expected him to take care of himself and to not take risks with his health.

Even now, nearly two years after his death, she railed against the injustice he'd done to her and the boys. Time with them should have mattered more than risking his life for transient adrenaline highs.

"I remember your wedding."

Prim blinked in surprise. "You do?"

He nodded.

She cocked her head, curious what exactly he recalled.

"I remember how beautiful you looked."

For a second she swore he blushed. But she must have been mistaken, because that cocky grin was on his lips as he continued.

"And the reception. Man, that night was a college boy's dream. A pig roast and all the beer you could drink. It was the talk of Good Hope for months."

It may have been the talk of Good Hope, but it hadn't been the wedding—and certainly not the reception—of her dreams.

"Rory loved barbecues and big splashes. I was hoping for something small and intimate. But Rory's mother encouraged me to let him choose." Prim smoothed the satin of her pale gold bridesmaid's dress with her palm. His mother had used his illness as an excuse to spoil him. "I swear, if Rory had been a girl, Deb Delaney would have been the quintessential stage mama."

"She was always in the stands for his games."

"I think she even went to the practices."

"Yep." Max finished off his champagne and grinned. "We used to razz him about having his mommy in the stands."

It was easy to forget that even though she and Max had shared so many scholarly interests in high school—chess club, math club, debate—Max had been an athlete, too. He'd played ball with her husband.

"How did Rory take it? The razzing, I mean." It felt strange to be asking such a basic question. Wasn't this something, as Rory's high school girlfriend, she should have known?

"He'd flip us off." Max grinned. "Rory could hold his own."

"You got that right." Following his example, Prim downed the last of her champagne.

Plucking the empty glass from her hand, he placed it along with his on a nearby tray. "Okay, enough reminiscing. There's a dance floor with our name on it. What do you say, Primrose? Are you ready to show your sisters you can boogie with the best?"

Prim hesitated. She looked for her sons, found them safe and sound on the edge of the dance floor with her father. What would be the harm in one dance? This was a party, after all.

Max's warm hand took hers. "It'll make your family happy to know you're enjoying yourself, rather than standing on the sidelines." His tone turned persuasive. "Ami, especially, will want to see you having fun."

Putting on a show for her family was something Prim had gotten used to doing over the past years. This was Ami's big day, and if there was ever a time to fake it until she made it, this was it. Besides, this was Max, and dancing with an old friend might be just what she needed to hold back the memories for a few minutes.

"Okay, you win. I'd love to dance." Her voice came out casual and offhand, just as she'd intended. "Thank you for asking."

Max's hand cupped her elbow, but instead of leading her onto the dance floor, she found herself standing with him in front of the raised dais that held the band. The loud beat of the Black Eyed Peas' "I Gotta Feeling" had the crowd rockin'.

Jerry, the sax player, smooth skinned and baby faced when they'd graduated high school, now sported a full beard. Though only in his late twenties, a few strands of gray ran through his dark hair, and fine lines now spread outward from the edges of his eyes.

When Max motioned to him, Jerry put down his instrument and came to crouch down at the edge of the dais.

"I'm bringing a rookie on the dance floor and we're going to need a slow song." Max spoke loudly in order to be heard above the vocals.

"You got it." Jerry winked at Prim, then turned to the band leader.

Heat flooded Prim's face. What had Max been thinking? Granted, she might not be a party animal, but she *could* dance.

"This is for calling me a rookie." She elbowed Max in the ribs and had the satisfaction of hearing a loud *oomph*.

"Same old Prim." Max chuckled and took her hand, pulling her deep into the crowd of gyrating bodies. Once they'd found a spot with a little extra space, Prim began moving in time to the beat, smiling smugly when his eyes widened in admiration.

Moments after the up-tempo song ended, strains of a romantic ballad filled the air. In seconds, he'd enfolded her in his arms. His shoulder was hard beneath her hand, his arms steady as they danced.

Although they were barely moving, her pulse picked up speed. Pressed this close, his delectable scent enveloped her.

"Prepare to be wowed."

The words had barely processed when Max spun her around, then dipped her low.

Prim laughed aloud, the sheer joy in the sound taking her by surprise. How long had it been since she'd felt so carefree? *Years*, she thought. "Think the Brewers will make it to the playoffs?"

"Not likely, but anything is possible." Max smiled down at her. "Just like I didn't think you could dance, but you were doing a good job keeping up with me a few minutes ago."

"I was rockin' the dance floor, Brody, and you know it."

"You are my dancing queen," he sang softly and swept her low once again.

For the next several minutes she lost herself in the music, so comfortable in his arms she barely noticed the song had ended and another was starting up. "Still doing the brackets for the College World Series?"

"Ah." Max lifted a brow. There was a spark of mischief in his blue eyes. "Do I sense a friendly wager in the works?"

"Maybe." Prim gazed up at him through lowered lashes. "You know I'll win."

"In your dreams, Red. I—"

He stopped speaking to stare. Prim followed the direction of his gaze and watched Gladys Bertholf sweep across the dance floor in Floyd Lawson's arms. The steps were so graceful and elegant it was like watching a 1940s musical come to life.

It was Prim's last thought before the tall woman and the portly man crashed into them.

Max turned at the last second in an attempt to shield her from the impact, but the force pushed him into Prim. She had a few seconds to enjoy the sensations of soft curves against hard flesh before Gladys shrieked.

"Primrose." The cadaver-thin older woman flung her arms around Prim, nearly clipping Max in the jaw.

With an agility honed during high school football drills, Max dodged the elbow with a quick move to the left.

"Sorry, Max." Looking over her shoulder, Gladys shot him a dazzling smile before returning her attention to Prim. Though they stood in the center of the dance floor, Gladys held her at arm's length and studied her. "You look incredibly lovely, my dear. I have to admit I felt like shooting off a few fireworks when your father told me you're moving home."

Max inclined his head. "Moving home?"

"I'm excited to be back in Good Hope." Prim noticed everyone was careful dancing around them as their impromptu reunion created a bit of a traffic jam. Impulsively Prim gave Gladys a quick hug. "I'll call you. We have to get together. Catch up."

"Gladys." Floyd Lawson, dance partner extraordinaire, stepped toward the older woman. "I believe we're creating a scene."

"I was seized with an urgent need to offer a personal greeting to my girl." Gladys leaned over and brushed her lips across both of Prim's cheeks. "Welcome back, sweet one."

"I'll be in touch," Prim called out as the couple twirled off.

Then Max's hand was on her arm and he was maneuvering them through the dancers.

"Where are we going?" she asked when they stepped off the hardwood.

"To get some fresh air." His gaze lingered on her face. Or was it her mouth?

Her lips tingled. What did it say that even now, all these years later, she remembered Max's taste, remembered how it had felt to have his mouth pressed against hers?

"Prim?"

"I—I could use some fresh air, too."

"You had the oddest look on your face. What were you thinking about?"

Kissing you.

Something almost primal flared in his eyes.

For a second, Prim feared she'd spoken her thoughts aloud. She took a deep breath to calm herself, but that only intensified her reaction to him. Gawd, she loved the way he smelled.

"Where are you two headed in such a hurry?" Approval underscored Ami's words.

Prim had been so focused on Max that she hadn't noticed her sister and Beck approaching.

Prim waved a casual hand. "We thought we'd get some fresh air."

Ami shot her the same disbelieving look she'd given last night when Prim had told her she didn't plan to date until her six-year-old twins were grown. Prim prayed her sister wouldn't read something into a simple stroll.

Beck's gaze remained on his best man. "Just remember Prim is my sister-in-law now."

Was that a warning she heard in that charming southern accent? Prim hid a grin, finding the thought of Beck embracing his new role as big brother rather sweet.

"If I compromise her, will it be dueling pistols at ten paces?" Max's lips twitched. "Or would you prefer swords?"

Prim rolled her eyes.

"Cut it out," she told the men, then turned to Ami for support. "Men can be so juvenile."

"Just remember," Ami told her. "If you decide to run off and get married, I want to be a bridesmaid."

Prim pointed at her sister. "You're as bad as your husband."

Ami's only response was to link her arm with Beck's and flash a bright smile.

"I'm sorry about that." Prim waited until she and Max were outside of the large white tent—and alone again—to speak.

"About what?"

"Ami is madly in love and wants that for everyone. Her sisters are her first targets."

"Can you blame her?"

"No. I understand she wants us to have what she's found with Beck." The music faded with each step away from the tent. "That's fine. She can matchmake to her heart's content with Fin and Marigold."

A slight frown furrowed Max's brow. "Not with you?"

"It would be a futile effort." Prim shrugged. "I've made it clear I'm not dating until the boys are out of high school."

"Might as well have waved a red flag in front of a bull."

"You're wrong." Prim lifted her chin. "Ami might not fully agree with my decision, but she respects it."

"Uh-huh."

Sometime while she'd been talking, he'd stepped closer. Her breath quickened. "What's that *uh-huh* supposed to mean?"

Instead of answering, he rocked back on his heels and studied her. "You're moving back to Good Hope."

"I am." She twisted her hands together, then stopped when she saw him watching. "My job was eliminated. I couldn't afford the house payments."

"I'm sorry, Prim." The brief touch of his fingers on her arm was soft as butterfly wings and oddly comforting. "I know you liked Milwaukee."

"It's a wonderful town. I had good friends there. It was difficult to leave them." Prim's voice wavered for a moment before she brought it under control. She stared into the darkness, realizing just how much Rory's death had affected her life and the lives of her boys.

"I think I'm ready for round two on the dance floor," she said, changing the subject.

She'd been enjoying the quiet, but Max was right. This was a party, and they should be dancing. She turned toward the tent, but he stopped her with a hand to her arm.

"We can dance here. It's crowded inside. And way too dangerous."

She laughed and shot him a quizzical look. "Dangerous?"

"Dangerous with Gladys Bertholf on the floor." He smiled, showing a mouthful of perfect white teeth. "It's safe here."

Prim let him tug her close, telling herself Ami would want her to have fun. She closed her eyes as they swayed in time to the distant music.

"Prim."

"Yes, Max?"

"It's good to have you home."

Home. Yes, Good Hope had always been home. It was that fact that had made leaving Milwaukee, and her friends, easier to bear.

"Did you buy a house?" he asked after another few beats.

"I rented a fabulous Cape Cod." Prim smiled against his shirtfront. "It has a large fenced backyard and is in a quiet neighborhood. It's perfect for me and the boys."

"Where is this gem located?"

"Coral Road."

He laughed. "You're kidding. I live on Coral."

Prim jerked back in his arms. "Seriously?"

His thumb and little finger came together in a gesture she recognized. "Scout's honor."

The thought of Max living so close made her traitorous heart flip-flop. She was a widowed mother of twin boys. She did not need the distraction of an old flame just a few doors down. "I thought you lived on Market."

"Old news, Primrose." Max grinned. "I moved last year."

Prim had known when she'd decided to return to Good Hope that her past would be waiting for her. So what if she and Max were neighbors? It was inevitable they would cross paths, living in the same town. She had to get herself together. It was not a good sign that less than a week into her fresh start she was going to let an attractive old friend throw her off track. She was an adult. She could handle this.

"Well, I guess there are worse people I could have for neighbors," she said, even as a jolt of anxiety coursed through her. "Ax murderers, for instance."

He gave her a spin before responding. "True. I'm nowhere near as dangerous as an ax murderer."

"I'm not so sure about that," she muttered.

Her pulse began to drum when he grinned broadly.

While certainly not as threatening as an ax murderer, there was no denying that living close to Max was a dangerous proposition.

Then why, Prim wondered, couldn't she keep from smiling?

Chapter Two

Max pulled khakis and a plaid button-down shirt from his closet. After a momentary hesitation, he grabbed a tie. There would be hell to pay if he met Eliza Shaw wearing his normal summer attire of cargo shorts and a T-shirt.

He added an extra shot of espresso to his travel coffee mug before heading out the door. His former high school classmate had insisted on meeting with him right away. Since he didn't have anything on his calendar other than returning phone calls and e-mails, he'd let her set the time and place.

Though he had time to respond to a few more e-mails, he left shortly after receiving the call. Not out of a desire to be on time—although Eliza *was* a stickler for promptness—but because he didn't like to rush.

He drove downtown with the windows down. Though he spotted a couple of open spaces on Main Street, he parked a couple of blocks away, leaving the prime spots for tourists. Good Hope merchants, which made up the majority of his clients, depended on money brought in by year-round visitors.

Max stood beside his car for a moment, breathing in the fresh morning air. One of the benefits of living in a place like Good Hope was being able to saunter instead of scurry from appointment to appointment. He'd done too much of that when he'd worked for a large CPA firm in Madison.

In this small community on the shores of Green Bay, there was plenty of time to stop and smell the roses. Or rather, be engulfed by the overpowering scent of jasmine wafting up from the large pot outside of the Enchanted Florist.

"Women love flowers. I suggest you take a moment and pick up a bouquet for your sweetheart."

The familiar male voice had Max turning, a smile already on his lips.

Dressed in a uniform of crisp, tan pants and a dark brown shirt, Sheriff Leonard Swarts rocked back on the heels of his shiny boots. Despite the large gap between his front teeth, Len was a handsome man who'd earned the nickname Silver Fox years ago because of his thick thatch of gray hair.

"Morning, sheriff." Max barely refrained from shoving his hands into his pockets. The sheriff had been a frightening figure when Max had been a boy. Even now, closing in on sixty-five, the man had an imposing presence.

For over two decades Leonard had patrolled the roads of Good Hope. At six feet four inches, with his broad shoulders and large hands, the man reminded Max of a sturdy oak.

"The sign says there's a special on roses."

Max glanced at the chalkboard set on an easel next to the front door, more out of form than interest. "Thing is, I don't have a sweetheart."

"Then what's this I hear about you and Eliza meeting up at the Bake Shop this morning?"

Though Max hadn't mentioned the meeting to anyone, he wasn't surprised Leonard had heard. The man had his finger on the pulse of the community. It was the speculative gleam in the sheriff's eyes that had Max spreading his hands. "Strictly business, lawman."

Even as Leonard chuckled, his gaze sharpened. "Heard Primrose Bloom Delaney is back."

This time Max's smile came easily. "With her two boys. They've rented the house next to mine."

"Seem to recall you two were tight in high school."

Max hesitated. "Prim and I were debate partners."

"Is that what it was?" Leonard grinned. "Well, you be sure and give your new neighbor my regards."

The sheriff's radio squawked. When he stepped away to answer, Max resumed his stroll.

Eliza had mentioned she wanted to discuss the Cherries' finances. He tamped down his annoyance. It was just like her to snap her fingers and not give him time to prepare.

It had been the same when she'd contacted him to do the annual audit of the Cherries' books two years ago. The previous accountant had made a last-minute move to Florida, leaving her scrambling for a replacement. Max hadn't let himself be pushed, though she'd certainly tried. In the end, Eliza had been pleased with the thoroughness of his report.

Not that she'd implemented any of his suggestions. The treasurer still used the old ledger method to keep track of accounts, the board still only met semiannually, and they'd yet to bring anyone on to pursue grants.

Those first two audits had been straightforward with no blips. This year, it hadn't taken long for him to become concerned, then alarmed.

Max assumed the meeting this morning was to discuss the steps the Cherries planned to take to remain solvent. He couldn't understand why Eliza had set such an important business meeting at Blooms Bake Shop, a business owned by a woman she barely tolerated.

Once again, he reminded himself that she was the client.

As it was a beautiful day, Max waited outside the bakery, enjoying the sunshine and the cool breeze from the bay. Although it was barely nine a.m., the quaint street already bustled with tourists. They scurried in and out of shops, reminding him of the pet mice he'd had as a kid.

From the number of people entering Beckett Cross's Muddy Boots café, Max wasn't surprised his friend's income had soared this year. He had no doubt these same tourists would be renting kayaks and sailboats later this morning before attending a fish boil or a performance at the Northern Sky Theater in the evening.

But this crush was nothing compared to how it would be in several weeks. Visitors and locals would swarm the streets at the end of June to enjoy all the festivities the Cherries had planned. The weeklong series of events would culminate with the big bash, the Independence Day parade, followed by fireworks over the bay.

All the merchants would benefit, including the woman clipping down the sidewalk in bright red heels and a white sleeveless dress with bold swaths of color across the front. Members of the Shaw family had been forces to be reckoned with in the Good Hope business community since Victorian times.

Max noticed several men checking her out as she passed by. Eliza didn't spare them a second glance. Though Max was usually drawn to dark-haired women, Eliza's beauty left him cold.

As she drew close, he lifted a hand in greeting. She gave an almost imperceptible nod of acknowledgment. The slight frown on her classically sculpted face disappeared when she stopped to speak with the Cherries board president, Lynn Chapin.

Oh, great, Max thought, *she's bringing backup.*

"Good morning." He smiled warmly when Eliza concluded her conversation and drew close. "Will Lynn be joining us later?"

"No," the brunette snapped. As if realizing she'd crossed the line into rudeness, she offered a smile and added in a cordial tone, "I asked Lynn to join us, but she had another meeting scheduled."

"That's too bad." Max liked Lynn, but dealing with Eliza was enough of a challenge. Opening the door to the bakery, he stepped aside to let her enter. "You're ready to discuss my recommendations."

Eliza's short nod sent her bob swinging like a dark curtain before falling back into place. "That and several other matters of importance. I'll be updating Lynn later today on the results of our conversation."

"What other matters do—?"

"Not yet." Her razor-sharp voice sliced the air.

Max clenched his jaw so tightly it ached.

"Sorry. I'm not fit for cordial conversation until I've got at least two shots of espresso in me." Eliza flashed a smile that didn't reach her eyes and moved directly to the counter. "A mocha and a cherry Danish."

Hadley Newhouse, Ami's second-in-command, manned the counter. Her long, honey-blond hair was pulled back in a low tail. Though he knew she often worked late at the Flying Crane, Hadley looked bright and cheery in a hot-pink T-shirt that proclaimed "Baking Up Some Love," the new slogan for Blooms Bake Shop.

"Coming right up. Have a seat and I'll bring it out to you," Hadley said with a pleasant smile.

"Fine. Just make sure the mocha is extra hot." With an imperious wave of her hand, Eliza turned on her stilettos and walked over to one of the brightly painted tables.

"Hey, Max, a mocha and cherry Danish for you, too?" Hadley said with a wink when he reached the counter.

"Yes to the Danish, but make it black coffee for me." Relaxing under the warmth of her smile, Max gestured with his head to Eliza. "You handled that like a pro."

"Well, she's just lucky the customer is always right. Besides, it's not like I haven't had years of practice dealing with difficult people." Hadley's shoulders lifted in a shrug. "Frankly, I'm surprised she has the nerve to show her face in here. I bet she only got her courage because Ami's away on her honeymoon."

The warm smile Hadley had bestowed on him disappeared as her gaze settled on Eliza.

Max turned to see the executive director of the Cherries tapping a perfectly manicured nail on the table in an impatient gesture. Something told him this was going to be a long morning.

He pulled out his wallet as Hadley placed their order on the tray. She gestured to a blue table off to the side. "That table would give you more privacy."

"The queen has already chosen." Max chuckled. "Don't worry. I'll keep her safely away from the rest of the customers."

"Thank you." Hadley mouthed the words, her blue eyes twinkling.

Picking up the tray, Max walked to where Eliza sat. He placed the cups and plates on the pink tabletop and set the tray aside before taking a seat opposite her.

After casting the pastry a calculating look, Eliza picked up the Danish. "It looks passable."

Personally, Max thought the pastry looked mouthwateringly good. One bite confirmed his assessment.

Eliza set down the Danish. "We'll start with your audit recommendations, then move on to several other matters. It's imperative we stay focused. I'm on a very tight schedule today."

In other words, no small talk. Fine with him.

"As I emphasized when we spoke previously, this matter requires immediate attention."

Max opened his briefcase. He slipped out the report he'd shared last week with her and the executive board.

Eliza shifted her gaze to the clock on the wall that proclaimed "It's Cupcake Time." From the distant look in her eyes, Max knew she wasn't admiring the various cupcakes that designated the hours.

Without warning, she refocused those steely gray eyes on him. "How did I miss it?"

Okay, so they'd revisit what went wrong. *Then* they'd discuss the changes that needed to be made.

"It's easy for boards of old, established groups to become complacent. When things run smoothly for so long, they grow lax in their oversight. Floyd, as board treasurer, should have caught what was going on. However, Gladys, as treasurer of the Cherries, bears the bulk of the responsibility. And—"

Eliza held up a hand, stopping him. "Although Gladys feels badly about what occurred, the responsibility is mine. I'm the executive director. I should have been scrutinizing the P&L statements. I should have asked myself how bills were getting paid when we'd scaled down our fundraising. I should have seen we were depleting our savings."

Max didn't argue. "You might have noticed if you were meeting quarterly."

"Semiannual meetings have been the practice for decades." Eliza lifted the cup of mocha but made no move to drink. "Per your recommendation, we'll now be meeting quarterly."

"You need to computerize the books."

"Gladys has always refused to embrace new technology." Eliza's inscrutable gaze gave no indication of her thoughts on the matter. She set down her cup. "That's not an issue now, as she handed in her resignation this morning."

"She what?" Max dropped his mug to the table with a clatter.

"She resigned. This is her seventy-fifth year as a Cherrie, and she figured it was a good time to bow out." Eliza frowned, then her expression cleared. "The official stance is she's leaving the organization in order to pursue other interests. It plays well as she's deeply involved in rehearsals for *George M.*"

Max knew all about the woman's involvement in the patriotic play put on by the local community theater. This year they'd chosen *George M*, the Broadway musical that had produced such favorites as "It's a Grand Old Flag" and "Yankee Doodle Dandy."

"What about the Independence Day parade?" He and Gladys were co-chairs for the event this year. Max couldn't say he was sorry to see her go. She'd been too busy with all her other social projects to be of any help. "Do you have a replacement in mind?"

"The person who replaces Gladys will take on the parade co-chair role. Which means you'll mentor them." Eliza's cool gray eyes met his. "It can't be helped. The other Cherries already have their assigned tasks."

Great. He would get the new person. Still, could whomever they chose be worse than Gladys? Max took a bite of Danish, considered.

"The parade is less than a month away." Max washed the pastry down with a gulp of coffee. "How soon will you have her replacement on board?"

"Our next meeting is Monday. My plan is to take nominations, vote, and confirm that same day."

"Make it someone with a strong accounting background."

"Who is chosen is up to the membership." Eliza's voice rose, garnering a curious look from a couple of tourists settling in at the other table. Visibly restraining herself, she continued in a softer, but no less determined tone. "It isn't your concern."

Max folded his hands on the table, met her determined look with one of his own. The knowledge that he had a duty to the organization kept him pressing forward.

"It *is* my concern. You hired me for my expertise. I'm telling you—" He paused to rein in his rising temper. When he spoke again it was in a pleasant, conciliatory tone. "I'm *recommending* you bring in someone with a strong accounting background."

Eliza absently broke off a piece of Danish, not appearing to notice the cherry filling dripping on her fingertips. "Off the top of my head, I don't know anyone with that particular skill set who would be suitable for membership in the Cherries."

"Having that background makes them eminently suitable," he said, hammering the point home while keeping the same pleasant tone.

Eliza dropped the pastry back onto the plate, carefully wiping her fingers with a napkin. "I'll take your recommendation under consideration."

Max was done playing nice. If he'd insisted on these changes three years ago, the organization might not be teetering on the brink of disaster now.

"Make an exception." He leaned forward, his gaze locked on hers. "Or the Cherries might not be around to plan another holiday event."

Chapter Three

Prim's stellar Monday morning came to a crashing halt when she approached the living room holding a basket of laundry still warm from the dryer and stepped into chaos.

Callum, the older—by two minutes—of her six-year-old twins stood in the middle of the room, fists clenched at his sides, a mutinous expression on his face. "I don't like it here. I want to move back home."

His brother, Connor, didn't bother to look up. He was too busy rolling on the floor with Boris, their Russian wolfhound.

Of the two boys, Callum was the one who had the most difficulty adjusting to change. Unfortunately, he'd experienced many changes in his young life.

Guilt washed over Prim. She should have fought harder each time Rory insisted on moving. Only after she'd convinced her husband to purchase a house had she been able to give her son a little of the stability he craved.

Six months later, Rory had died and their lives had been plunged into turmoil. That had been two years ago.

Though none of the recent changes had been preventable, Prim understood Callum's pain. Change didn't come easily to her, either. Connor seemed to be the only one undisturbed by all the upheaval.

Prim placed the basket on the table and pulled out a shirt. She expertly folded the Spider-Man T-shirt while keeping her gaze focused on Callum. She resisted a motherly urge to tell her son that *this* was home now. "Why don't you like living here?"

Her son's answer came quickly, in a tone one step up from a whine. "Sean isn't down the street."

Next to his brother, Sean Flannery had been Callum's best friend.

Picking up another shirt, Prim offered her son a sympathetic smile. "I spoke with Sean's mother before we left. She promised he could come and visit you as soon as we're settled."

Callum's jaw jutted out at a stubborn tilt. "It's not the same."

Prim upended the basket, dumping the rest of the contents onto the table, and considered her response. Unlike Callum, she already loved this house. Loved the open floor plan. Loved the fact that from where she stood in the kitchen, she had a good view of the living room.

The way the two rooms ran together allowed her to keep a better eye on her three boys—two rambunctious twins and one wolfhound—all with a penchant for trouble.

"It might not be the same, but living here will be so much better than Milwaukee." She refocused on the laundry. Picking up a sock, she frowned at the hole in the toe. She set it aside and waited for Callum's response.

A suspicious look settled over her son's face. "How better?"

"Well, Grandpa has a boat." She spoke in a deliberately offhand tone and picked up another sock. "I don't know many boys in Milwaukee who get to go fishing in a real boat. And that's not all."

Rolling on the floor, Connor and Boris tumbled into Callum. Without taking his eyes off his mother, Callum shoved them back. "What else?"

"Aunt Ami owns a bakery. When Sean visits we'll be able to walk downtown and get him any kind of cookie he wants."

A boyish giggle split the air.

"Help." Laughter filled Connor's voice. "Boris won't stop licking me."

"Boris." Callum's quiet murmur was enough to stop the slobber bath. Once the dog sat on its haunches, Callum turned to his brother. "Want to play ball?"

The sable-and-white hundred-pound wolfhound leaped to his feet and wagged his tail, a hopeful gleam in his golden eyes.

"Boris says yes." Connor scrambled to his feet, wiping the dog's spit off his face with the back of his hand. "I say yes, too."

Callum grinned and took off running. He'd nearly reached the door when he paused and tossed over his shoulder, "Race you outside."

His brother gave a war whoop and sprinted. And just like that, the I-hate-my-new-life discussion came to an end. Prim sighed in relief.

"I'll let you know when lunch is ready," Prim called as her boys tumbled out the screen door, an ecstatic Boris at their heels.

The fenced-in backyard was another favorite feature of the house. The boys could play outside and she didn't have to worry.

Yes, this house was practically perfect. Except for the fact that Max Brody lived next door.

She wasn't certain why she found the thought of him being so close disturbing. It wasn't as if they'd been *involved*, unless, of course, you counted the kiss he'd given her in that hotel hallway when they were seniors.

Her fingers rose to her mouth, to lips that began to tingle at the memory of Max's kiss.

A car door slamming made her rear back. She slipped to the front window and glanced out, wondering if her dad had decided to stop by.

Instead of her father, she spotted Loretta Sharkey, high school choral director and across-the-street neighbor, stepping from her ancient Chevrolet. Prim watched Loretta round the back of the Impala, open the passenger-side door, and retrieve several sacks of groceries.

She wondered if the neighbors got together for backyard barbecues. Would Max be there? Blood surged through her veins at the possibility.

Prim hadn't seen him since the wedding reception. Though he'd made it clear she should let him know if she needed help moving, she hadn't contacted him. Relying on herself was familiar territory. She was more than capable of handling the details of her and her sons' lives.

Even when Rory was alive, Prim had carried the bulk of the load. While her husband had been off scaling mountains and zip-lining across canyons, she'd been working, taking care of the twins, and handling all the day-to-day concerns that came with a household.

She couldn't begin to count the number of times she'd pleaded with him to think of the strain he was putting on his body, the toll his exploits were taking not only on him but on his family. She and the twins needed him. They wanted to spend time with him.

For a few weeks after one of those talks, life would be better. He'd be around more. But inevitably some new adventure would beckon and he'd be off again. His need to prove he was stronger than his illness took priority over everything else. Over his job. Over the boys. Over her.

A familiar resentment flared. She could have dealt with bearing the brunt of the responsibilities at home, but not his selfishness. They were already dealing with a shorter amount of time together, and the fact that he would risk cutting short even a second of that time infuriated her.

Even when his lung function had decreased, instead of scaling back his activities as his pulmonologist recommended, Rory had pushed himself even more.

When he'd left on that last trip, she'd been so angry. She'd said hurtful things. So had he. Prim closed her eyes and felt the pain of those last few minutes they'd shared wash over her.

Despite the fact that no one should have to die because of a manufacturing error in a climbing harness, she was grateful Rory hadn't suffered. The fall had killed him instantly.

Early in their marriage, they'd talked about what he wanted to happen if he died. His mother, he told her, wanted him buried in the family plot. So she could keep vigil, he'd said with a flash of a grin. Then he'd sobered, looked her in the eye, and told her what *he* wanted—to be cremated and his ashes scattered to the winds.

Prim's gaze slid to the black ceramic urn on the upper shelf of the corner curio cabinet. Despite pressure from Deb and Mike, she'd gone ahead with the cremation. But she hadn't scattered him to the wind. She'd kept him close in a way not possible when he was alive.

A knock at the door pulled her from her reverie. Swiping at a couple of stray tears, she hurried to the door. Instead of her father, Ami stood there.

With a loud whoop, Prim pulled her sister tight against her for a hug. "I didn't realize you were coming back so early."

"We're taking a longer honeymoon in January." Ami looped her arm through Prim's as she stepped inside. "To somewhere warm and tropical. Where they have beautiful beaches and drinks with little umbrellas."

"Sounds like heaven."

Ami heaved a happy sigh. "Anywhere with my Beck would be heaven."

"Now you're getting mushy." Prim grinned. "I might have to slap you."

Ami giggled, the sound so joyful Prim joined in.

"Where are my nephews?" Ami glanced around. "It's way too quiet in here."

"They're playing with Boris in the backyard. I can get them?" Prim had already turned when Ami placed a restraining hand on her arm.

"While I'd love to see them, I need to scoot."

"Oh." Puzzled, Prim shifted from one foot to the other and tried not to whine. "But you just got here."

"There's something I needed to discuss with you. I thought it best to do it in person."

Prim's heart gave a hard thump. "Is it something with Dad? Marigold? Fin?"

"No. No. No. Nothing like that, the family is all fine," Ami quickly reassured her, the words tumbling out one after the other. Then she gestured to the sofa. "Can we just sit for a minute?"

Prim plopped down, her gaze scanning Ami's face. "It must be important for you to come here right when you get back from your honeymoon."

"I have a Cherries meeting later this morning. I wanted to speak with you before I went."

"Nearly out of patience here, Am." Prim made a rolling motion with her hands. "Cut to the chase."

"Gladys is retiring from the Cherries. I want to nominate you."

———————

Ami Bloom Cross sat in the center of the semicircle in the parlor of Hill House, waiting for just the right moment. The meeting, as far as meetings went, had been interesting.

Eliza had broken the news about Gladys's "retirement," and there had been lots of hugs and tears. They'd then moved on to the updates. Plans for Fall Fashion Week had been discussed as well as a couple of tweaks to the Twelve Nights celebrations in December. The majority of the talk had centered around the progress on the upcoming Fourth of July events.

"It sounds like there's still a lot of work to be done on the parade," Ami whispered to Gladys, who sat on her left.

Gladys's bright red lips curved. "Like I said on the phone, in the weeks ahead there will need to be a *lot* of coordination between Max Brody and the person who replaces me. Lots of tête-à-têtes. Business meetings. You know. Like the kind you and Beckett used to have when you first started dating."

Recalling the outcome of some of those meetings, Ami felt her cheeks warm. She cleared her throat. "You're going to back me?"

"Count on it. It's a brilliant solution. You were so wise to think of it."

Though Gladys's innocent expression didn't fool Ami in the least, she played along. "When you called to tell me you were stepping down and the Cherries would be looking for a replacement with an accounting background, Prim was the first one who crossed my mind."

No need to mention she'd nearly discarded that thought. After all, her sister had just moved back and had a lot of settling in to do.

"Of course, in the interest of full disclosure I was compelled to mention that whoever replaced me would be spending *hours* of time *alone* with Max."

Had Gladys really just wiggled her brows suggestively?

"That was kind of you to mention that fact." Ami patted the older woman's arm. "It might be a problem for some."

Or a blessing. Ami hid a smug smile. She'd been horrified when Prim had told her she didn't plan to date until the boys were out of high school. That was crazy talk. No way was Ami letting that happen. Her younger sister had so much love to give. She shouldn't have to wait another twelve years for her prince.

Especially when that prince lived right next door.

"Ladies." Eliza raised her voice to be heard above the chatter.

The room immediately silenced.

Ami straightened in her chair, exchanging a conspiratorial smile with Gladys.

"This is the part of our meeting where we accept nominations from the floor. As we discussed earlier, Gladys will be impossible to replace, but we'll do our best to fill her shoes." Eliza gestured to Gladys and everyone applauded. Again.

When Gladys started to rise, Ami nearly groaned. They'd already been treated to several lengthy farewell addresses from their departing treasurer.

Eliza must have sensed another speech coming on because she spoke quickly. "Please raise your hand to offer nominations. Wait to be recognized. I'd like both the person's name and qualifications."

Ami shot her arm high in the air.

Eliza's gaze swept right past the waving hand as if it weren't there.

"Eliza," Lynn Chapin called out. "I believe Ami has her hand up."

The smile on Eliza's face never wavered. "Thank you, Lynn."

Eliza glanced at Ami and made an impatient go-ahead gesture.

"I'd like to nominate my sister, Primrose Bloom Delaney." Ami spoke in a loud, clear voice. "Prim has a degree in accounting, worked as an actuary for many years in Milwaukee, and has recently moved back to Good Hope to stay. She's very organized and can be counted on to get things done. Thank you."

Applause broke out in the room, quieted by one swift slice of Eliza's hand.

"The problem is," Eliza said, that phony smile still on her lips and her voice sugary sweet, "Prim is new to our community. I think we'd like someone with a little more investment in Good Hope for this opening."

"I have a friend—" Katie Ruth Crewes began, then halted when Gladys shot her the stink eye. "On second thought, I don't think she has time right now."

Gladys raised one bony hand, the jewels gracing each finger sparkling in the light.

"Yes, Gladys?" Eliza's expression brightened. "Do you have someone you'd like to nominate?"

"Indeed I do." The older woman's tone was as regal as the swath of silver in her dark hair.

"I love that you're nominating someone," Eliza said. "If you feel this person would make a good Cherrie, I'm confident she's who we should select. After all, she'll be taking your spot."

Eliza settled her gaze on Ami for a second, then smiled to the group. "I think that would be best."

The murmur of voices indicated agreement.

Eliza clasped her hands together and leaned forward. "Tell me, Gladys, who is it you want to be the next Cherrie?"

Ami felt as if she were at some political party's national convention when Gladys rose, lifted her arm as if holding a torch, and bellowed in a voice guaranteed to reach the third-floor rafters, "I throw my support behind Primrose Bloom Delaney."

Chapter Four

Prim dropped the phone into her pocket and wondered just when she'd lost her mind. But it was too late to back out now. According to Ami, her being a Cherrie was a done deal. She moved to the window and stared, unseeing, into the sunshine.

For better or worse, she was going to spend the next month working with Max Brody.

Tap. Tap. Tap.

Prim yelped and jumped back.

As if summoned by her thoughts, Max stood on the other side of the picture window. He jerked a thumb in the direction of the front door.

Face burning, Prim moved swiftly to unlatch it.

Before she could attempt to explain why she'd had her face glued to the window, Max strolled past, not quite able to hide his grin. "Happy to see you've taken up Jeannie Alcorn's flag."

The odd response drove away any excuse she might have been conjuring up in her head.

Prim saw him glance around the room and stifled a groan. The boys had gotten out of the house before she could insist they pick up the large pads of paper they'd been drawing on earlier. The pads, as well as a dozen colored pencils, were scattered across the floor.

Boris had added to the mess. In the dog's enthusiasm to lick Connor like an ice cream cone, the wolfhound had upset his basket of toys. But she couldn't blame all the clutter on the twins or the dog. Her gaze lingered on the shirts and socks scattered across the top of the kitchen table. At the moment, an open floor plan no longer seemed like such a fine thing.

"Who's Jeannie Alcorn?" Prim asked in an attempt to distract him.

Max's gaze returned to her, his expression faintly amused. "She used to rent this house. She was also captain of the neighborhood watch committee. Nothing happened on the block without Jeannie knowing about it."

"What does she have to do with me?"

His lips twitched. He gestured with his head toward the spot where she'd been standing only moments before.

Prim flushed. "My dad had mentioned he might drop by. He—"

The words stuck in her throat when Max took her hand. The feel of his skin, so warm against hers, brought back the memories of the reception and how good it had felt to whirl across the floor in his arms.

Even now, his light touch made her quiver. She couldn't make herself pull away.

"I was teasing you, Prim." Max's thumb absently stroked her palm. "It's good to have someone watching out for the neighborhood."

Her cheeks heated. She jerked back her hand. "When you saw me at the window, I was seeing if—"

"Your dad had stopped over." As if sensing her embarrassment, Max's voice remained steady as he finished the sentence for her. "I'm here because I have a proposition for you."

Without warning, he moved close. So close the delicious scent of his cologne made rational thought difficult. "Pro-proposition?"

"Yes. A proposition." He gazed into her eyes and she found herself drowning in the liquid blue depths. "And Prim, I need you to say yes."

Her heart fluttered as if a thousand butterflies were trapped inside. She moistened her lips with the tip of her tongue.

When he took her hands in his, she forgot how to breathe. Finally she found her voice. "What do you want?"

For a long moment Max simply stared into her eyes. Then he shook his head and took a step back, dropping her hands. She could almost see him doing a reset as he collected his thoughts.

He cleared his throat. "I want you to be the next treasurer of the Cherries. Gladys is retiring . . ."

Prim barely listened to his next words as relief surged over her like a crashing wave, leaving her weak and trembling. It had to be relief she felt, because there was no reason, no reason at all, for her to be disappointed.

He continued to talk, but her brain had shut down several minutes earlier and was taking its sweet time restarting.

Finally, she held up a hand. "Stop right there."

The explanation of all that would be entailed if she accepted his "proposition" ceased, but the determination in those baby blues still shone brightly.

He immediately launched a second offensive.

"You know how much Good Hope merchants depend on tourist dollars. Merchants like Ami and Beck." He shot her a smile that had her insides turning to mush. "Events planned by the Cherries bring millions of dollars into the Good Hope economy. They—"

"Yes."

He stopped. "What did you say?"

She smiled, a full-blown smile that felt as good, as right, as the decision she'd made. "I told Ami this morning she could nominate me, for all the reasons you've outlined. Just before you got here, she called to tell me I'd been voted in."

Prim knew boys could be unpredictable, men too, but she was unprepared when Max snatched her up and twirled her around, hollering, "Thank you, God," or maybe it was, "Thank you, Prim."

Her head was still spinning when he set her down, framed her face in his hands, and kissed her.

A yearning so strong it nearly toppled her rose up as the kiss gentled, then ended.

"M-Max," she stammered. "I—"

She wasn't sure what she planned to say, because the boys were suddenly there, demanding to know what the shouting was about.

"Mr. Brody and I were celebrating some good news," Prim said, not looking at Max.

Callum narrowed his gaze. "Your face is red and your hair is sticking out."

Connor studied her for a moment, then nodded agreement with his brother's assessment.

Great, Prim thought. Red-faced with hair sticking out. Now, didn't that paint a pretty picture? Resisting the urge to sigh or simply run to her room and put a pillow over her head, she smiled brightly instead. "It's because of the twirling."

"What's that?" Callum tilted his head, not appearing convinced.

"It's when you pick someone up and spin them around," Max said in a calm, matter-of-fact tone that inspired confidence. "Want me to show you?"

Callum considered.

"I want to try," Connor said.

"Okay. I pick you up under your arms." Max stepped toward the boy, then lifted him. "Then we do this."

All of a sudden Connor was spinning round and round and calling out, "Woooooo."

"My turn," Callum demanded, stepping forward.

Despite his protests for more, Max put Connor down near Prim. She set her hands on her son's shoulders to steady him, just in case he was dizzy.

She still felt unsteady from her twirl.

Callum shrieked for more, his small body almost parallel with the ground as he spun around.

When the two finally stopped twirling, Max rested his own hand on the top of a nearby bookshelf. Perhaps she wasn't the only one a little unsteady from their . . . twirl.

"It's Mommy's turn," Connor told Max.

"I've already had my turn, sweetheart," Prim reassured him.

"Mommy's turn. Mommy's turn. Mommy's turn," Callum chanted, and his brother joined in until finally Max held out his arms and Prim stepped into them.

They'd only made one rotation when the front door opened with a clatter.

"Why didn't someone tell me you were having a party?"

The abrupt halt to the twirling had Prim stumbling slightly when Max put her down. His hand closed around her arm for the briefest of moments as she steadied herself.

"Dad." Flushed and out of breath, Prim crossed the room to her father. Steve Bloom was a tall man with a lanky frame and a perpetual smile on his face. His pewter hair matched his wire-rimmed glasses.

She gave him a quick hug. "I didn't realize you were here."

"I knocked, but with all the commotion . . ." Her father's speculative gaze scanned the scene, taking in, no doubt, her red face and disheveled hair and the boys' happy grins.

In the center of it all, Max.

"Steve." Max moved forward, and the two men exchanged a one-armed man hug. "Prim told me you might be stopping by."

"I haven't had a chance to tell you how much comfort it brings me to know that you're right next door to my girl." Steve's gaze shifted to his grandsons. "And to these two monkeys."

"Mr. Brody twirled us, Grandpa." Connor lifted his arms. "Way high in the air."

"We were cel'brating," his twin added.

Callum may have stumbled slightly over the word, but it came out clear enough to have her father raising one eyebrow, his gaze shifting between her and Max.

"I'm a Cherrie, Daddy. Like Ami." Prim hooked her arm through his. "Come into the kitchen. I'll make some tea and tell you all about it."

Steve glanced at Max's briefcase sitting on the floor, then back to her. "If you've got business to attend to, I don't want to intrude."

"You're family," Prim chided. "You could never intrude."

"If anyone is intruding, it's me." Something in the way Max said the words told Prim he believed them.

"You're not intruding, either. You're as close to a Bloom without carrying the name." In saying the words she knew to be true, Prim felt herself settle, as if she'd stepped off shifting sand onto solid ground. Years earlier, way back in middle school, Max had been matched with her dad by the Big Brothers Big Sisters organization in Good Hope. "I swear you spent more time at our home than your own."

"Prim's right. You're family. Always have been. Always will be." Steve's tone brooked no argument. "And forget about the tea, Primrose. I'll take my grandsons out back to play some ball and you two can get down to your business."

Prim hesitated. "Are you sure, Daddy?"

"Positive." Steve's gaze shifted to his two grandsons. "Ready to hit it out of the park, boys?"

"Yay," they cheered until Prim had to put her hands over her ears.

"Let's take some of that energy outside." Putting a hand on each boy's shoulder, he guided them to the door.

Just like that, she and Max were alone.

Prim glanced at the briefcase her father had noticed. "You have some specifics you want to discuss?"

"If you have time." He shoved his hands into his pockets, making no move to retrieve the case. "Prim, about the kiss."

She waved a dismissive hand. "Temporary insanity. No biggie."

He nodded, but the look in his eyes told her he didn't believe the explanation any more than she did, but thankfully he would let the matter ride, at least for now.

"Shall we sit out here? Or would the kitchen table be better?" Prim gestured to the sofa, drawing Max's attention to her green stretchy shirt that showed off high, firm breasts. When her hand dropped, he admired the way the denim hugged her shapely thighs.

Something stirred in him, a familiar yet altogether new sensation. Masculine interest, to be sure, but something more. "Here will be fine."

He didn't know whether to be relieved or not when she settled herself in a nearby chair rather than sitting next to him on the sofa.

Clearing his throat, Max fought to recall the subject needing to be discussed. *Ah, yes, the Cherries.* "I'm serious. You're a perfect fit to be the Cherries treasurer."

Prim's eyes turned soft. "You always did have confidence in me, Brody."

Hearing his last name on her lips, spoken in a teasing tone that was once so familiar, took him back to high school days. Back to a time when he and this widowed mother of two had been a team.

"Often, more than I had in myself," Prim murmured.

Max realized with a jolt that while he'd been tripping down memory lane, she'd continued to speak.

"The Cherries desperately needed someone with your accounting expertise." Max resisted the overpowering urge to cover her hand with his. Which made no sense. Just like the kiss. That had made no sense, either.

Temporary insanity.

Hadn't he learned his lesson when his last girlfriend had gone back to her ex? There were major risks when you got involved with a woman whose heart still belonged to another.

"I never wanted to be a Cherrie," she admitted in a soft voice, as if imparting a confidence. "But they do such good work for the community. While I don't have money to donate like MarJean Thorpe, I do have the time."

"Giving of your time, lending expertise, can be just as valuable as a monetary donation," Max assured her.

"Is the rumor true?" Prim lifted a brow. "Did Mrs. Thorpe really leave the Cherries a hundred thousand dollars in her will?"

"One hundred and three thousand, to be exact."

"Same as her age." Prim leaned back against the seat cushions and shook her head. "She always did have a great sense of humor."

Max clicked open his briefcase. "While the unstipulated gift was very generous, it's also at the root of the group's current difficulties."

"I'm aware there are . . . issues."

"That's why I strongly advised Eliza that Gladys's successor have a strong accounting background."

He didn't quite know what to think when Prim's lips curved.

"Successor?" Those beautiful hazel eyes took on a faraway expression. "It'll take someone more special than me to fill Miss Hannigan's shoes."

"Miss Hannigan?" Max frowned. "I thought we were talking about Gladys."

Prim's hazel eyes sparkled. "Don't tell me you've forgotten my big acting break?"

Baffled, he could only shake his head.

"Back when I was in grade school, Gladys starred in *Annie*. I played one of the orphans." Prim sighed. "I was terrified, but Gladys went out of her way to be nice to me. She taught me the value of sticking with a commitment. I love the woman."

"By the way she greeted you at the reception, the feeling is mutual." Max shifted uncomfortably. "You know that Gladys made critical mistakes."

Prim's smile vanished.

So she knows some, Max thought, *but not all*.

"What did she do?" Prim's voice matched her serious expression.

"Let me show you." Max opened his briefcase, and she moved to sit beside him as he placed the last year's and the current year's profit and loss statements and balance sheets on the coffee table.

After several minutes of studying the figures, she lifted her head.

Satisfaction rippled through him at the understanding he saw in her eyes. "You see it."

Prim lifted her hands. "The current year total expenses are higher than their income. The balance sheet shows the savings account is dwindling. Money is being transferred from the savings to the checking account to pay the current-year bills."

"No one on the board caught it." Max shook his head. "Not even Floyd Lawson."

"But Floyd is an accountant. He had his own CPA firm until he retired." Her brows pulled together in puzzlement. "He should have spotted the problem the first month they had to pull money out of savings to pay the bills."

"Even when I pointed it out, he acted as if he didn't think it was important." Max kept his voice even, not letting his frustration show.

"You did your job. You found the error. Now that the problem has been identified, corrective measures can be taken." Prim's gaze settled on the papers. "Gladys doesn't bear sole responsibility. There should have been checks and balances. I can't believe the board—"

"Had only been meeting semiannually."

Prim gave an incredulous snort. "An organization of their size should meet quarterly."

"Finally, someone who gets it." As his hand slapped hers in a high five, satisfaction surged. Bringing Prim on board had definitely been the right move. "I've also recommended that the new treasurer computerize the record keeping. Bring the Women's Events League into the twenty-first century."

"Aren't you forgetting something?"

He tilted his head, thought for a moment. "I don't think so."

"Isn't Gladys co-chairing the parade with you?"

He offered a sheepish smile. "Oh, yeah, that's part of the deal, too."

"So many tasks, so little time," she murmured, then lifted her gaze. "I'm willing to dive into all of this, but I need something from you."

"Tell me what you need." Max stared into those beautiful hazel eyes. Whatever she wanted, it was hers.

Her lips curved as if sensing how far he was willing to go. She said nothing for several heartbeats, and his heart began to hammer.

Then she extended her hand. "Be my backup babysitter."

Max felt a surge of disappointment, though he wasn't sure why. He reached out and closed his hand around hers, smiled. "Deal."

Chapter Five

Prim rolled her shoulders, then followed the move with a cross stretch. Last night she'd had difficulty settling. She blamed the restlessness on too much caffeine. Her tossing and turning certainly couldn't be the result of THE KISS she'd shared with Max.

The brief melding of their mouths had been too brief to stir up such intense . . . longings.

"Throw the ball, Mommy," Connor called out, punching his small fist into the pocket of his glove. "I'm ready."

Saying a little prayer, Prim gave her best MLB pitcher imitation and flung the ball at him. She grimaced as it curved to the right, so far out of reach her son didn't even try to catch it.

Then he was scrambling after it, his skinny legs churning.

Callum, who'd already run after his share of overthrown balls, merely watched as his brother passed him. Standing on a decorative boulder between her property and Max's with his eyes squinted, he reminded Prim of a sea captain at the bow of a ship. He pointed. "Is that Mr. Brody's wife?"

Startled, Prim turned to see an attractive, dark-haired woman standing on the porch of Max's home. Decked out in a white dress covered with red, saucer-size poppies, the brunette's attire was definitely a step above Max's T-shirt, cargo shorts, and hiking boots.

Callum still stood on the rock, studying the woman with the intensity he usually reserved for large, black bugs.

"She has red sparkly shoes," he announced. "Like in *The Wizard*."

Prim adjusted her gaze downward. The woman's shoes were indeed red and sparkly. Unlike Dorothy's shoes in *The Wizard of Oz*, these kicks had three-inch heels. And the legs they were attached to weren't those of a little girl but the shapely ones of a grown woman; a beautiful, adult woman with lips as bright as her shoes.

"Think she can throw a ball?" Callum asked when his brother returned, the ball clutched tightly in his glove.

"Who?" Obviously confused, Connor glanced around.

"Mr. Brody's wife." Callum gestured with one hand toward Max and the woman.

"Mr. Brody isn't married." Prim tried to place the visitor but came up empty. "She's probably just a friend."

Friend with benefits?

Prim shoved aside the disturbing image of Max and the statuesque beauty with hair the color of rich walnut and legs up to her neck, naked. In bed. Together.

At the moment, the two stood a respectable distance from each other. Prim wondered if Max would kiss her good-bye. She expelled the breath she hadn't realized she'd been holding when he merely extended his hand. The woman laughed, gave it a shake, and flashed a brilliant smile.

Once the brunette's roadster disappeared from sight, Max turned. His gaze met Prim's and her heart stuttered.

Prim returned his smile and lifted her hand in a friendly wave.

Apparently taking the polite gesture as invitation, Max sauntered over. The first thing she noticed was that his shirt—advertising last year's 5K Spring Color Run—made his eyes look as blue as the walls in Muddy Boots, her brother-in-law's café. The second was those eyes held more than a hint of amusement.

When his gaze dropped to her mouth, she felt a punch. Prim moistened her suddenly dry lips with her tongue and forced herself to breathe. As their gazes remained locked, her heart began to thud against her ribs.

Not until Callum shoved his brother against her did the fog lift. She stumbled and might have fallen without Max stepping forward.

After shooting Max a grateful smile, Prim whirled on her son. "Callum, how many times have I told you not to shove your brother?"

The boy's lip jutted out. "He wouldn't give me the ball."

"It's mine." Connor held the glove protectively against his chest. "Mom threw it to *me*."

"She threw it to the sidewalk," Callum corrected.

"If I'd known there was baseball action going on in the neighborhood, I'd have brought my glove." Max rocked back on the heels of his battered boots and shot Prim a wink. "You know how I feel about playing."

She'd loved watching Max on the baseball field. He always gave one hundred percent, whether it was fielding a pop fly, solving a difficult equation . . . or kissing her with a sweet tenderness that took her breath away.

Heat flooded her cheeks. She cleared her throat. "You still play?"

"Second base for the Hawks," Max said, referring to Good Hope's amateur team.

The boys exchanged a glance.

"You could get your glove," Callum suggested. "We can wait."

His brother nodded. "Yeah, we can wait."

Max appeared to be hiding a smile when he turned to Prim. "The glove is in my garage." He angled his head. "I could have them get it for me?"

"That's fine." Her heart did a slow roll. He actually *wanted* to play catch with her boys. "I'll be able to see them from here."

Max looked from one twin to the other. "My glove is hanging on the garage wall. It's not far up. You should be able to reach it."

"I can jump high," Connor told him, his thin face serious.

"I can jump even higher," Callum boasted.

"No jumping necessary." Max slipped the phone from his pocket, tapped a couple of buttons. The garage door slowly rose.

"I'll get it." Excitement reverberated through Callum's voice. The words had barely left his lips when he took off running.

"He was looking at *me*," Connor protested, sprinting after his brother.

"You don't have to play ball with them." Prim touched Max's arm. "I'm sure you've lots to do."

"Have you forgotten I was Good Hope High's standout second baseman?" His teasing tone had her relaxing. "Baseball and I, we go way back. In fact, she was my first love."

Prim realized she was staring at his mouth and lifted her gaze to those amazing blue eyes. "I thought your first love was math."

"Anytime you fall in love with something new it's a first time." Something she couldn't quite decipher flickered in those liquid blue depths. He cleared his throat. "You know what I recall about those days? You cheering in that short skirt."

She tilted her head. "Were you looking at my legs, Mr. Brody, when you should have been keeping your eyes on the ball?"

"Guilty as charged." His lips lifted in a slow smile.

Prim's blood turned to warm honey. The yearning became an ache. Though she told herself to look away, her eyes remained locked on his. "I was the worst one on the squad."

Max didn't bother to dispute the assessment, which only confirmed she'd been right. "I never understood why you did it."

"I know." She sighed. "I wasn't the type."

"Cheerleading—" He paused as if searching for the right words. "Just never seemed in your wheelhouse."

He was right. While Fin and Marigold loved performing, for her being in front of crowds had been pure torture.

"My mother was big on us girls trying everything from dance to cooking to cheer. I tried out the year my mom was diagnosed with cancer." Prim swallowed hard against the sudden lump in her throat. How odd that after all this time, the fear and grief of those days could appear out of nowhere, the pain just as swift and intense as it had been back then. "I knew it would make her happy to see that I was willing to at least try out. Never in a million years did I think I'd make the squad."

"You brought elegance and grace to the field," he said gallantly.

"Yeah, right." She rolled her eyes. "You're being way too kind."

"Not at all." Max waved aside her protests. "In addition to elegant and graceful, you're smart and kind and beautiful. You, Primrose Bloom, are a rare blossom."

It was obvious by the way he pressed his lips together that he'd said more than he'd planned. But the sweet words lingered in the air.

His eyes were dark as midnight, and, as she stared into their depths, Prim forgot how to breathe. She forgot how to think. She forgot why she should keep her distance.

The loud chatter of a squirrel perched on a tree branch, the strong scent of lilac from the row of bushes across the street, all disappeared.

All she knew was him. All she wanted was him. Her heart agreed, pounding out a primitive rhythm.

Kiss him. Kiss him. Kiss him.

As if he heard the seductive beat, Max stepped closer until he was right. There.

Her heart was a sweet, heavy mass in her chest.

Max held out a hand to her as if asking her for . . . something.

Prim held her breath and waited. For what, she wasn't sure, but the moment seemed important, monumental even. Almost as if the years that had passed had fallen away, and they were being given another chance to be—

Callum's voice echoed across the yard. "I got it!"

Max's hand dropped to his side.

Prim hid her disappointment behind a Mona Lisa smile.

The twins raced toward them, Max's glove held high in the air as if it were an Olympic torch. They came to a skidding stop directly in front of Max.

"Good job." Max grinned and took the glove, slipping it on, then giving the pocket a punch. "Now, let's have some fun."

Prim rested her back against the solid oak and watched her boys soak up Max's undivided attention.

He lobbed the ball straight to Callum, the move so slow and easy Prim was sure *she* could have caught it.

The ball wobbled in the pocket, but Callum gripped it tightly, a big smile spreading across his face when the glove fully encased it.

"Toss it back to me."

The boy did as Max instructed. Though it veered to the side, Max easily snagged it from the air. "Good throw. You have a strong arm."

Callum beamed.

Despite her son's often-cocky bravado, Prim knew he wanted so much to please. They both did. They wanted male approval. Needed it.

Tears filled Prim's eyes. Rory was missing so much. A pang of regret for what never would be was followed by a hot burst of anger. Had climbing another mountain really been that important?

She shoved aside the ugly thought and refocused in time to see Max gently toss the ball to Connor.

The boy stood in the ready position but his gaze had shifted to Boris. The wolfhound had gotten up from his nap on the porch to put the noisy squirrel on notice with a series of staccato barks.

The ball hit Connor square in the chest, then dropped with a thud to the ground. The boy glanced down, a look of surprise on his freckled face.

Callum hooted.

Prim shot her eldest a warning look while her youngest flushed.

"It's important to keep your eye on the ball," Max reminded Connor, his tone kind and almost . . . fatherly.

After thirty minutes of playing catch, Max called a halt.

Prim held up a hand when the boys began to beg. "Tell Mr. Brody thank you, then go inside and wash up for lunch."

"Thank you, Mr. Brody," the boys called over their shoulders as they raced to see who would reach the door first.

Prim shook her head and chuckled. "Boys."

The word said it all.

"They're great kids."

"I know." Prim smiled. "I think I'll keep them around."

"I'm going to be coaching a T-ball team through the Y every Wednesday." Max picked up the ball the boys had left on the ground and tossed it to her. "There may still be a couple of spaces left on the team. Katie Ruth is the contact person."

"Katie Ruth Crewes?"

"She's the only Katie Ruth in Good Hope." Max grinned and tucked the glove under his arm. "She's the youth activities coordinator. Call her. If you're interested, that is."

"Thanks. I'll definitely consider it."

Max started to walk away but turned when Prim called his name.

She'd tried to put the brunette out of her mind. She'd tried to tell herself who Max associated with was none of her business. But that was pure malarkey. Max was her neighbor. And a friend. "I didn't recognize the woman in your driveway. Is she from around here?"

"Her name is Charlotte McCray. And you're right, she's not from around here."

"But she lives here now?"

He hesitated. "Sort of."

"What's that supposed to mean?" Prim raised her hands when he started to speak. "Forget I asked. Not my business."

"It's okay." His mouth relaxed into a slight smile. "She owns Golden Door but also has a salon in Chicago. That's what I meant by 'sort of.' She has an apartment here but spends most of her time in Highland Park."

Golden Door Salon and Spa.

Though she'd never been inside, Prim was familiar with the pricey salon and day spa that catered to wealthy tourists and residents. "She's not married. Doesn't have a family."

A curious look filled Max's eyes. "You sound so certain."

"Two salons. Two states. Two homes. You couldn't have a family and do all that traveling. It wouldn't be fair." The second the words left Prim's lips, an image of Rory carrying his duffel to the car, ready to take off on another *adventure*, surfaced. "But then, I could be way off base. Some people don't care about fair. Some don't care about the family left behind."

Prim regretted bringing up the subject, regretted the bitterness she hadn't been able to keep out of her voice. Whatever problems they'd had in their marriage, Rory was Callum and Connor's father. Her smile suddenly felt brittle, ready to break in a thousand pieces. "Thanks again for—"

"You were right. Charlotte is divorced."

There was a beat of silence.

Max leaned toward her and lowered his voice. "Though you haven't asked, I'm her accountant. We've gone out once. No kids in the picture. But that kind of goes without saying. I'd never be in a casual relationship with a single mom."

Prim inhaled sharply, then covered it with a cough. The Max she knew loved children. Seeing him with her sons told her that hadn't changed. She'd even found herself thinking how nice it would be if . . .

She stopped herself. *Not going down that road. No point.*

Still, she couldn't help wondering, couldn't stop herself from asking the question. "Why no single moms?"

He paused for so long she wondered if he was going to answer.

"You remember how it was at my house." There was a hesitant quality to his voice.

Prim's heart pinged. She remembered his mother's revolving door of men.

"For a long time I thought I was the reason none of them stuck long." A muscle in his jaw jumped. "I won't do that to someone else's kids."

She understood the do-no-harm mentality, admired the protective streak. That's why she knew he'd understand *her* decision. "The potential upheaval dating brings to a child's life is the reason I won't date until the twins are out of high school."

"That's what you said at the reception." His inscrutable expression gave no indication of his thoughts on the matter.

Then again, what had she expected him to do? To say?

Did she really think he'd slap her on the back and tell her it was a wise decision? Had she thought he'd argue and try to change her mind? She wouldn't have wanted that, not at all.

"I spoke with Eliza this morning." He glanced at his phone, checked the time. "She said you plan to start entering data today."

Prim took up the conversational ball, finding comfort in the familiar. "Computerizing the Cherries' financial records will be a piece of cake. I figure I should be able to get all the data keyed in before dinner."

Max shoved his hands in his pockets. "I have a few things I need to handle, but I can stop over after lunch, help you get started."

"I appreciate the offer, but like I said, this is pretty basic stuff."

"That's not how Gladys felt."

"At this stage in her life, Gladys's heart is with the theater." Prim lifted her chin. "If I had even half her talent, I'd be focused on the stage, too."

"Spoken like a loyal friend."

"Just calling it like I see it." A self-conscious laugh escaped her lips. "Now, coordinating the parade is a whole different animal. I definitely need you to guide me."

"You can count on me, Prim." His steady gaze shot tingles down her spine. "Always."

Chapter Six

"What did Dad have planned for the boys this morning?" Ami asked, turning around to lock her front door.

Since Hill House, where the Independence Day planning meeting would be held, sat just down the street from her sister's home, Prim had parked in Ami's drive and retrieved her sister for the short walk over. Once they reached the home, instead of immediately heading inside they paused on the porch.

"Actually, the boys aren't with Dad, they're with Max." Prim tossed the words out there with all the attention one might give to flicking a piece of lint off a summer dress. A casual disregard that said the twins spending time with Max was no. Big. Deal.

"You and Max are together?" Her sister practically squealed the words. "Of course you're together. Why else would he be watching the boys? Oh, I can't wait to tell Beck the good news."

"Slow down. He's watching the twins because I'm helping him with the parade. He owes me."

"If you say so." Ami's tone was irritatingly cheery.

"I can't believe you." Prim threw up her hands in frustration. "I just moved back and you already have me hooking up with my hunky neighbor. In what universe does that make any kind of sense?"

Ami waved the question aside. Or perhaps she was waving to Katie Ruth, who was striding down the sidewalk, ear buds obviously hooked to a phone in her pocket. Either that or the pretty blonde had taken up talking to herself.

"So you think Max is hunky, huh?"

"Oh, for goodness' sake." Prim started toward the porch steps, but Ami grabbed her arm and dug in her heels.

"Not so fast. Really, tell me what's up with you two." Her sister's tone was lighthearted, but the flare of hope she saw in Ami's green eyes tore at Prim's heartstrings.

It wasn't in Prim's nature to burst anyone's bubble, but she didn't understand why clarifying was even necessary. Ami knew where she stood on dating and romance. Prim had made that quite clear. And not all that long ago.

The wine and chocolate the four sisters had consumed two nights before the wedding hadn't been enough to dull anyone's senses. But it appeared she needed to say it again, and keep saying it, until Ami accepted it as fact.

"Nothing is between Max and me, other than neighborly friendliness." Dismissing the kiss they'd shared as a simple momentary lapse, Prim kept her tone easy and conversational. "I meant what I said. I'm not going to date until the boys are out of high school."

Ami was so busy checking her bag, pulling out one umbrella then another before dropping them back into the cavernous depths that Prim wondered if her sister was listening. Then Ami looked up. "I thought you were joking."

"You knew I was serious, *am* serious," Prim quickly corrected.

From their position on the massive porch, she and Ami waved to a couple of Cherries members hurrying past. One of them was Max's mother, Vanessa Eden.

Rain had been forecast, but the clear, brilliantly blue sky mocked that prediction. There was, however, a slight mist in the air from the bay, and Prim felt her hair expanding by the second.

"Shouldn't we get going?" Prim attempted to smooth the frizz with the palm of her hand. "I don't want to be late."

"Once we take a step into the inner sanctum"—Ami's voice lowered to a spooky whisper—"we must remain silent. Or risk Eliza's wrath."

The cackling sound that burst from Ami's throat was a mix between a squawking chicken and a deranged madman.

Prim shook her head, unable to keep from smiling. "You're crazy. You know that, don't you?"

"That's the word." Ami wagged a finger. "I believe *crazy* was what Fin dubbed your twelve-year no-dating plan."

"I believe her actual words were, 'Primrose, have you lost your mind?'" While Prim had laughed along with her other sisters, she'd wished they'd been more supportive of her decision.

"We want you to be happy." Ami spoke softly, as if she'd read her mind. "That's a long stretch of time to be alone."

"I have the boys."

"It's not the same."

Prim couldn't argue that point. Having children in the house *wasn't* the same as having a husband by your side when you needed a shoulder to cry on or wanted to celebrate a success. "You can be alone even when you're married."

"Was it that bad?" Sympathy filled Ami's voice.

Prim hesitated, then realized she was tired of covering for Rory, tired of lying—especially to her own family—about her marriage. "I wouldn't call it *bad*, but my marriage was different than I imagined it would be when I spoke my vows. Different than what I watched Mom and Dad share. Different from the way I see it is with you and Beck."

She glanced away, not needing to see the pity in her sister's eyes to know it was there. "I knew Rory had CF when I married him. I just didn't realize how much his passion to live every moment, to experience every adventure, would impact our life together, and the lives of our sons."

She stopped, realizing even now she was making excuses for his self-centered behavior.

"I'm angry at him, Am." Prim's voice shook with emotion. Because they were sisters—and close—she didn't need to add that underneath the hot, molten anger flowed a river of sadness.

"I'm sorry, Prim."

"I made my choice." Taking a deep breath, Prim pulled out her phone and glanced at the time. "We really should get going. I don't want to walk in late."

Prim made it all the way down the steps before Ami caught up with her.

"Just remember, not all marriages are like what you had with Rory." Ami kept her voice low. "With the right person, it can be amazing. Max is a wonderful guy."

"I'm happy for you and Beck." Prim willed her sister to see that truth in her eyes. "But I'm content with my life just the way it is."

"We'll talk more about this later." The determined note in her sister's voice made it a statement, not a question.

"Sure." Prim knew whether she agreed or not, her decision would be questioned, debated, not just by Ami but by Fin and Marigold. Heck, her dad might even weigh in on the matter.

But Prim already knew what her response would be—what it *had* to be. The welfare of her boys came first.

"I dropped an extra umbrella in here for you." Ami changed the subject, patting her large bag as they reached the sidewalk. "Remember how Mom always carried an umbrella in her purse? Even when there were blue skies and zero chance of rain?"

"I miss Mom and her umbrellas," Prim said with a sigh.

Ami reached over and squeezed her hand. "It helps having you back. I mean, Dad is great, but lately he spends so much time with Anita."

Anita Fishback, her dad's *girlfriend*. Just the thought of the two together made Prim ill.

Prim paused for traffic at the corner of Market and Main. "I keep hoping Anita will show her true colors, do something that will be such a turnoff that he'll never want to see her again."

"Your mouth to God's ear," Ami muttered and made Prim grin.

Prim touched her sister's arm as the two started up the walkway toward the doors of the majestic Hill House. "Tell me how this will play out."

"We'll follow the agenda we received. Basically we're just going to be updating Eliza—and the others—on where we are in regard to our part in the upcoming Independence Day festivities." Ami continued in a matter-of-fact tone, "As I'm coordinating the Cherries' involvement in the pancake feed the morning of the Hometown Heroes parade, I'll report on those efforts."

"What will I do?"

"Just listen, get a feel for how everything works." Ami offered a reassuring smile. "Since you recently came on board, no one expects you to know much of anything yet."

The explanation sounded logical and made perfect sense. But Prim's unease still grew with each step.

The house hadn't changed. The massive staircase to the left was still impressive, and the ornate crown molding still drew the eye.

Hearing the click of heels on the hardwood floor, Prim looked up and caught the heavy scent of designer perfume just before Eliza stepped into the foyer.

"Everyone is in the parlor waiting." Eliza's gaze fixed on Ami. "We're ready to get started."

If the barb had struck its target, Ami gave no indication. Her sister merely glanced at the grandfather clock, which showed the time as 12:55. "The meeting is still set for one?"

"It's always at one."

"Just wanted to make certain nothing had changed," Ami said equitably.

"If we're late, it's my fault," Prim interjected. "It took me longer to—"

"We're not late," Ami snapped, then softened the words with a smile. "We still have five minutes."

When the executive director remained silent, Ami's head tilted. "Isn't that right, Eliza?"

"As long as you are seated and ready to proceed at one."

Her sister may have appeared unfazed, but Prim knew Ami had tender feelings. Since Ami was apparently determined to act as if Eliza's barbs didn't matter, Prim let it go.

She wanted to say more but they'd reached the parlor. As her gaze took in the scene, Prim was surprised how many of the women she knew around the semicircle. Katie Ruth was there as well as Lynn Chapin and Max's mother.

If Prim remembered correctly, the two women had been high school classmates and were still good friends.

Catching the warning glance sent by Eliza in her direction, Prim stifled the urge to greet everyone and slid into an empty chair next to Katie Ruth. Ami slipped in beside her.

The clock in the foyer chimed the start of the meeting. Eliza made a few announcements, including a brief welcome to Prim.

The executive director cut off the words of greeting with one slice of her hand. "Lynn, would you like to report on the state of the Fourth of July preparations?"

Lynn Chapin, dressed in white pants and a royal blue camp shirt, rose with an easy grace Prim envied. Unlike Prim's unruly 'do, Lynn's silvery-blond bob brushed the tops of her shoulders, silky smooth.

"In addition to what is already in the works for the Independence Day and Hometown Heroes parades, the pancake feed, and the Music in the Square events, we'll be adding a children's parade on July third. Prizes will be given for the best-decorated bicycle, wagon, et cetera. We—"

"There was no money earmarked in the budget for prizes," Eliza interrupted, startling Lynn, who simply stared.

"I was about to explain that the prizes will be covered by the merchants." Lynn's tone turned as cool as her eyes. "Katie Ruth got the buy-in from the business owners because any child who is in town during the festivities can participate. The merchants see this as a win-win for the community."

Some of the tightness bracketing Eliza's mouth eased. "I hope they're not offering their support for this but pulling back on other planned donations."

A startled look crossed Lynn's face, as if that thought had not occurred to her. "Absolutely not."

"Are you certain?" Eliza pressed.

Lynn's lips pressed together for half a second but her voice displayed no irritation. "As a matter of fact, while I was discussing this addition, I confirmed their donations to the main celebrations."

"Good." A look of relief crossed Eliza's face. "That's fine, then."

"Are donations of time, money, or supplies down, Eliza?" Katie Ruth raised her hand but spoke before being acknowledged. "You seem concerned."

"We haven't done as much fundraising this year as in the past. As each year we attempt to up our game, it doesn't take much to deplete our coffers." As if dismissing any further questions from Katie Ruth, Eliza shifted her body toward Prim. "Primrose, I'd like you to report on the progress of the parade on Independence Day."

Startled, Prim glanced at Ami, who looked equally perplexed.

"Primrose is co-chairing the Independence Day parade with Max," Eliza explained to the others. "As this is one of our most attended events of the year, it is critical that the parade go off without a hitch."

The glint in those hard gray eyes told Prim the executive director was well aware she'd put her on the hot seat. Not only that, Eliza hoped she'd get scorched.

If Prim explained she'd only taken over the duties in the past forty-eight hours or protested that the brief agenda e-mailed to her hadn't indicated she'd be expected to give a report, Eliza could make her appear incompetent with a few carefully chosen words.

Judging by the cat-got-the-canary look on Eliza's face, that's exactly what the executive director had in mind.

"Thank you for the opportunity to report, Eliza." Prim rose, plastering a serene smile on her lips. "Max and I have all of the participant entry forms. We will be reaching out to the contact person for each entry to verify their participation and make sure they understand the parade guidelines."

Her assumption was, at this late date, they had all the entry forms. By the nods, she'd assumed correctly.

Now the slippery part.

Last night—another restless one—she'd opened her laptop and pulled up everything she could find on parade planning. The information on how to best organize a parade had proved to be a better sleep aid than warm milk or melatonin. Still, Ami wasn't the only Bloom sister with an excellent memory.

Prim wasn't certain exactly how the parade in Good Hope was organized, but as she continued her report, she focused on common tasks cited in the articles.

"Our focus for this week is to fine-tune the lineup." The way Prim figured, a lineup could always be adjusted to make it better. "We want to—"

"The lineup is the same every year," Eliza interrupted, obviously determined to squish her like a bug under those pretty black heels.

"The parade is one of the Cherries' biggest events," Prim continued without breaking stride. "For instance, just because fire trucks normally come later in the parade doesn't mean we shouldn't move them closer to the beginning."

"What would be the advantage of moving them up?" Katie Ruth asked, genuine interest on her face.

"They'd be able to leave more quickly in an emergency." Several of the articles Prim had read with smaller communities in mind had stressed that point.

"That makes sense," Katie Ruth said.

The other women seated in the room nodded.

"Max and I will be viewing the videotape of last year's parade to analyze problematic areas," Prim added.

"That should have been done long before now," Eliza said.

"Prim just took over this position." Lynn Chapin spoke up, shooting Eliza a pointed look. "I don't know about all of you, but I'm impressed by the strides our newest Cherrie has made in such a short time."

A ripple of applause sounded.

"Yes. Thank you, Primrose. Good job." Eliza's sweet tone didn't fool Prim. Still, she'd spoken the words.

Heels O. Bug 1.

Though she wanted to jump up and do a happy dance, Prim listened quietly while Katie Ruth, Vanessa, and Ami gave their reports. She couldn't wait to go home and tell—

The thought brought her up short.

Tell who? Callum and Connor? They'd listen for maybe ten seconds, not understanding a word she said, then ask if they could watch television or go out and play.

Fin and Marigold were too far removed from Good Hope business to understand the significance.

There was only one person who would understand, who would truly celebrate her victory over Eliza's machinations.

Her lips curved into a smile. Wasn't it lucky she knew just where to find him?

Chapter Seven

Prim shielded her eyes from the sun with one hand and watched Max and her sons build a sand castle. Or what she assumed would eventually be a castle. Another little boy she didn't recognize crouched beside Connor, helping pack sand.

They all looked like they didn't have a care in the world. Which was exactly how Prim felt at this moment. She couldn't stop smiling as she started down the steps leading from the parking lot to the sandy beach . . . just as Clint Gourley started up them.

Clint was older than Prim by a good seven years. She vaguely recalled him being cute in his younger days. But the blond good looks had faded, leaving him middle-aged and paunchy with a receding hairline he tried to hide with too much gel.

One thing hadn't changed: he still had that leering smile that made her skin crawl.

"Hey, Primrose, lookin' good."

Prim gave him a perfunctory smile and brushed past him. He deliberately bumped her. She heard him laugh but didn't turn around. Instead she hurried across the sand, weaving in and out of the sunbathers with their beach towels and umbrellas and floaties.

In her one-piece navy swimsuit and shorts, she fit right in with the crowd. The intensity with which the boys were patting sand on their castle-in-progress made her glad she'd gone with impulse and swung by the house to change. She'd had a feeling the twins might be having too much fun to want to leave immediately.

Max glanced in the direction of the now-empty steps. "What did Clint say to you?"

Behind those sunglasses, he'd been watching her, she realized. The thought added another layer to her happy mood. She didn't want to chance bringing it down by discussing creepy Clint. Prim waved a dismissive hand. "Nothing important."

"Mommy, Mommy, look what we're building." Connor jumped up and grabbed her hand, tugging her to the mound of sand.

Callum lifted his head from where he sat on his knees, hands buried deep. "Can we stay longer?"

"Please can they stay?" the tow-headed boy, the unknown part of the construction crew, added his pleas.

Prim scooped up a handful of sand, intensely aware of Max's scrutiny. "Absolutely. For a while, anyway."

The boys cheered, then went back to working on their masterpiece.

Prim dusted the sand off her hands. "Two wasn't enough?"

Max tilted his head. "Huh?"

Prim pointed toward the third boy. "You picked up another one."

Max grinned. "That's Chris. He's Cory and Jackie White's son. They live just down the street from us."

"The names ring a bell."

"Your sister was involved in several Giving Tree fundraisers for the family. Cory was diagnosed with leukemia, but he's in remission now and doing great."

"I hope that continues." Prim thought of her mother. For six years she'd been cancer-free. Then it had come back with a vengeance.

Max motioned to her. He took a couple of steps away from the boys and lowered his voice so they wouldn't be overheard.

"Jackie, Cory's wife, has MS." Max gestured with his head toward a couple with two younger children sitting in the shade. "They're good people. You'll like them."

"You'll have to introduce me before you leave."

"Before I leave?"

"You're off the clock. I'm ready and willing to assume sand castle duty." She gave him a mock salute, then glanced doubtfully down. "I assume that's what that blob of sand is supposed to be."

He quirked a brow. "What if I'm not ready to leave?"

"Then stay." Her heart quickened. "It's a public beach."

"Do you want me to stay?"

"Sure." She spoke quickly, too quickly, then added, "If you want to, I mean, that's your decision."

His smile slowly widened until Prim felt tingly all over. She was trying her best not to stare but it was becoming increasingly difficult. While she'd seen a lot of men in swimming attire, the sight of Max in striped board shorts made her mouth water. His skin was a light golden brown, and his broad, taut chest held just the slightest dusting of hair.

She'd let her eyes drift downward, admiring the cut of his suit . . .

"Have you been in the water yet this year?"

She jerked up her gaze. He'd lifted his sunglasses, and she flushed at the knowing look in his eyes. "Is it cold?"

He held out his hand. "One way to find out."

With the surface a vivid blue and smooth as glass, the water did look enticing. But she wasn't a single female out for a day of fun at the beach. She had responsibilities, and they were sitting at her feet, covered in sand. "I can't leave the boys by themselves."

"Cory will watch them." Waving broadly, Max caught the man's eye and gestured for him to join them. "You can trust him. He teaches with your dad at the high school."

Prim hesitated. "It's not that, it's the boys. They're very fast and—"

"He's also the father of three little ones. He knows how slippery they can be at that age. He won't let them out of his sight."

In his early-to-midthirties, Cory had short, sandy-brown hair and a ready smile. After the introductions were complete, he made a shooing motion with his hands. "Enjoy the water. I've got this under control."

"Thanks, Cory." Prim shifted her gaze from one twin to the other, her voice stern. "You listen to what Mr. White says."

She got two impatient nods in response.

Max crouched down, put a hand on each of her sons' shoulders. "Don't forget the moat."

"We won't," Callum said. "That's my favorite part."

"Listen to Mr. White." As she'd done only moments before, he focused on one boy and then the other. "Promise?"

"We promise," they said in unison.

Prim breathed a little easier as she slipped off her shorts and placed them on top of the towels.

She smiled at Max. "I'm ready."

"Then let's get wet."

Prim waited until she reached the water's edge to tell Max the news that had been on her tongue since she'd arrived. "You should have been at the meeting today. Eliza was in rare form."

As she stepped farther into the water, she gave him a blow-by-blow account. By the time she finished with Eliza's compliment, they were chest deep in cold water. Max raised one hand and high-fived her. "I'm proud of you, Prim. I wish I could have been there to see you shine."

Despite the coolness of the water, Prim felt warm all over.

They swam nearly to the buoy, putting needed distance between them and all the inflatable rafts, water toys, and jostling bodies.

The sun, high and hot overhead, warmed her face as she treaded water. It had been a long time since she'd been able to relax in anything other than a bathtub. And that was for five minutes at best.

"My arms are getting tired." She shot Max a sheepish smile. "But this is so pleasant I don't want to get out. Not just yet, anyway."

"I'll hold you up." Without waiting for an answer, Max moved closer. "Arms around my neck."

"Bossy, much?"

He grinned and repeated, "Arms around my neck."

After only the briefest internal struggle, Prim did as he'd instructed.

They were nearly eye to eye and his were gorgeous. Flecks of gold glistened in the blue depths. Her heart gave a sudden leap and desire pooled low in her belly. She realized only a thin piece of material—that now clung to her like a second skin—separated her from the hardness of his body.

"You have beautiful eyes," he said unexpectedly.

"Thank you." Even though she knew this was dangerous territory, pleasure rippled through her at the compliment. Apparently she wasn't the only one who'd been doing some surveying.

Focus, she told herself. On anything but his handsome face, broad shoulders, and muscular legs. "Want to know how my conversation with Ami before the meeting went?"

A wave broke over them but Max held her tight. "Not particularly."

"Strange," she managed to stammer. "All she wanted to do was grill me about you."

His lips curved. "I do have a way with women."

Max said this as if it were a joke, but the statement made Prim wonder. Max was no longer a gawky adolescent boy with a passion for math and baseball. Though he seemed totally unaware of his charisma, he definitely had a quality that made a female take a second look.

The thought had her tightening her hold on him. "Ami thinks you're *wonderful*."

He stilled as if waiting for the punch line.

Prim leaned close. "Want to know what I think?"

Red flags popped up faster than kernels in a hot skillet, but Prim paid them no mind.

After a glance at the shore to confirm the boys were fully engaged in the building of their castle, she slid her fingers into his hair and brushed a kiss across his cheek. "You're a good guy, Max Brody. The best."

He'd given her a compliment; now she was giving him one. She was grateful for what he'd done to protect Gladys, grateful he'd taken time to play with the twins. Yes, she was very grateful.

"Prim."

How could he make her simple name sound so sexy?

"Yes?"

"I apologize in advance if I'm misreading the situation."

She tilted her head back and studied him. "What are you talking about?"

"Let me show you." He lowered his head and covered her mouth with his.

His lips were warm from the sun. The tenderness in the touch stirred a part of her that had been cold and dark for a long time.

As she clung to him in the waters of Green Bay, Prim was forced to admit what she'd tried so hard to deny: the fire that once burned for this man still smoldered.

Now she just had to figure out how to put out the embers before it burst into flame and consumed them both.

Prim stood in the shower and let the warm spray soothe her sore muscles. She tried not to think of Max and the kisses they'd shared.

Instead, she reflected on all she'd accomplished in the past twenty-four hours. Thirty minutes ago, she'd reached the finish line. At least in terms of the house. The last of the moving boxes had been brought in from the garage and emptied. All contents were now neatly stowed in closets, drawers, and cabinets. Her new house finally felt like a home.

She stepped back from the pulsating spray to squirt coconut-and-lime-scented gel onto the loofah. She sang along with the radio while smoothing the light green soap over her skin.

Though way too many freckles dotted all visible surfaces, Prim was generally pleased with her body. She'd once feared her stretched-out belly would never recover after delivering two seven-pound baby boys.

She slid the loofah across her lower abdomen. While that section of her body might not be as flat as it had been when she'd gotten pregnant at twenty-one, a slight pooch was a small price to pay for her wonderful sons.

As she moved the sponge upward, she recalled how Max's gaze had lingered on her chest when he'd seen her in her swimsuit.

The tips of her nipples hardened with the memory and a tightness filled her belly. Prim could no longer deny the electricity between her and the handsome CPA.

Back in high school she'd done her best to explain away the connection. She'd told herself the kiss they'd shared after their mathlete win was simply due to excitement over the victory. When she'd been unable to completely silence the doubt in her head, she'd blamed it on Calvin Klein Eternity. The totally awesome scent *had* to have contributed to her losing her head and kissing Max back.

"M-om." A pounding sounded against the bathroom door, making it rattle.

Startled, Prim whirled. The loofah spurted from her hand.

"Callum won't let me have any grapes." The whine in Connor's voice came clearly through the closed door.

Prim closed her eyes and counted to five.

"Tell your brother I said he has to share." She leaned over and scooped up the pouf. "I'll be out in a minute."

She'd put in a movie and sat the boys down with a bowl of grapes hoping for fifteen minutes of peace. She'd gotten five.

With a sigh, Prim quickly finished her shower. She wrapped her freshly shampooed hair in one thick towel while drying off with another. Turkish bath towels, soft and known for their incredible wicking ability, were leftovers from her life with her husband.

Nothing but the best for Rory.

Prim brought the fluffy towel to her cheek, sighed again. One thing about Rory was he'd helped her see that life should be lived to the fullest, whether that be using premium towels or seizing every moment.

It was sadness, not anger, she felt today. Genuine sadness at the loss of a good man who'd still had so much life to live. Sadness that his adventures had always mattered more to him than her. Sadness that despite her efforts to keep his memory alive through pictures and stories, his sons' memories of their dad were few and faded with each passing day.

With a towel wrapped snugly around her, Prim opened the bathroom door and listened. Hearing only the movie and childish chatter, she slipped back into the bathroom.

She took a few minutes to blow-dry her hair, a rare luxury. Since Callum and Connor were still occupied when she finished, Prim padded into the bedroom and flung open the closet door. Normally, she put on the first thing she grabbed. But she had a few minutes now and could be selective.

It was silly to be so concerned with what to wear to a community barbecue where you'd likely see more jeans and flip-flops than anything else.

When Ami had called to remind her of the event, Prim had to stop herself from asking her sister if she knew if Max was coming.

It shouldn't matter if he was at the party or not. It wasn't as if the kisses they'd shared had meant anything more than she was young with a healthy sex drive. And Max was an attractive man. And a sweet guy.

She danced her fingers across her lips. There had been tenderness in his kiss, but also an underlying passion.

It had been two years since she'd been intimate with a man. But when Max kissed her, she yearned for more. The fact that she kept imagining Max naked simply showed she was normal. End of story.

But just because any romantic dreams he stirred would remain untapped for the next twelve years didn't mean she had to show up at a party looking like someone's dowdy maiden aunt. Prim gave the closet her full attention.

Her hand settled on the hanger of a dress she'd purchased on a whim last summer. The fit-and-flare sleeveless cotton of distressed ivory covered with carnations in varying shades of pink had made her skin look peaches-and-cream pretty.

Prim remembered that day well. She'd been feeling blue and, with the boys at an all-day birthday party, she'd been on her own. Instead of moping at home, she'd called a friend and gone shopping.

After slipping it on, she impulsively decided to straighten her hair. The primping had nothing to do with Max and everything to do with the fact she was a Bloom. Bloom women took pride in looking their best. Which was why, when the twins' attention remained focused on the movie, Prim grabbed her makeup bag and used the opportunity to work a little additional magic.

Chapter Eight

"Look at all the cars." Charlotte McCray glanced around the nearly full parking lot, a look of stunned surprise on her pretty face. "This is like Grant Park on the Fourth."

"There are probably about as many people here. Tonight is for anyone—and I mean anyone—involved in the planning or execution of this year's Independence Day celebration." Max stepped from his vehicle into the late afternoon warmth. The surrounding land, owned by the Rakes family for generations, was some of the most beautiful on the peninsula. "Lots of community events are held at Rakes Farm. I'm surprised you haven't been to one."

"I may own a business here, but I spend far more time in Chicago than in Good Hope." Charlotte stepped from the vehicle and smoothed the front of her dress. The deep purple made her blue eyes look almost violet in the light and was the perfect foil for her brown hair and ivory complexion. "Even after four years, I still feel like a tourist."

Max could believe it. Until that night at the Flying Crane, his path had never crossed hers. That wasn't especially surprising, considering he didn't frequent high-end salons and she had yet to join any of the service organizations on the peninsula. Still, they'd become acquainted over drinks and pretzels, and a friendship of sorts had developed. Last month he'd started handling the tax work for the Golden Door, the pricey salon and day spa she owned.

Weeks ago they'd agreed to a date to explore the possibility of expanding their friendship. He'd actually forgotten all about that promise until she'd called and told him she was available tonight for a movie and the barbecue.

What would Prim think when she saw him with Charlotte?

A knot formed in the pit of Max's stomach. It was ridiculous to feel as if he were cheating on Prim when they weren't dating. Heck, he and Prim didn't even have *plans* to date.

But the kisses they'd shared had meant something to him. If he wasn't mistaken, they'd meant something to her as well. None of that changed the fact that Prim had made it clear she wasn't dating until her boys were grown.

And even if Prim was open to exploring a relationship with him, after his breakup with his previous girlfriend, Lori, he was wary of starting up with someone whose heart wasn't free.

He'd known Lori was on the rebound last year when they'd started dating, but she'd insisted she was ready to move on. When she went back to her ex-boyfriend six months later, he realized she hadn't been ready. Unfortunately, knowing that hadn't lessened the pain of their breakup. Max wouldn't knowingly put himself in that position again.

"Do you have any idea?"

Max slowed his steps. Though he was as good as any guy at multi-tasking, he'd obviously let his mind wander too far off course.

Pasting a smile on his face, he turned to Charlotte. "Pardon me?"

"Not important." She gave a laugh, waved a dismissive hand, but he saw hurt in her eyes.

Instantly contrite, he gave her hand a squeeze. "Tell me."

She hesitated only a second.

"I was simply wondering if you could tell me some people I might know who'll be here tonight." Charlotte brought a finger to her brightly painted lips, effectively drawing his attention to her mouth.

Nice enough lips, though they lacked the pouty fullness of Prim's.

With great effort, Max pulled his attention back to the conversation, determined to stay focused. "You'll likely see many of your clients. And you said you've met Jeremy Rakes. He's hosting the event."

"Excellent." Charlotte looped her arm through his as they strolled up the sidewalk toward the sound of music and laughter.

Jeremy's three-story home blazed with lights. Though his backyard was the size of a football field, the Good Hope mayor had also opened the main level of his home tonight.

As they passed lilac bushes heavy with flowers, Charlotte's fingers tightened around his bicep. "Blue is a good color on you."

Max glanced down at his short-sleeved twill shirt, then back up. He shot her a wink. "I aim to please."

"You do." She gazed up at him through lowered lashes. "You please me very much."

Having a gorgeous woman openly flirt with him should have made his evening. Instead, Max shifted his gaze and said nothing as they rounded the house.

Jeremy Rakes, current mayor and a friend since childhood, had gone all out this year. Chinese lanterns in a variety of vibrant colors had been strung across the endless, perfectly manicured patch of green. Red-and-white-checkered cloths covered numerous picnic tables that held side dishes ranging from the commonly seen watermelon slices, deviled eggs, potato salad, and baked beans to the more unusual grilled pineapple and mac 'n' cheese bites.

For those who didn't like pork, Floyd Lawson, Cherries board member, manned one of several large grills that included shrimp-and-vegetable skewers in addition to burgers and brats. The retired CPA, wearing an I Like Pig Butts and I Cannot Lie apron, lifted tongs in greeting when he spotted Max.

Though Max firmly believed Floyd could have done more to keep the Cherries out of their current financial difficulties, he liked the man and admired his civic involvement.

Steering Charlotte in that direction, he stopped by the grill. "Great apron."

"It's a favorite. And who's this lovely creature?" Without giving Max a chance to perform introductions, Floyd wiped one hand on the apron, then stuck it out to Charlotte. "Floyd Lawson, retired CPA. Most around here call me Santa."

"Ah, Charlotte McCray, business owner." The brunette's lips twitched. "Most call me Charlotte."

Floyd did his ho-ho-ho laugh while patting his jiggling belly.

Noticing Charlotte's perplexed look, Max explained Floyd played Santa Claus every Christmas.

"I can see you as Santa." Charlotte studied him thoughtfully. "Your beard is the right length and color, but the hair is too short. Do you let it grow out or wear a wig?"

Floyd appeared startled, as if no one had ever asked him that question.

"Charlotte is a hair stylist. She owns Golden Door," Max explained.

"Ah." Floyd nodded and fingered his hair. "That's why you're so focused on the white stuff."

"Occupational hazard." Charlotte studied him through lowered lashes. "If you ever need a trim, stop and see me."

She was actually flirting with the old guy, Max realized, bemused.

"If I could afford your prices, I'd take you up on that offer."

Charlotte just laughed and turned, obviously ready to move on.

"One thing, Max, before you leave." Floyd's serious tone stopped them both. "I'd like to ask you to keep an eye on Primrose. She's been special to me ever since I taught her in Sunday School and she asked more questions about math than Jesus."

Max chuckled but Floyd didn't crack a smile.

"The thief hasn't hurt anyone yet, but most of us think it's just a matter of time until he surprises someone at home. She's alone in that house with those boys."

"Prim is cautious and very safety minded." Max kept his tone light but felt a chill at Floyd's words.

"The burglar is becoming bolder." Floyd pointed the tongs at Max. "He entered the last house when the family was out for dinner."

"Burglar? In Good Hope?" Charlotte appeared more curious than distressed. Not unexpected, considering her home base was a city of three million where crimes like this were an everyday occurrence. "I heard a couple of customers chatting about a string of burglaries, but I thought it was happening somewhere else."

"Nope." Floyd lifted a couple of brats to the warming rack. "This crime spree is happening right here in Good Hope. And I'm serious about you watching out for Primrose, Max. This guy could be dangerous."

"Primrose?" Charlotte arched a brow.

"She's my neighbor. She and her sons recently moved back to town."

"Promise you'll watch out for her," Floyd pressed, a bulldog tilt to his whiskered jaw.

"Of course, I'll watch out for her."

A look of relief crossed Floyd's face. "Good. That's good."

"Come on, Charlotte." Max took her arm. "There are lots of people here I want you to meet."

"It was nice visiting with you, Mr. Lawson." Charlotte gave Floyd a jaunty wave as Max pulled her away.

Once they were out of earshot, she tugged him to a stop. "I think Santa Claus is into matchmaking. Is Primrose young and pretty?"

"Floyd may be many things, but not a matchmaker. Prim lives next door. In Good Hope we look out for each other."

Charlotte merely lifted a shoulder, let it fall, then turned to survey the scene spread out before them.

Groups of men in shorts, jeans, and khakis and women in bright summer dresses dotted the lush yard. Scattered tables, strategically placed, held guests who preferred to eat sitting down.

In the far back of the yard, men tossed horseshoes while children played badminton or croquet. Callum and Connor were part of a group of children at the net. Instead of attempting to hit the birdie, the two redheads held their rackets like swords and fenced with each other. The exuberance of their play made him smile.

He searched for Prim and spotted her by the beverage tables speaking with her father and sister. Beck wasn't there, but it was a given that where you saw Ami, her husband wasn't far away.

"Thanks for inviting me." Charlotte's hand returned to his arm in a gesture that felt a little too proprietary. She slanted him a flirtatious look that he was beginning to realize was as much a part of her as those bright red lips.

"Max Brody," Cory called loudly from several feet away, a smile breaking over his face. "I hoped we'd run into you tonight."

Out of the corner of his eye, Max saw Prim whirl at the sound of his name.

Their gazes collided.

His heart stumbled.

She was breathtakingly beautiful this evening in a dress covered in pink flowers. The reddish cast to her strawberry-blond hair glistened in the glow of the lanterns.

She'd straightened the wiry strands into a sleek style worthy of a fashion model. While he preferred the wild and untamed look, Prim was a rare beauty either way.

Regaining his inner balance, Max offered her a smile, but she'd already turned her attention back to Steve.

"We went to a movie earlier," he heard Charlotte say to Cory and his wife, Jackie. "A chick flick with a happily ever after. Max indulged me." She tightened her hold on his forearm.

Max forced an easy smile. "It was a good movie."

Jackie sighed. "I love the ones with happy endings."

That didn't surprise Max. He imagined life was hard enough for this family without being depressed at the movie theater. Now that his hair had grown out, no one looking at Cory would ever guess he'd been near death last year. He always had a smile on his face as if he didn't have a care in the world.

Jackie's unsteady gait and reliance in recent months on a cane gave some indication of her declining condition. But she'd never let MS define her.

"We enjoyed spending time with you at the beach the other day." Jackie paused, then appeared flustered, as if realizing Max had been with another woman that day. "I love the weather we've been having lately, don't you?"

Charlotte ignored the weather comment and smiled up at Max. "You went to the beach during the week?"

Max shrugged. "My schedule opened up for an afternoon."

"Next time your schedule opens up, call me." Charlotte batted her heavy lashes. "I've got a new bikini I've been dying to show off."

Cory chuckled. "You're a fool if you don't take her up on that offer, Brody."

Jackie gave an exaggerated sigh. "I switched to a one-piece this year. After three children, it seemed time."

"You're as beautiful as the day I married you." Cory looped an arm around his wife's shoulder, leaned over, and kissed her cheek.

Max smiled at the easy display of affection, but Charlotte appeared to have grown bored with the conversation. She shifted her gaze, then stilled, like a hunting dog spotting its prey. "Isn't that Jeremy Rakes?"

Following the direction of her gaze, Max saw it was indeed Good Hope's mayor helping Floyd flip burgers. Tall and lanky with blond hair just a little too long, Jeremy was friendly, approachable, and extremely intelligent. All those characteristics, plus the fact that he sprang from one of the peninsula's oldest families, explained how he'd been able to win the mayoral race last year though he wasn't even thirty.

He was also single, although in recent years he'd been seen frequently in the company of Eliza Shaw. Max looked for the Cherries' executive director in the crowd but came up empty.

"Let's go say hello," Max offered.

"No. You mingle. I'll discuss my business with him, then hunt you down." She wiggled her fingers in a casual gesture. "Back soon."

"Sounds good," Max murmured, though Charlotte was already too far away to hear him. He turned to Cory and Jackie. "Floyd mentioned there's been a lot of talk about the burglaries."

"It's kind of scary, not knowing where this criminal will strike next." Jackie glanced at her husband. "I was worried it might be a gang thing, but Sheriff Swarts told Hadley he's convinced the break-ins are the work of a single individual."

Floyd had been right, Max realized. People *were* talking.

He decided it'd be a good idea to mention to Prim he wanted her to call him day or night if she heard or saw anything suspicious.

"We're going to hit the barbecue line." Cory took his wife's arm and glanced at Max. "Want to join us? Or can we get you anything?"

"I'm fine. Thanks. I'll catch you later." Max turned and meandered in the direction of the beverage tables.

After being stopped several times by friends and people wanting to talk about the parade, the tables holding large galvanized tubs filled with ice, beer, and an assortment of soft drink bottles grew near.

"Max."

With a resigned smile, Max turned.

Eliza, stunning as a scorpion in a red dress, stared at him through slitted eyes. A bottle of Corona dangled between her thumb and forefinger, moving like a pendulum back and forth. "Going to see your girlfriend?"

Max tilted his head.

"Primrose." Eliza gestured with her head to where Prim and her family stood. "Your *girlfriend.*"

She emphasized the word, a malevolent gleam in her eyes.

Max remembered when he'd have given anything to hear those words. But not from Eliza. And not now. "What do you want?"

The executive director lifted the bottle and took a delicate sip, her smile easy, those gray eyes hard as steel. "I'm sure by now she's told you all about her performance at the planning meeting."

"Prim mentioned she gave our report."

"I'm warning you." Eliza's voice held an icy edge. "This parade is important. Not only to the Cherries and to Good Hope but to me. For both your sakes, you'd better be giving it the attention it deserves."

"Is that a threat?" His tone could have frosted glass.

"You shoved her down my throat, getting her sister and Gladys to team up and sway the vote." Eliza's eyes never left his. "Let me speak frankly, Max. If anything goes wrong with the parade, I'll make sure it's your and Prim's ass in the sling, not mine. That's not a threat, that's a promise."

Chapter Nine

Prim watched Max approach and, conscious of Anita's watchful gaze, schooled her features into a pleasant smile.

Her father greeted Max warmly, slapping him on the back. "How've you been, son?"

"Keeping busy." Max slanted a sideways glance at Prim and offered a smile.

Her traitorous heart gave a little leap.

"I'm glad I ran into you tonight, Max." Ami stepped forward to give him a quick hug. "I'm hosting an impromptu housewarming at Prim's house tomorrow night. I'd love it if you could make it."

Beck had just walked up, and though his expression gave nothing away, because Prim was facing him, she saw the brief flash of surprise in his eyes.

Apparently the housewarming Ami was hosting was news to him. Just like it was to Prim.

"I'm not sure—" Max stopped when Beck placed a hand on his shoulder.

"He'll be there." Beck's tone brooked no argument. Surprised or not, he was backing his wife's wishes.

"I told you that a housewarming isn't necessary," Prim demurred, giving her sister a pointed look.

"And I told you it is." Ami's tone, while pleasant, was as firm and unyielding as her husband's. "It'll be great fun. I'll bring the food, so you don't have to worry about a thing."

Something was going on here; Prim just couldn't figure out what it was yet.

"This seems awfully last-minute to me." Anita pursed her lips, a suspicious gleam in her eyes. "Lindsay and I are spending the weekend shopping in Milwaukee, so I won't be back until Sunday night."

"I know, that's what you said." Ami's face was all sympathy. "It's too bad you'll have to miss the housewarming."

"It could be rescheduled." Anita glanced at Steve.

"Not my party, honey." He patted her shoulder in a comforting gesture, then glanced at Ami, a question in his eye.

"Unfortunately this is the only time that worked." Again, her tone oozed sympathy and regret, but Prim wasn't fooled.

Unless she was misreading the signs, Ami had specifically set this time so the family could be together without Anita. But why was Ami so insistent Max come? What if he had plans with his new girlfriend? "Max, you don't have—"

"I thought we could show the videotape of last year's parade," Ami interrupted. "You mentioned at the meeting you and Max were planning to review it. We can all munch on popcorn while we offer suggestions for possible improvement."

"That's a good idea." Max turned to Prim. "We do need to move ahead on the parade. If changes are going to be made, it needs to be soon."

Prim nodded, surprised at the fervor in his tone.

"I still think you could find another time," Anita huffed.

"Let it go, honey," Steve said in a low tone they all heard.

Anita's hazel eyes flashed, telling Prim she was poised for battle. Prim wondered who would feel her wrath. It wouldn't be her dad. Anita was smart enough to know she could only push him so far.

"I don't believe I've met your date." Anita pinned Max with a take-no-prisoners gaze. "Who is she, anyway? And why is she chatting up Jeremy Rakes instead of staying with the man that brought her?"

"Her name is Charlotte McCray." Though he responded to Anita, Max's eyes remained on Prim's face. "She's a friend."

"A friend you brought to one of the biggest social events of the summer." Anita's lips lifted in a sly smile. "Sounds like more than a friend to me."

The anger that slammed into Prim told her Anita's barbs had achieved the desired result. While it was true Prim had no claim on him, why had he kissed her with such sweet emotion? The way he'd acted had made her believe she was someone special to him.

As if afraid she might lash out, Ami looped her arm through Prim's. After a warning squeeze, her sister smiled at Max. "I can't wait to speak with her and get acquainted."

"Looks as if you're about to get your chance." Anita's eyes glittered in the glow of the Chinese lanterns. "She's on her way over here now."

Everything about Charlotte McCray was high-end: hair, makeup, clothes . . . even the confident smile that showed a mouthful of straight, white teeth.

When Charlotte zeroed in on Max like a homing pigeon come to roost, it took all of Prim's self-control to paste a welcoming smile on her lips.

Once again Prim told herself she had no claim on Max. He was free to attend barbeques with whomever he liked. But why did he have to bring Charlotte? Hadn't Max seen that for every minute she wasn't batting her eyelashes at him she was busy making eyes at Jeremy? Apparently a tight wrap dress that barely covered her cleavage was more than enough to excuse Charlotte's nonexclusive flirting.

And who in their right mind would even consider Jeremy when they were on a date with Max? Prim couldn't trust the sanity of a woman who didn't realize she was already on the arm of the best man in Good Hope.

It doesn't matter. Prim's anger deflated like an untied balloon. If it wasn't Charlotte, it would be someone else. A great guy like Max wouldn't stay single forever.

Prim wanted him to be happy, to find that special someone.

Just not Charlotte.

Just not now.

"It was sure nice of Ami to arrange this housewarming." Max took a sip of wine and gazed around the comfortable living room. Though Prim had barely moved in, the place already had a homey feel.

He tapped the edge of a picture to straighten it, then turned back to Steve. The two men stood by the front window.

"I'm glad you could make it. It wouldn't have been the same without you here." Steve clapped Max on the shoulder. "It's just too bad Anita couldn't have joined us."

The older man appeared serious so Max merely nodded, though he knew the evening wouldn't have been nearly so pleasant with Anita in attendance.

"That looks like something off a Hallmark card." Max gestured with his glass of wine to where Beck sat on the floor building a Lincoln Log fort with the twins.

Prim's father tilted his head, considered. "Better if there was snow falling outside and a fire blazing in the hearth."

Max studied the scene, grinned. "And Beck should be wearing one of those red sweaters with a bunch of dancing reindeers across the front."

At the sound of his voice, his friend looked up and started to rise.

"Go back to playing with the kids." Steve waved him down. "Max and I are just planning a Christmas card."

After a quizzical look, Beck shook his head and picked up another log.

"Boris needs reindeer antlers." Max swore the wolfhound, crouched down and waiting for an opportunity to steal a log, got a pained expression.

"That would complete the picture," Steve agreed, chuckling as he took a sip of wine.

"You've got a wonderful family, Steve." Max spoke in a matter-of-fact tone, ignoring the emotion that kept trying to clog his throat. The Bloom family was special, always had been, and always would be.

They genuinely enjoyed spending time together. Conversation and wine had flowed freely while they'd feasted on prime rib, au gratin potatoes, and spinach salad with cranberries and blue cheese crumbles. Max had enjoyed himself so thoroughly he'd forgotten for a moment he wasn't one of them.

Oh, he knew how to play the part. Just like when Sarah was alive, when dinner ended, he'd gotten up with the other men to clear the table. Prim and Ami had chased the men out of the kitchen so they could load the dishwasher. From where Max stood in the living room, he could hear the sounds of their laughter.

What would it be like to truly be part of this family? To be Prim's husband and Callum and Connor's father? The fact that he could so easily see it gave Max a little jolt. Was it too much to hope Prim was over Rory? It *had* been two years . . .

"I've missed seeing you."

Max looked up to find Steve's gaze on his face.

"You don't come all that often."

"You know how it is, life gets in the way." Max kept his tone light. "You're busy, too. You have Anita. And your family."

"Stop right there. You're family as much as anyone here." The older man stabbed Max in the chest with a pointed finger. "When you and I were matched all those years ago, you became my son. You've shared this family's ups and downs, and you were there for me when Sarah died. I don't want to hear any more of that kind of talk."

Max nodded. The lump that now filled his throat prevented him from commenting. He shifted his gaze, searching for something, anything, to discuss that didn't involve emotions. He found it on the top shelf of the corner curio cabinet. "That's an interesting vase."

It was sleek and black with a white Aztec design. Oddly, instead of being open at the top, it held some kind of stopper.

"That's Rory."

"Rory bought it?"

"No." Steve smiled slightly, though his expression remained serious. "That's an urn, Max, not a vase. It holds Rory's ashes."

Max had fallen off his bike when he was ten and had the air knocked out of him. He remembered that feeling. He felt that way now.

"I-I'd have thought he'd want to be scattered to the winds." Max cleared his throat. "Maybe from the observation tower in Peninsula Park. Or around Good Hope."

"That's what he did want."

Prim's voice sounded behind him. Max whirled. Her eyes were as flat as her voice.

"Deb didn't want him cremated, but that's what he wanted. I followed his wishes."

Her father offered a sympathetic smile. "Knowing Deb, she probably wanted him in a spot where she could go and visit, keep vigil."

Prim gave a slight nod. "I don't know if you remember, but she pushed to have him buried in the family plot at the Lutheran cemetery. I don't believe she's forgiven me for not following her wishes."

Steve squeezed her shoulder, his hazel eyes, so like hers, dark with sympathy. "You had to do what Rory wanted. She'll come to realize that one day."

But Steve didn't mention, and neither did Max, that Prim had only followed Rory's wishes so far. Yes, she'd had him cremated. She hadn't scattered his ashes.

Was it her way of holding on to him?

Max didn't ask. He wasn't sure he wanted to know. But it gave him pause, made him wonder.

"Five-minute warning," Ami called out. "I'm loading the video of the parade."

"Time to pick up." Beck reached for the large plastic container where the logs were stored.

"Nooooo," the twins whined in unison.

Normally Max would have found their exaggerated protests amusing, but right now, nothing amused him.

He touched Prim's arm, kept his voice low. "May I speak with you a minute?"

Surprise flicked in those hazel depths. "Sure."

She stepped closer to the window and looked up at him, that gorgeous freckled face framed by a mass of red-gold curls. "What is it, Max? If it's about Charlotte and last night, truly it's none of my business who you date."

"Charlotte is a friend of sorts, not even that, really. More of a business associate." Max had made that clear when he'd taken Charlotte home. Thankfully, she'd told him she hadn't felt a connection, either. "That isn't what I want to discuss with you . . . "

Prim looked up at him with that sweet, trusting expression. What did it matter if she still had Rory on the shelf? It wasn't his business. She'd made it clear she wasn't wanting to date.

She touched his hand. "Max?"

His heart swelled with love, and he knew that even if she never loved him back, couldn't love him back, he would do whatever he could to protect her. "About the burglaries. If you see or hear anything unusual, I want you to call me. Day or night."

"No one is going to—"

"Promise me, Prim."

"I promise." She smiled that bright, sunny smile that always warmed his heart, then tugged on his hand. "Now, let's go watch the video. Eliza won't be happy unless the parade is a smashing success."

"You don't know the half of it," he muttered and let her lead him to the sofa.

Boris's barking yanked Prim from a sound sleep. She opened one eye and found a hundred pounds of fury standing beside her bed. The ruff on the wolfhound's neck stood straight up, as if he'd just received an electrical shock.

He gave three more staccato barks, then raced from the room. She scurried out of bed, her heart slamming against her ribs.

Had something happened to one of the boys?

Bile rose in her throat, but when she flung open the door to the room, she found both sleeping peacefully.

Thank you, God.

Boris had disappeared down the hall and the barking continued, sounding as if it was coming from the kitchen now. Prim lifted the baseball bat leaning against the wall, hugging it to her while she gently closed the door.

Keeping her eyes on the hall, she zipped into her room. Prim scooped up her phone, then stood guard outside her sons' room.

Call me, Max had said.

As she hit his number, she hoped he'd meant it when he'd empha-sized *at any time*. She supposed she could call the sheriff, but if it ended up being a skunk or a possum that had gotten Boris riled, she'd feel like a fool.

Max answered on the third ring, his voice groggy with sleep. "Hello."

"It's Prim," she whispered. "Boris is barking like crazy. I think there might be something—or someone—in the backyard."

"Where are you and the boys?"

"They're sleeping. I'm in the hall outside their room."

"Go in there now. Lock the door. Take your phone."

She could hear him stumbling around, swearing. "I'll be right there. Don't leave that room until you hear my voice."

"Be careful." She slipped into the bedroom and locked the door. Setting her phone on a nearby dresser, she stood at the end of the boys' beds, bat in hand.

Prim couldn't have said how much time went by before she heard footsteps in the hall and a quiet voice on the other side.

"It's me, Max. You can open the door."

The breath she must have been holding came out in a whoosh. With trembling fingers Prim set down the bat. She stepped out of the bedroom and right into his waiting arms.

"I'm sorry," she murmured against his shirtfront. "This burglar thing has me more spooked than I realized."

"It's okay." With gentle fingers he stroked her hair and held her until she quit shaking. "I'm here. I'm not going to let anyone hurt you."

She breathed in the scent of him, shampoo and soap and that inde-finable male scent. The strength in his arms gave her comfort, and she found her world steady. Finally, she eased back and gazed up at him.

His cheeks were shaded by golden stubble. His jeans were worn and the faded red T-shirt he'd tossed on had clearly seen better days. He looked magnificent.

"Was it an animal?" Even as she asked the question, Prim saw the answer in his eyes.

"It was a man."

Her heart gave a solid thud against her rib cage. "You saw him?"

"No. You called me. I called the sheriff. They were here before I got out my door, searching your backyard. They found footprints."

"I don't understand." Prim's heart had begun to hammer, so fast she felt light-headed.

"Let's sit down." Max took her arm and guided her into the living room, taking a seat beside her when she collapsed onto the sofa. "I'll tell you everything I know."

Boris rose to his feet, came to her, his tail swishing from side to side.

Prim leaned forward and buried her face in his fur. "You're such a good boy, such a good watchdog."

When she sat back, she had to wipe tears away. "You should have heard him barking."

"Once you called, I did hear him." Max gave the dog a rub. "He did a good job keeping the guy at bay."

"It was him, then? The burglar?"

"Yes. They almost caught him tonight. The Rhodes family down the block are visiting family in Illinois. He tripped their alarm system. The sheriff and several deputies were there in minutes, but he ran. From the boot print they found out back, it looks as if he was hiding in your backyard for a few minutes."

"He could have broken inside." She shivered, running her hands up and down her bare arms. Only then did Prim realize she wore only an oversize tee.

"He'd have to get through Boris first." Max grabbed the crocheted throw from the back of the sofa and tucked it around her. "Better?"

The concern in his eyes and the strength she saw there warmed her more than any blanket. "Yes. Thanks."

"Sheriff Swarts is confident the guy is no longer in the neighborhood."

"I'm okay, now that I know he's gone." Prim forced a brave smile but the effect was ruined when her lips trembled. "If he would have gotten inside . . . the boys . . ."

She closed her eyes as her voice broke.

Max placed his hands on her shoulders. "Look at me."

She met his gaze.

"You need me, you call. Understand?" His intense gaze remained on her face. "What did I tell you in Milwaukee?"

Confused, Prim cocked her head. She didn't recall Max ever visiting her in Milwaukee. "You didn't tell me anything. You—"

He gave a lock of her hair a little tug.

"Hey," she protested.

"The math competition, Red. I told you that you could always count on me." The eyes focused on her face were clear and very blue. "That hasn't changed."

Fatigue and the events of the evening must be getting to her, Prim decided. Blinking rapidly, she cleared her throat. "That trip is my favorite memory from high school."

"Mine, too."

The air grew heavy as a curious tension filled the space between them. It was a kind of watchful waiting.

"I still have my medal," she blurted, seized with a desperate need to fill the silence.

The gold medals they'd received from winning the mathlete competition had been modeled after Olympic medals, circles of faux metal hanging from red-white-and-blue ribbons.

"You had yours around your neck when I ran into you in the hotel hallway," she reminded him.

He studied her for several seconds, his steady gaze shooting tingles down her spine. "The fluorescent lights made your reddish hair look like spun gold."

He'd said those words to her that night. For the first time in her life she'd felt beautiful.

A self-conscious-sounding laugh escaped him. "I knew you were Rory's girl, but I took a step toward you anyway."

As if to illustrate, he slid closer.

Prim's heart gave a lurch.

"And I," Prim inhaled the intoxicating scent of his shampoo and soap, "took a step toward you."

"Then I," Max gently brushed a strand of hair back from her face with the palm of his hand, "did this."

He pressed his lips against hers, and she found his mouth just as warm and just as sweet as it had been back then.

Prim slid her arms around his neck, weaving her fingers through his silky hair. When his tongue swept across her lips, she opened for him and he deepened the kiss.

The pressure of his arousal through the thin fabric of her shirt should have been a wake-up call. Instead it was as if kerosene had been tossed on an already roaring fire.

"You're so beautiful," Max murmured against her mouth as his fingers cupped the nape of her neck.

His other hand flattened against her lower back, drawing her up against the length of his body.

Prim gave in to impulse and planted a kiss at the base of his throat. His skin was salty beneath her lips.

She didn't care if this made sense or not; right now being in Max's arms was the only place she wanted to be.

"M-om. Boris won't move."

Prim stiffened. It was Connor's voice. The dog had obviously sought refuge in the boy's bed. Prim had been down this road enough times to be confident if she didn't respond, he would keep calling and wake his twin. Callum would not hesitate to search for her.

"I should go." Max's hands dropped to his side but he made no move to get up.

Prim drew in a steadying breath. With the last ounce of common sense she possessed, she stood and moved to the door, opening it for him. "Thanks for everything, Max."

When he stepped onto the porch, he raised a hand as if to cup her cheek, let it fall without touching her. "Anytime."

Before he could turn away, Prim lunged at him, wrapping her arms around his neck, holding him tight, so tight. She buried her face in his shoulder.

His hand cupped the back of her head and his cheek rested against her hair.

Prim let herself cling, let herself lean, let herself believe this was a man who would stick.

A man worth taking a chance on.

Chapter Ten

Prim was the only thing on his mind when Max awoke the next morning. Still in bed, he rolled over and grabbed his phone from the nightstand.

Everything okay? he texted.

All good, she texted back. Thanks for coming to my rescue last night.

Always.

Once he'd confirmed all was well in Prim's household, Max was up and out the door. He'd promised to help Beck set up tables in the town square for a pancake feed that would follow the popular Hometown Heroes parade.

This parade, intended to honor those who'd served in the military as well as those currently serving, always made him think of his father.

Brian Brody had been killed in action in Bosnia when Max had been in kindergarten.

The sad thing was, he didn't remember his father. But he would honor him and all other soldiers today. Max's patriotic pride stirred the second he stepped from his house and saw all the American flags flying from porches.

The Independence Day celebration was a month-long event in Good Hope. The gazebo that anchored the town square had already been decked out with patriotic fan bunting. Strategically placed red and white geraniums in bright blue pots encircled the perimeter of the white-lacquered wood building. Small American flags on pencil-thin sticks had been placed in each pot.

Typical small-town stuff, Max thought, experiencing a surge of pride in the community he called home.

The large flag, which fluttered year-round from a twenty-foot flag-pole, was currently being raised by members of Boy Scout Troop #1022. A lump formed in Max's throat as he watched the pint-size flag bearers salute the stars and stripes.

As far as Max was concerned, every boy should be a scout. Like his father, he'd made it all the way to the rank of Eagle Scout. He wondered if Prim planned to get the twins involved in scouting. Because of their adventurous spirits, Max had no doubt Callum and Connor would enjoy the varied activities the organization had to offer. At six, the twins were the right age to start. He would mention the possibility to Prim the next time he saw her.

Max turned his attention away from the scouts and focused on the activities around him. The pancake machine had been set up and was being checked. The warming ovens had been turned on in preparation for the sausage links that would be brought from the Muddy Boots kitchen at regular intervals.

Stacks of vinyl-covered tablecloths striped in red and white and edged in blue with white stars sat piled on chairs, ready to cover long, rectangular tables. That, of course, couldn't happen until the truck came and he and Beck got the tables unloaded.

As if thinking about the task had conjured up the vehicle, a truck bearing the logo of a local rental business rolled up and parked. For the next hour he and Beck removed eight-foot-long banquet tables from the back. The tables, with their folding legs, ended up being more awkward than heavy.

Unfortunately, the physical labor didn't keep Max's mind as occupied as he'd hoped. His thoughts kept returning to Prim.

What had he been thinking, kissing her that way? If one of the boys hadn't called out, clothes may have hit the floor, along with his common sense.

Though Max ached to make love to her, he didn't think that would be wise. But damn, he wanted her.

"Something on your mind?"

Max jerked his head to the side and found Beck's dark eyes on him. All around them people hustled, including nearly eighty high school band members. High-pitched teenage chatter and laughter mingled with the squeaks and squawks of instruments being tuned.

"Are there more tables to unload?" Max blurted out the first thing that came to mind, then realized it was a stupid question considering the truck was now empty.

He expected Beck to laugh. Instead a thoughtful look crossed his friend's face. "Let's get some coffee."

"And food." Filling his empty belly seemed something positive to focus on.

"Ami sent me off this morning with a bag of scones."

"What kind?"

Beck grabbed a white sack and glanced inside. "Looks like lemon blueberry."

"That works."

Grabbing a cup, Max filled it from one of the commercial coffee machines that had been set up near the refreshment area.

"Is there anything else that needs to be done before we take a break?" His stomach growled as he fixed his gaze on the sack Beck held between his fingers.

"We've completed our assignment. The first one, anyway." Beck motioned to a couple of chairs under a large shade tree. "Once the parade starts we'll move to our stations for the pancake feed. For now, it's relax and recharge."

Max dropped down into the empty chair and accepted a scone from Beck. One quick bite told him the pastry was up to Ami's high standards. "Where is the little woman this morning?"

Beck grinned. "I dare you to call her that to her face."

"No way." Max chuckled. "She'd cut me off at the knees."

They both laughed, knowing that sweet, good-natured Ami Bloom-Cross would never cut anyone off at the knees. But she might restrict access to her mouthwatering pastries and desserts. That was an even more frightening prospect.

"I just wondered where she was keeping herself this fine morning." Max took another bite of scone and chewed. "You and she are usually joined at the hip."

"My *wife*," Beck lingered on the word as if simply saying it brought him pleasure, "and I enjoy spending time together. But she had a couple of things to finish up at home. She'll be here shortly to man the pancake machine."

"If Ami is cooking, I'll skip a second scone and save room for a real breakfast." Max popped the last piece of pastry into his mouth and glanced around, his gaze drawn to the group of women who'd just arrived.

He recognized them as Cherries. Apparently they'd been assigned the task of setting up chairs and spreading tablecloths. Disappointment surged when he didn't see Prim among them.

"I just got a text. Prim finally called Ami and told her about the trouble in your neighborhood last night." Beck's casual tone didn't fool either of them.

Beck had been as upset as Max about the almost break-in at Prim's home. Max had given him all the details while they'd put up tables, but it appeared Beck wanted to revive the topic.

"I'm glad you were there for her."

"I'll always be there for her."

If Beck found anything odd about the statement, it didn't show. He rubbed his chin. "Makes me think I should get a dog."

"Might not be a bad idea."

"This guy still being on the loose isn't good." Beck tapped a finger against his leg. "If he isn't caught by the day of the big parade, people might not show up to watch or might cancel their participation. Empty homes are ripe for the picking."

Max swore. "That never crossed my mind."

"We'll just have to hope Len catches the guy before then." Beck brushed some crumbs from his lap, then stood. "Those were some good thoughts you and Prim had on the parade."

"Yours about having the lineup crew wear caps that say 'parade' for better identification wasn't half bad."

Beck grinned. "Just another moment of brilliance."

"Who said anything about brilliance?" Max asked, then dodged a punch.

"You showed your own brilliance"—Beck grinned—"by not getting involved with Charlotte. She and Prim aren't even in the same league."

Max just smiled. It didn't matter that Beck was operating under the delusion that what he and Prim had could turn serious. Despite the strong attraction, after seeing the urn Max feared he and Prim had as much chance of ending up together as Fin and her old high school flame, Jeremy Rakes.

And that was no chance at all.

———————

After leaving the boys happily playing with their grandfather, Prim drove straight to her sister's home. Later that morning she and Ami would work the pancake feed. Before they made the trek to the town square, she'd agreed to spend an hour helping her sister sort through their mother's recipe cards.

Prim was of the mind that if her older sister hadn't found the recipe for lavender cookies with rose water icing in the four years since their mother's passing, it was not to be found.

After parking in the driveway, she followed the sidewalk around to the front porch. She still found it difficult to believe that her sister now called this grand house her home.

The stately Victorian sat at the corner of the highway and Market Street, an immense two-story white clapboard with green shutters. Stained glass topped each window. A black iron fence enclosed a yard that spanned two lots. Mature trees shaded a spread of sprawling green accented with clusters of colorful flowers and perfectly manicured bushes.

Red, white, and lavender-blue impatiens mingled with wax begonias and variegated ivy in the hanging baskets that decorated the porch. The scene was so charming that Prim found herself smiling as she climbed the steps and rang the bell. The chimes had barely sounded when the door flew open and she was enveloped in a hug.

"Ohmigoodness, I was so worried about you." Ami hugged her tight. "I can't believe that horrible man was in your backyard."

"Boris and the deputies ran him off."

"And Max made sure you were okay."

Prim's lips lifted. When she'd called and told her sister the whole story that morning, Max's role had been Ami's favorite part of the story. And, Prim had to admit, hers as well.

"All's well that ends well. I doubt the burglar will be visiting our neighborhood again anytime soon." Prim followed her sister deeper into the house, taking in the shiny hardwood floors that gleamed as if they'd been hand polished.

The dark wood paneling that had graced the foyer at Christmas had been painted a bright white. The Anaglypta paper that Ami had said was impossible to remove had been painted a blue gray. The color added a contemporary twist to the hall, while the antique rug retained the feel of an older era.

Prim lightly danced her fingers over the hand-painted porcelain bowl gracing an elegant foyer table. "Callum and Connor would have this on the floor in under three minutes."

"I know better than that." Ami chuckled. "My nephews are exceptionally well-behaved."

"Keep your delusions." Prim patted Ami's arm.

She tried. God knew she tried hard to teach the twins manners. But they were rambunctious boys and could benefit from a man's influence. Another plus for being back in Good Hope and near her father.

"Even though he'd just seen them last night, Dad was superexcited to have the boys over. When I got to his place, he was making them scrambled eggs. He said they needed protein to tide them over until the pancake feed."

They reached the back of the house and Ami paused by the kitchen. "Did you have some?"

"I'm not hungry." Prim stepped into the dining room and let her fingers trail along the massive sideboard graced by a multicolored floral arrangement that not only filled the air with sweet perfume but provided a nice splash of color. "Last night, well, everything threw me off."

"The burglar? Or Max?"

She'd told her sister how kind Max had been, but knowing Beck had been with Ami when she'd called, Prim had kept the explanation of the events that had unfolded pretty basic. Taking a seat, Prim gazed unseeingly at the tabletop strewn with recipe cards and books and sighed heavily. "Both."

"As I plan to drag every last detail out of you and I am hungry, I'm going to bring in some lemon chia oat bars for us to munch on." Ami smiled. "And coffee. I just brewed a pot. Then the interrogation will begin."

"Oh, goody," Prim drawled, but found she was eager to share her confusing feelings with her sister.

While she waited for Ami to return, Prim picked up a recipe book. Flipping it open, she found pages of recipe cards tucked into little plastic slots, all transcribed in her mother's neat, precise handwriting.

Tears stung the backs of her eyes. Prim hadn't completely blinked them away when her sister swept into the room. The folk art serving tray she carried held a carafe, two mugs of coffee, and a plate of bars.

Ami paused, her gaze dropping to the book Prim still held. A look of understanding filled her eyes. "The cards bring back memories. See the ones with the stars in the corner? Those were the ones everyone in the family liked."

"I miss her." Prim stared at the card in her hand. "I wish I could talk with her now."

Ami placed the tray on the table, handed Prim a mug, then nudged the plate with the bars closer. "It's hard when there's something in your life you want to share with her. I think of all those confusing feelings I had when I first met Beck. I really wanted her at my wedding."

"We were lucky to have had her for our mom." Prim sighed. "We could talk with her about anything."

Ami nodded. After taking a slow sip of coffee, she wrapped her hands around the cup.

"I used to believe that things would make more sense when I got older. I've discovered sometimes life just gets more confusing." Prim ran her finger around the edge of one of the recipe cards, her thoughts returning, as they had all morning, to Max.

"Mom may be gone, but you can talk to me. About anything." Ami reached over and gave Prim's hand a squeeze. Instead of releasing it immediately, she held on, those green eyes steady on Prim's.

"I think I'm falling in love with Max," Prim blurted out. "Or maybe I always have been, just a little."

If the admission shocked Ami, it didn't show.

"He's so great. So good to me and the boys. We share so many interests and we have fun. He seems to genuinely like spending time with me."

"Of course he does, why wouldn't he?"

"Rory didn't." Prim dropped her gaze to the recipe cards. "Or, he did, but not as much as he liked his adventures with his friends."

"Max isn't Rory."

"I know, but I'm still scared."

Ami's fingers tightened on her hand. "Tell me what you're scared of?"

"That Max will grow tired of me." Prim whispered the words though she and Ami were alone in the house. "That I won't be enough to keep his interest."

"Oh, honey." Ami reached up with her free hand to brush a lock of hair back from her sister's face, the gesture reminding Prim of something their mother might have done. "You're a wonderful woman, and any man would be lucky to have you in his life."

"I'm scared, Ami. It's not just me this time, it's Callum and Connor who'd suffer if things go bad."

"They'll also benefit from having a father in their life."

"I'm not sure if Max even wants a serious relationship."

Ami sat back, startled surprise blanketing her features. "What makes you say that?"

"He told me he doesn't do casual relationships with single moms."

Ami brought a finger to her mouth. "I believe the key word here is 'casual.' Max isn't the kind to go in and out of a child's life. He knows what that feels like."

Prim was embarrassed to admit the thought gave her a spurt of hope. She flipped the recipe card over in her hands.

"And it isn't as if you're walking down the aisle tomorrow."

Prim dropped the card to the table as if it had suddenly turned red-hot. "I didn't say anything about marriage."

"First comes love, then comes marriage . . ." Ami said in a singsong tone, her eyes dancing before turning serious. "All I'm saying is give it time, trust your heart."

"Okay. I'll think about it." Prim began riffling through the loose recipe cards. "We're looking for the recipe for lavender cookies with rose water icing, right?"

Ami sighed, obviously sensing the heart-to-heart had come to a close. She picked up one of the recipe books but didn't open it. "I've been through these dozens of times. I'm hoping it'll be like that bottle of ketchup you're searching for in the grocery store aisle you can't find. You ask for help and discover it's been right in front of you all along."

The cookies had been Sarah Bloom's favorite. Though Ami and their mother had made them every year together, once their mother died, Ami had struggled to recall the exact ingredients. None of the variations she tried measured up to the original.

For several minutes, the two women worked in companionable silence as they pored through the books and individual cards.

"I hope you found a way to suitably thank Max for coming to your rescue last night."

Seeing where this was headed and knowing she couldn't stop it, Prim set down the cards in her hand. "I said thank you."

"That's all?" Ami put a hand to her chest and adopted a faux-shocked expression. "You pull the guy out of bed in the middle of the night and all he gets is a peck on the cheek and a thank-you?"

"It was a nice kiss," Prim muttered. *A very nice kiss.*

"I'll be the judge of that." Curiosity danced in her sister's eyes, and for a second Prim was reminded of the nosy older sister who was always trying to steal her diary. "Open mouthed or closed?"

Prim's lips twitched. "MYOB."

"Open. Good."

Prim laughed. She couldn't help it. "I don't know how your husband puts up with you."

Ami leaned forward. "I'm great in bed."

"Oh, for goodness' sakes."

"Don't be such a prude. And don't tell me having sex with Max didn't cross your mind." Ami's tone invited confidences.

Prim flushed. "Regardless of how, ah, enticing that might sound, you forget I have two little boys in my house."

"You forget you have a sister in town." Ami shot her a sunny smile. "Anytime you get the urge, bring them here. Beck and I would love to watch them while you have sex with Max."

Prim rolled her eyes. "Ami . . ."

"I'm serious. It's time to put all those lascivious thoughts into action."

Prim swallowed past the sudden dryness in her throat at the thought. She lifted the mug to her lips, took a long drink, and picked up a recipe card.

Chapter Eleven

"Finally." Beck dropped the plastic utensils in his hand on the table and rose.

"What is it?" Max kept his eyes focused on the task in front of him. Who knew rolling silverware took such concentration?

"The womenfolk cometh."

Max's heart gave a lurch. He scrambled to his feet to stand beside Beck. He'd been waiting all morning for Prim to show up.

Maybe it was the blue-green color of her dress or the way her hair hung loose around her shoulders, the hints of red in it as vibrant as the rising sun, but as Prim made her way across the courtyard, she reminded him of a sea goddess rising from the mist.

"If they didn't keep stopping to talk to everyone and their dog, they'd be here by now," Max sputtered. "How many times can two women stop and start?"

"The problem is, between the two of them they know practically everyone here," Beck said in a resigned tone. "They have to stop and say hello."

That may have been true with all the others, but they did more than simply say hello to David and Clay Chapin. Granted, Prim spent a minute speaking to Brynn, David's young daughter.

But when she shifted her attention and smiled at Clay, a tightness gripped his chest. Clay had always been popular with the ladies. You'd never see the high school principal spending time on a sudoku puzzle or a magic cube. For a second, Max forgot he considered Clay to be a friend.

Beck slapped Max on the shoulder and jerked his head toward Prim and Clay. "They make a nice-looking couple."

Two could play this game.

"David and Ami?" Max slammed the ball neatly back into Beck's court. "They do look good together. Too bad they're both married."

Beck's scowl had him grinning. When he saw Prim walk away from Clay, he relaxed and returned his attention to rolling plastic silverware into paper napkins.

Despite staying focused on the task, Max knew the instant Prim walked up. He inhaled the fresh citrus scent he was coming to associate with her and lifted his head.

She stood before him, two spots of color high in her cheeks. "Hi, Max."

"Hi." He searched her face. "How are you feeling this morning? I hope you were able to get some sleep last night."

"I'm fine. I, ah, had a little difficulty drifting off." She waved a vague hand. "All the excitement and everything."

Her gaze met his, and he found himself wondering, hoping, some of that difficulty was because of him.

Prim turned to her sister. "I know you're making the pancakes. What's my assignment?"

Before Ami could respond, Beck stepped forward and greeted his wife by pulling her into his arms and kissing her soundly. "I missed you."

Ami looped her arms around his neck. "I missed you, too."

Max made a gagging sound. When they turned to him, he lifted a hand to his mouth, as if covering a cough.

Beck scowled.

Ami looked amused.

Max swore he heard Prim chuckle.

Beck kissed his wife's forehead, then stepped back. "While you make pancakes, I'll supervise the sausages coming from the kitchen. Dakota is going to be the roving troubleshooter. She'll let us know if any position requires additional help."

Beck turned to him. "You're in charge of adding sausages to the pancake plates."

Max shrugged. "Wherever I'm needed."

Ami picked a clipboard off a nearby table, frowned. "Prim is on the list to supervise the refreshment table."

"Okay." Prim glanced around.

"You'll be way over there." Ami pointed to a freestanding oasis a good distance from the food tables. About as far from Max and his sausage duty as she could get. "You job is to make sure we don't run out of coffee and juice."

Prim glanced at Max, lifted her shoulders, and let them fall. "Sure."

Steve arrived with the twins to grab Prim for a few minutes before the pancake feed commenced. Max watched the end of the parade with the Chapin family.

Brynn, David's daughter, was a pretty little girl with blond hair and big blue eyes. She wore a short, pink ballerina skirt and a T-shirt displaying the face of a princess holding a glittery wand.

"Brynn is looking forward to starting T-ball." David smiled down at his daughter, then back up at Max. "It was nice of you to step up and agree to coach."

Max smiled at the child in the frilly skirt eating a wad of rainbow cotton candy.

"Katie Ruth called me three times to ask if I'd volunteer. The last time she said she was desperate." Max cocked his head. "I'm surprised you didn't do it. You have a child on the team and you're more than qualified. If I recall correctly, you played varsity ball in college."

David glanced at his daughter, who'd stuffed the last of the cotton candy in her mouth, obviously anticipating the candy-tossing clowns who were now less than a block away.

"I considered it, but practice is during a time when I'm usually on a conference call." David, a successful architect and partner in a Chicago firm, worked primarily out of his home.

"Let Whitney know I can take Brynn to practice when she's out of town," Clay told his brother.

"I'm not counting on Whitney. These days she's gone more than she's home." Irritation mixed with frustration in David's tone. As if he'd said more than he'd intended, he clamped his mouth shut. "I appreciate the offer, Clay. But I've already arranged for Camille to take and pick up."

Max cocked his head. "Camille?"

"Brynn's nanny," David explained. "The woman is a gem."

"I didn't realize Whitney worked outside of the home." Max tried to recall what he knew about the socialite whom David had met and married nearly a decade earlier while living in Chicago.

"She doesn't." David's tone was measured and gave no indication of his feelings on the matter. "She travels a lot and doesn't like being tied down with the day-to-day."

A voice over the PA system gave a five-minute warning for pancake feed volunteers to take their stations. Max looked for Prim as he took his spot, but people had already begun lining up, and they blocked his view of the refreshment table.

Gladys Bertholf nudged him not-so-softly with one bony elbow. "Those plates are going to need sausages on them."

Max had been startled when he'd learned Eliza had assigned the ninety-six-year-old to sausage duty. As volunteer jobs went, it was a relatively fast-paced one.

As the feeding frenzy began, he quickly discovered Gladys was more into supervising than doing any actual work. When she wasn't telling him to pick up the pace, she was socializing.

"See and be seen" appeared to be her mantra.

She definitely stood out in her leopard-print dress and filmy purple cape. No mundane red, white, and blue for the woman with the jet-black hair and bold skunk stripe. But it wasn't just Gladys's flamboyant appearance that drew people to her; her vivacious personality made her stand out in any crowd.

She chatted and preened while Max rushed to do her job and his, too. But she was so obviously enjoying the day that he couldn't hold her lack of initiative against her.

"How's it going here?" Dakota, holding a clipboard and looking festive in blue shorts and an Uncle Sam tee, took in the situation.

Since Max was on a dead run, Gladys spoke with the girl. After a couple of minutes Dakota nodded and moved on.

"Is she getting another person to help us?" Max asked, grabbing another pan of sausages as the line backed up.

Surprise skittered across the woman's face. "I think two is more than adequate," she told him. "Although I did mention to Dakota—isn't that a lovely name?—that I was getting fatigued."

Can a person get worn out from too much talking? Max dismissed the uncharitable thought the moment it arose.

Gladys was elderly—though he'd never use that word within her hearing—and right now her cheeks appeared a bit flushed. Although it might be simply a case of too much rouge.

"I requested Dakota send over another volunteer," Gladys continued, then stepped forward to greet another friend.

Five more minutes passed. Gladys continued to socialize, although she seemed to now be hyping *George M*, the musical that would open at the community playhouse next week. A musical in which she had a starring role.

"Dakota said you needed me?"

Max's head jerked up at the familiar lilting voice, then he realized Prim wasn't speaking to him. Her gaze was focused on Gladys, who was all smiles.

"Thank you so much for coming." The older woman held out both hands to Prim, air-kissed each of her cheeks. "You're just in time."

Prim smiled hesitantly. "What can I help you with?"

The line had backed up again, so Max didn't wait for the answer. He returned to adding sausages to the platters of pancakes.

Suddenly Prim was beside him, grabbing sausages with the extra set of tongs Gladys hadn't once touched.

He slanted a sideways glance. "What are you doing?"

"What does it look like? Gladys asked me to exchange places with her. She said the pace was too slow for her."

Max couldn't help but grin. Almost immediately he and Prim fell into a comfortable rhythm that kept the food lines flowing smoothly. Working side by side with Prim had turned the overcast day bright and sunny.

"Max. Prim. Big smiles."

Heads close together, they glanced up at the same time.

Gladys snapped a picture. After glancing at her phone to check the shot, the older woman beamed. "You two make the cutest couple."

Without another word, the star of community theater swept off into the crowd.

"What just happened?" Max asked.

"I'd say we were punked." Prim laughed and shook her head. "By a real pro."

"How was the pancake feed?" Steve Bloom leaned back in his deck chair, the picture of contentment in a madras shirt, Bermuda shorts, and slip-on sneakers.

"Judging by the crowds, I'd say a huge success." Prim lifted the glass of sun tea her father had pressed on her when she'd arrived to pick up the boys.

"The boys wanted to come home and play, so we didn't stay long." Her dad's gaze settled on his soaking-wet grandsons, a fond smile on his lips. "I'm glad you brought their suits."

"I thought they might want to run through the sprinkler." She winced as a water balloon hit Connor square in the face. But her youngest only laughed with glee and pelted his brother in the chest. "I'm sure this is much more fun."

"They're great boys, Prim." He slanted a glance at her as he sipped his tea. "I'm so happy you moved back. Three hours away was three hours too far."

"You know I loved Milwaukee." She leaned back in the Adirondack chair and smiled. "But Good Hope is home."

"Losing that job of yours ended up being a blessing in disguise."

"It did." When the company she'd worked for since college had been bought out and she'd been offered a severance package, she'd taken the money and run . . . straight back to Good Hope.

Prim took a long drink of tea and lifted her face to the sun, reveling in the warmth on her skin. "I hated to uproot the boys, but this way they can grow up surrounded by family."

"With the money from the insurance settlement, you'll be able to stay at home with the boys."

"I'll probably find something part-time once they're back in school, but you're right, it does give me some options." Prim sighed. "I just wished it didn't feel like blood money."

"Your husband lost his life because someone in that factory didn't do his job. You should be able to count on a climbing harness doing its job." Steve's face turned grave. "Rory should have been able to count on it."

"I know. That's why I pursued the case." Prim had let her lawyers do their best, not just for Rory but for his sons. Because of the money she'd soon receive, instead of rushing the twins to day care every morning, then picking them up with just enough time for dinner, baths, and a bedtime story, she was able to be at home with her boys.

"Earth to Prim."

Her father's teasing words had her turning in his direction.

"Sorry, Dad." She offered an apologetic smile. "I didn't sleep well last night after all the commotion, and I'm a bit spacy."

"I wished you'd called me. But I'm glad Max was there for you." He studied her for several seconds. "There isn't anyone I trust more."

Prim wasn't sure how to respond to that pronouncement. "He's a good neighbor."

A smile tugged at the corners of her father's mouth. "I got the feeling at your housewarming he may be more than just a neighbor."

Prim felt her face warm. "We're, ah, close friends as well."

Her father absently rubbed the condensation off his glass with a thumb. "Going through life without someone you love beside you can be lonely."

Thinking of Rory—and how distant he'd been the last year before he died—she was tempted to tell her dad it could be lonely even when you were with someone you loved. But something in his eyes had her reconsidering. This conversation wasn't about her anymore.

"You and Mom were always so close. You did everything together." Prim spoke softly, hoping to soothe. But when the lines on his forehead only deepened, she reached across the table to squeeze his hand. "I can't imagine what it'd be like to lose a spouse who was also your best friend."

Only after the words left her mouth did she realize that she'd dissed Rory by the thoughtless comment. Thankfully, her dad didn't appear to notice.

His fingers tightened around hers for the briefest of seconds, then relaxed.

"It helped having Ami here. Watching her find her soul mate reminded me of all the good times your mother and I shared. And Beck is a good man." Coming from her father, that was high praise. "Now I have you and the boys. With children, everything seems new and fresh again."

His eyes softened as his gaze shifted to where the twins were now taking turns pointing the sprinkler at each other. Tattered remnants of what once were brightly colored balloons lay scattered at their feet.

"I love those boys." Those hazel eyes, so like her own, returned to her. "I love *you*, Primrose."

"I love you, too, Daddy." A lump rose to her throat. "Very much. I want you to be happy."

"I know you do." Steve took a long sip of tea. "Anita is a good woman."

"You've been dating for a while now." Prim kept her tone conversational.

"We have fun together." Her father's lips quirked in a lopsided smile. "Most of the time, anyway."

"Relationships aren't always easy."

"Tell me about it." He laughed, a low, pleasant rumbling sound. "I never imagined I'd be dating again at my age. But we all need someone."

Was that what was going on here? Could it simply be that her father was lonely for companionship and Anita filled that void?

"I'm lucky that way." Prim's gaze settled on her dad and her heart filled with love. "I have my boys and my sisters. And you."

"Sometimes a person needs more," her dad said.

"Not always." An image of Max surfaced but was quickly shoved aside. "I'm perfectly happy with my life just the way it is, at least for right now. I don't need more."

Chapter Twelve

Maybe she did need more, Prim thought to herself as she strolled down Good Hope's Main Street with her father and Anita. The boys ran ahead, but close enough she could keep her eyes on them.

There was something a bit pathetic about being twenty-eight years old and being the fifth wheel on your father's Saturday-night date with his girlfriend.

Until he'd hooked up with Anita, her dad had displayed good judgment in all parts of his life. Prim slanted a sideways glance at the divorcée, dressed casually—but seductively—in a clingy jersey dress with a scooped neck that showed an ample amount of cleavage.

It was easy to see how her dad had been sucked in. Anita was an attractive woman and she could be charming. At fifty-nine, her father still had a lot of life to live. While something in her rebelled against her *dad* having any kind of sexual needs, she wondered if that was a large part of his attraction to Anita.

Prim frowned. Could that be what was going on between her and Max? Simple physical need between two people with a lot of life to live? It felt like so much more, but then what did she know?

"What in the world are they doing?"

Anita's irritated voice had Prim's head swiveling. By the woman's shrill tone, Prim expected Connor and Callum to be swimming in a mud puddle or climbing onto the hood of a parked Mercedes. Instead, one of the boys must have brought a rubber snake with him. When one twin tossed it high into the air, the other would catch it.

Since they seemed to be avoiding bumping into anyone—a miracle—Prim had no problem with the harmless game. Neither, apparently, did her father.

"They're being boys, Anita." The affection in his tone warmed Prim's heart. "Having fun."

"I always made my girls stand right beside me whenever we went out." Anita's tone was milder than it could have been, but the censure came through loud and clear.

When the muscle in her father's jaw jumped, Prim knew he'd caught it, too.

"Sounds like we have another good band this year." This time Steve spoke directly to Prim.

"Music in the Square is one of my favorite pre-Fourth activities." Prim let her gaze linger on the red-white-and-blue street banners that decorated each light pole.

Festivities were planned for every weekend leading up to the main event. The businesses they passed, as well as the ones up ahead, already sported patriotic themes and colors.

Because of the crowds swarming the square, they'd had to park several blocks away.

"I can't believe you couldn't find anything closer, Steve," Anita griped. "By the time we get to the square my feet are going to be killing me."

Personally, Prim thought Anita complained just to get her father to look at her shiny red toenails and strappy heeled wedges. Unlike Anita, this evening she'd gone for comfort.

She'd tossed on a white eyelet dress and let her hair go wild, then grabbed a pair of her most comfortable shoes. Though her father had wanted them to all ride together, she'd driven separately, compromising by parking next to him and Anita. She wanted the flexibility of being able to leave whenever the boys got too rowdy or she could no longer take Anita's whining.

The crowds around them began to thicken and Prim called the boys back to them. They came willingly, showing their grandfather the realistic-looking snake and chattering how their mom had promised them a snow cone if they were good.

As the twins fell into step beside the older man, one grandson on each side, Prim found herself stuck beside Anita.

Make an effort, Prim told herself. "How are Lindsay and Cassie doing?"

Although Prim had been younger than either of Anita's two daughters, she'd been acquainted with both of them.

"Lindsay is still working as a floral designer at the Enchanted Florist." Anita's tone conveyed mild disapproval. "I told her on our shopping trip this weekend that she should be owning her own shop, not working in one."

It took all of Prim's self-restraint not to bring up Bernie, the Bagel King. It was Anita's divorce several years ago from the bagel magnate that had given her the money to start her own business.

"Dad works for the school system and he's perfectly happy." Prim kept her tone light. "He certainly doesn't feel the need to have his own business."

Prim glanced pointedly at her father, but he was wiggling the snake and making the twins squeal.

"That's totally different." Anita sniffed but cast a worried glance in Steve's direction.

Satisfied her point had been made, Prim smiled and changed the subject. "Is Lindsay dating anyone?"

"She's barely thirty." Anita bristled. "Not everyone jumps into marriage directly out of college."

Prim absorbed the punch and wondered if the boys would prefer going for ice cream over hearing the band. Only because she knew leaving so early would stress her dad, she tried again. "How's Cassie? Her daughter, Dakota, seems like a lovely girl. She was a big help at the pancake feed this morning."

Anita adjusted the purse strap on her shoulder. "Cassie and I have been estranged in recent years. Because of that I've been kept from my grandchildren."

That comment fell squarely into the bucket of "the truth according to Anita." Prim recalled quite clearly when Anita had washed her hands of Cassie—and her children—when her daughter had refused to follow her dictates. In deference to her father's fondness for Anita, Prim chose not to muddy the waters with any pesky facts. "I'm sorry to hear that."

"It happens in even the best families." Anita's hands fluttered like a bird in the air. "Now that Cassie has kicked that loser, Clint Gourley, out of her house, I'm hopeful we can reconnect."

Prim decided it best not to mention she'd run across loser Clint at the beach.

"Did Dad tell you the boys will be visiting Rory's parents in a couple of weeks?" Prim kept her tone conversational, still searching for neutral ground.

"I don't believe he mentioned it." The tension on Anita's face eased. "I've always enjoyed Deb Delaney. A wonderful woman and so devoted to her son. I remember when Rory was diagnosed. Deb and Mike were devastated. But of course, what else would you expect? Their only child had received a death sentence."

While the medical community had made great strides in recent years with CF treatment, back when Rory had been diagnosed, the outlook had been grim. As a parent, Prim couldn't imagine getting such news.

"I can't imagine what a relief it was that neither of your boys has CF. It being genetic and all." Anita exhaled a heavy, melodramatic breath. "That was quite a risk you took. Well, I guess that's why Rory had never planned on having children. But what's meant to be will be, right?"

People, Prim thought, *need to keep their mouths shut.*

It was true Rory hadn't been planning for children. Neither of them had. When he told her he would have a vasectomy, she'd understood completely. They'd both been terrified when they found out she was pregnant. For weeks Rory had been beside himself with guilt over the thought he might have passed his disease on to his child.

From the moment they heard those twin heartbeats, there was never any question that her getting pregnant was the best thing that had ever happened. Rory wanted the babies as much as she did, and not even the worry that the boys might have inherited CF was going to dampen their joy. After all, hadn't Rory been living proof that you could have a life bigger than your disease?

Deb had blamed her for the pregnancy, obviously forgetting it took two to tango.

Prim could still hear the hurtful words Deb had hurled at her when she found out. Rory had quickly put an end to that, and ever since, Deb had been civil to her, but Prim wasn't sure she could ever completely forgive or forget.

The boys had been a blessing then and they were a blessing now.

"Walking this far is ridiculous," Anita whined, limping a little.

Prim was about to suggest Anita sit on one of the benches and they could pick her up later when Connor shouted and waved wildly. "Hi, Mr. Brody."

Prim shifted her gaze from a sulking Anita and found herself staring directly into Max's vivid blue eyes.

"This is quite the party crowd." Max extended a hand to Prim's father and smiled at Anita and Prim before turning his attention to the boys. "What's that I see peeking out of your pocket?"

Quick as a ninja, Callum jerked the snake from his pocket and shoved it into Max's face.

"Whoa." Max jumped back, hands raised as if ready to fend off an attack. Though he did his best to look startled, he couldn't keep from smiling.

"It's not real." Connor moved forward and touched Max's hand. "It can't hurt you."

Max pretended to wipe sweat from his brow. "That's a relief."

Callum jeered. "You were scared."

"Connor. Callum. Oh, whichever one you are." Anita tossed up her hands in frustration. "You need to apologize to Mr. Brody. That was not amusing."

"Easy, there." Steve put a hand on Anita's shoulder. "It was a boyish prank. No harm done."

His tone might have been mild, but there was a distinct warning in his eyes.

Anita pressed her lips together. If she were a teapot, Max had no doubt she'd be spewing steam right about now.

He turned his attention to Prim. She'd appeared to be fighting a smile when the snake had made its appearance. In the simple, white dress with her hair tumbling around her shoulders, she looked as refreshing as a cool glass of lemonade.

He'd always had a particular affinity for lemonade.

"Are you here with a date?" Anita's question broke through his thoughts.

He cocked his head and casually blocked the punch Callum aimed at his midsection.

"Callum," Prim said sharply. "What are you doing?"

The boy lifted a skinny shoulder and let it drop.

"Being a boy." Max placed a hand on the child's head and gave him a noogie.

He squealed with delight.

"Charlotte seems like such a lovely woman." Anita glanced around as if expecting the brunette to walk up at any moment. "Both beautiful and successful."

Max sensed Prim's watchful gaze.

"Where is she this evening?" Anita pressed, much like a dog bent on a particularly delectable bone.

"I believe Charlotte is back in Chicago."

Anita raised a skeptical brow. "You don't know?"

"She mentioned something about catching a flight to Midway this morning."

Anita's eyes brightened. "Oh, so you're saying she spent the night."

Max blew out an exasperated breath, wondering how Steve stood this woman. "What I'm saying is that Charlotte and I are casual acquaintances, nothing more."

Rolling his shoulders against sudden tightness, Max cast a glance at the twins. They'd lost interest in the conversation and were running circles around each other on the sidewalk.

Even though the boys seemed fully occupied with the impromptu game, Max lowered his voice and focused on Steve, ignoring Anita.

"What did you think about the excitement in my neighborhood last night?"

"I don't like it one bit. It worries me that Prim and the boys are in that house alone." Steve's gaze met his. "Thank you again for coming to my daughter's assistance."

"Prim should have called the sheriff before she called Max." Anita glanced at Steve. "Don't you agree?"

"I don't." Steve's eyes were cool. "I believe my daughter responded appropriately."

"I agree," Max said, his tone as cool as Steve's eyes.

Anita opened her mouth, then closed it, appearing to reconsider what she'd been about to say. She offered a bright smile. "Tom Larson, who cooks part-time for Beck, came into my shop this morning. We got to chatting."

From the self-satisfied gleam in the woman's eyes, Max had no doubt it had been Anita doing the majority of the talking, probably pumping the poor guy for information about Beck and Ami.

"Tom brought up the burglaries. We are both very concerned that one of these times someone is going to get hurt." Anita continued without taking a breath, "When Steve told me it was your house that had been targeted, I got the heebie-jeebies."

As if to illustrate, Anita visibly shivered.

"He broke into my neighbor's house," Prim clarified. "He just hid out in my backyard."

A slight frown slipped over Steve's face and worry filled the gaze he leveled on his daughter. "Maybe you and the boys should stay with me until this guy is caught."

"That's very kind." Prim reached over and gave her father a hug. "I appreciate the offer, but the boys and I will be fine. The door has a dead bolt and Boris is on duty."

Anita made a scoffing sound.

Prim's gaze pinned her. "Most articles say the best deterrent for robberies isn't a top-notch security system, but a loud, barking dog."

"Boris barked and barked last night." Connor looked up from a crouched position. "Woke me up."

Max exchanged a glance with Prim.

"I didn't hear anything," Callum announced.

"He was real loud," his twin insisted.

"Oh, sweetie." Prim leaned over, ran a hand across his hair. "I'm sorry he woke you."

"'s okay. Boris came back to bed and we went to sleep again."

"Sheriff Swarts should start thinking about retiring soon." Anita pursed her lips. "Before people run him out of town."

"Len Swarts is a good man." Steve, who Max knew considered the sheriff a friend, sounded impatient. "He's a very competent sheriff with good deputies. They'll catch this guy. We all need to be patient."

"I'm merely telling you what I hear in my shop, Steven." Anita's hazel eyes flashed. "Citizens are fed up with his excuses. If the public gets wind that Good Hope has criminals running wild in our community, well, I don't have to tell you what that could do to the tourist trade."

"He's a *burglar*, not a rapist or murderer." Prim's gaze narrowed on the woman. "Burglars target homes when the people who live there are away. The thief gets what he wants and no one gets hurt."

"Unless someone happens to be there when he breaks in and gets in his way," Anita warned. "Trust me, one of these times that's just what is going to happen."

Chapter Thirteen

"I'm gonna hit a home run," Callum announced from the backseat of the family car, bouncing up and down.

"Me too," Connor chimed in, though looking decidedly less confident than his older brother. "Will we really get to hit a ball?"

"I don't know." Prim and her sisters had played softball for fun, but T-ball for six-year-olds was a new experience.

As she drove to the ball field, she was grateful for the diversion. It kept her mind off Anita and her troubling comments. Prim told herself the odds that the burglar would return to a neighborhood where he'd nearly been caught were slim to none. The odds he'd come back to her house were even less.

Still, when leaving the house this afternoon, she'd not only secured the doors but had taken a few minutes to shut and lock the windows.

That hurt. No one should have to shut their windows in Good Hope. The breeze wafting in through the windows had been heavenly, and she loved the way fresh air made a house smell.

But Prim would take no chances. Not with the safety of Callum and Connor at stake. Shortly after the twins were born, Rory had made her promise she'd always look out for his sons. At first she'd been insulted. Until she'd taken a breath and seen beneath her husband's confident—often cocky—facade to the man who knew he wouldn't be around to watch his boys grow, to be their protector.

The promise he'd asked for didn't have anything to do with her and her abilities, but with him and his inability to protect. Rory had seen his future more clearly than she ever had. With a heavy heart, Prim had hugged him tight and made the promise.

During that last year, when his CF had worsened, instead of scaling back, Rory had pushed himself more. It had been a pattern since childhood.

Prim could have blamed his parents for his refusal to accept the limitation of his disease, but she knew they'd done their best. Guilty over the knowledge they'd both passed a defective gene to him, Deb and Mike had overindulged him. Yet because of their efforts, Rory had done better with his CF than most afflicted with the disease.

He'd been able to play sports, go to college, and marry. For four short years he'd even been able to experience the joys—and challenges—of fatherhood.

"We're here." Callum's shout filled the car as she made the turn into the parking lot.

"Save it for the outfield, buddy." Prim couldn't begrudge him his excitement when her own bubbled up inside her.

The twins were already out of the vehicle by the time Prim got out. They were both practically dancing with anticipation, and she could tell they would have loved to bolt full speed ahead to the field. "Stay right beside me. Drivers sometimes don't watch as closely as they should in parking lots."

"But we're late," Callum whined, shifting from one foot to the other.

She stopped the whine with a well-practiced stare.

Only when they reached the edge of the ball field did the boys break into a run, gloves flapping. The twins stopped at the edge of the kids gathered around Katie Ruth Crewes, suddenly unsure. The pretty blonde smiled when she saw Prim.

Seeing the excitement on the faces of her sons and hearing the chatter of the other children brought a wave of sadness. Despite Rory's preoccupation with his own extreme sports adventures, Prim knew he'd have enjoyed spending time with the boys as they got older, especially if the activity involved sports.

Prim gave a little wave to Gladys's granddaughter, Penny, and several other women she recognized. Her purse held the printed-out registration form and a check for the fees. She'd attempted to complete and submit the form online, but because the deadline had passed, the system wouldn't accept it.

"The receptionist I spoke with at the Y said it was okay that the boys didn't preregister, that there was room on this team. She said to print out the forms and bring them with me." Prim held out the papers and the check to Katie Ruth.

Katie Ruth took them both and fastened them to her clipboard. "Of course, we're happy to have the boys. We had room for two more. Now we're full."

The tension in Prim's shoulders eased. "Callum and Connor have been looking forward to this all day."

"Appears they're fitting right in."

Prim slanted a glance and saw the boys, or rather Callum, animatedly telling some story—undoubtedly a tall tale—to Brynn Chapin. "He loves to talk."

Katie Ruth grinned. "I was the same way at that age."

"Are you helping Max coach this afternoon?"

"Actually, I'm here as the overall coordinator for the YMCA's youth activities." Katie Ruth gestured with her head toward the man coming out of the clubhouse. "This is Max's first time coaching for us. I'm sticking around to make sure it all goes smoothly."

Prim swore Max's eyes lit up when he spotted her. When a slow smile spread across his lips, everything in her went warm and gooey. Her eyes remained glued to him as he strode across the ball field.

When he drew close, she stepped forward, but the kids immediately surrounded him, eager to get started.

Prim moved to sit in the stands with the rest of the parents. She didn't know when she'd enjoyed an hour more. The kids were a hoot to watch. Dropped balls. Stopping to play in the dirt. Brynn running after a butterfly.

Her plan to head straight home after practice changed when Max offered to stay behind and help several children with their batting. Her two were among the ones needing help.

"Your boys show talent," Katie Ruth commented.

"Thanks." Prim appreciated the compliment, but while her sons showed great enthusiasm, they'd dropped as many balls as they caught. Not to mention they'd yet to hit one.

Katie Ruth smiled as if she'd read her mind. "They're a little rough around the edges. All kids are at this age. But I see Rory's boldness and willingness to take risks in them."

Prim thought of where that bold fearlessness had gotten her husband. Where it had left her—alone with two boys to raise.

"Why are you two looking so serious all of a sudden?" Max had wandered over, a clear signal the extra practice time had come to a close.

Her boys remained on the ball field, amusing themselves by taking turns throwing the ball high into the air, then laughing like a couple of hyenas when it fell to the ground with a loud thud.

Safe and in sight. Prim's shoulders relaxed.

"I was telling Prim I see Rory's bold nature in his sons." A smile hovered at the corners of Katie Ruth's lips. "Mark my words, they're going to be equally fearless."

Panic wrapped around Prim like a snake, squeezing the air from her lungs.

Max glanced at Prim, then back at Katie Ruth. "A little caution isn't always a bad thing."

"I can totally see them following in their father's footsteps." Katie Ruth shifted her gaze back to Prim. "Wasn't he involved in a lot of extreme sports as an adult?"

"He was a rock climber. That's what got him killed." Prim hadn't meant to sound bitter, but she felt bitter.

"I, ah, thought it was a malfunction of his climbing harness." Katie Ruth kicked the ground with the toe of her shoe. "That's what it said in the paper."

"The bottom line is, if Rory hadn't given in to the need to climb that particular piece of rock, he'd still be alive." Though Prim's face felt stiff, she forced her expression to relax and motioned to her sons. "Regardless of what you call it—fearlessness or recklessness—he's just as dead."

The next morning Prim rose at six. By seven thirty she'd fed the boys and done two loads of laundry. Her phone rang just as she emptied the dryer the second time. She set the laundry basket on the table and pulled out her phone, smiling when she saw the readout. "Morning, Dad. You're up early."

"Hello, sweetheart." Brimming with warmth and affection, her father's voice never failed to brighten her day. "How's my girl?"

"Doing well." She put the phone between her ear and shoulder and pulled out a handful of socks and underpants. "Just trying to get some things caught up around the house before our trip to Appleton."

"That's right, I forgot the boys will be spending some time with Deb and Mike." There was a pause on the other end of the line. "All the more reason for a fishing day with Grandpa."

"Excuse me?" Prim dropped the socks she'd just rolled into a ball, then picked up two more.

"I'd like to take my grandsons fishing today, if that's okay with you."

"They'd love it." Another ball of socks hit the tabletop. "When do you want to pick them up?"

"Have they eaten breakfast?"

"Just finished."

"I can be there in five minutes."

"Five minutes?" Prim turned and glanced out the sliding glass door to where the boys played in the backyard.

"I'm just down the block."

"Ah, sure, I'll get them ready."

Within fifteen minutes, the boys were strapped in their car seats and headed toward Egg Harbor Marina.

During her years with Rory, Prim had learned to go with the flow. Besides, what her father said when he arrived made sense. Summer wouldn't last forever. All too soon he'd be back teaching in the classroom, and the time he could spend with the twins would be more limited.

Prim had never enjoyed fishing, not even as a kid. Surprisingly, it had been her sister Delphinium, the most girlie of the four, who'd been their dad's fishing buddy. With Fin now in LA, her boys appeared to be taking on that role.

As the taillights of her dad's car disappeared around the corner, Prim considered her options. She could finish the laundry and clean the house. Perhaps give Boris a bath. She grimaced at the thought of manhandling the hundred-pound wolfhound by herself.

Or she could enjoy a latte and a Danish at a wonderful coffee shop downtown that just happened to be owned by her eldest sister. After closing up the house, Prim stepped out into the bright summer sunshine. She'd nearly reached her car when she heard her name.

"Hey, neighbor." Max crossed his lawn in several long strides. "Aren't you forgetting something?"

"What would that be?" Despite the thousand butterflies beating their wings against her throat, her voice remained calm.

"They're about this high." Max held a hand about four feet from the ground. "They have red hair and like bugs and baseball."

"I think I know the two." She couldn't keep from smiling. "Callum and Connor just left. They're spending the day fishing with my dad."

"I knew it." Max lifted his hands, let them fall. "I've been replaced."

She grinned at his dramatically pained expression. "What are you talking about?"

"Your father used to call me whenever he got in a fishing mood." Max expelled a heavy sigh. "I guess we're both castoffs. Which means we must stick together."

Pleasure washed over her at the thought. "We must?"

"We must." He gestured toward her car. "Where are you headed?"

"I thought I'd grab a latte and something sweet at Ami's bakery."

He cocked his head. "Want company?"

"You said we must stick together, so sure, come along, cast-off fishing buddy."

Max chuckled. "Interested in mixing business with pleasure?"

Prim gazed suspiciously up at him. "Maybe."

"I'd like to review the parade lineup with you." He gave her a sheepish look. "And, in the interest of full disclosure, if you have time, I'd also like to walk the parade route."

"I'll definitely review the lineup with you." Prim pulled her brows together. "But I don't understand the walking-the-route thing."

"We could drive it. But it's a nice day and I know you like to walk." Max took a step closer.

She inhaled the clean, fresh scent of him and angled her body to him. "No, I mean what's the purpose?"

Without taking his eyes off her, Max gestured widely. "To look for obstacles that may have popped up since the route was selected, that kind of thing."

Prim lifted her face to the warmth of the sun, moving even closer in the process. "Actually, a walk sounds good."

"Wow." Max rocked back on his heels and grinned. "That was quick."

She winked. "You caught me in an agreeable mood."

"In that case . . ." He paused. "Will you do my laundry?"

"Nope." She laughed. "My agreeability has limits."

"Would you have done it if I'd brought it up before I asked for the parade stuff?"

"No." She tilted her head. "In the interest of full disclosure, I will, however, bake you a pie."

A look of startled surprise crossed his face. His eyes lit up like the sky on the Fourth of July. "What kind?"

"Cherry."

"I love cherry." His slow grin had her insides melting like butter.

"Of course you do. It's a requirement if you live in Door County." Prim gestured to her car. "I can drive."

Max glanced back at his house. "Let me grab the papers and lock up the house. No more leaving doors unlocked during the day."

Resting her back against the warm metal of the car, Prim watched Max jog back to his house and disappear inside. The day wasn't going the way she'd planned, but that was okay.

That was one of the benefits of being back in Good Hope. Each minute of every day was no longer regimented. She could spend time with family and good friends . . . and even bake a pie if the mood struck her.

She smiled as Max returned, a leather satchel dangling from one hand. Yes indeed, this was turning out to be a stellar day.

"Your sister needs to give some serious thought to expanding," Max told Prim when they stepped inside Blooms Bake Shop.

A line snaked from the front counter across the dining area. Max noted most of the congestion came from a group of tourists having difficulty making a decision.

He shot Hadley a sympathetic smile before he and Prim ventured to take their place at the back of the line.

"Hey, Brody, shouldn't you be working?"

Max easily dodged David Chapin's quick jab.

"I could say the same about you," Max volleyed back, but the architect had already shifted his gaze to Prim.

"Primrose. I'd say this is a surprise, but given this is your sister's bakery, it's really not."

David's daughter, Brynn, stood at his side. Max remembered her as the one who'd chased a butterfly during T-ball practice. He didn't hold that against her. He could imagine Prim doing something similar at the same age.

"Hey, Brynn." Max offered the little girl a warm smile. "Good to see you."

The girl smiled shyly and gripped her father's hand.

"What did you think of T-ball practice?" Prim asked. "Did you have fun?"

"I hit the ball twice." She glanced up at her father for confirmation.

David nodded. "Camille said you did very well."

Brynn thrust out one hand. "My mommy painted my fingernails last night."

"If I had a daughter, I'd paint her nails, too." Prim studied the outstretched fingers. "Very pretty."

"Whitney is home catching up on her sleep," David said in answer to the unspoken question. "She's got a weekend trip with friends to Las Vegas coming up."

Prim kept her face impassive. Hadn't the woman just gotten home? How could she be leaving again so soon?

Not your business, Prim reminded herself. But she could empathize. She knew what it was like to shoulder the parenting burden alone, especially when the spouse was alive and well.

"Mommy is going to fly on a plane again," Brynn announced. Her lips drooped and she kicked the floor with the tips of her red sneakers. "I asked if I could go with her, but it's only for big girls."

"Mommy isn't going anywhere until Saturday, sweetheart. You and she will have plenty of time to spend together before then."

David and his daughter had reached the front of the line, so there was no opportunity to say more.

"Love the pink polish with glitter, Brynn." Hadley's gaze lingered on the child before shifting up to her father. "Good to see you again, David."

"You're busy," David observed. "Working solo this morning?"

"Just like you." Hadley's smile remained pleasant, but there was something, a look in her eyes, Max couldn't quite decipher.

"Whitney is home." David rested a hand on his daughter's shoulder. "We thought we'd surprise her this morning with some of her favorite pastries."

"That's very considerate of you." While Hadley filled the white box with an assortment large enough to feed an army, Brynn regaled the clerk with details of her T-ball practice.

Hadley asked questions as she boxed up the order. When she praised the little girl for hitting the ball two times in a row, Brynn was all smiles.

As David and his daughter left the store, Hadley's eyes followed them until they were out the door before refocusing on Max and Prim.

"You just missed Ami," Hadley explained. "She's over at Muddy Boots. They got slammed and Janey and Tom were having difficulty keeping up."

"They must be busy if they needed to pull Ami from the bakery." Max knew both cooks were seasoned and could usually handle even the stiffest rush.

"What can I get you?"

"A kouign amann and a medium skinny latte," Prim answered without hesitation.

What was it with women and their fancy drinks?

"Same except black coffee for me."

Hadley nodded her approval and placed two round, crusty cakes containing layers of butter and caramelized sugar onto pretty flowered plates before lifting a matching cup for the latte.

When they turned around with their plates and drinks, they had the place to themselves except for Clint Gourley, who sat on a stool by the window.

Prim chose the same pink table Eliza had picked when he'd met her here.

"It's like at the grocery store," Prim announced.

Max inclined his head, pulled out a chair.

"Everyone comes in at once, then leaves at once." Prim gestured to the nearly empty shop.

He chuckled. God, he was glad he'd invited himself along.

"Oh, before I forget, seeing Brynn reminded me that the boys are going to miss a few T-ball practices. I'm taking them to visit my in-laws in Appleton."

"That's too bad." Only after the words left his lips did Max realize how they'd sounded. "I mean there are so many events for children at this time of year that it's a shame they'll have to miss them."

"I know, but Rory's parents want to spend time with them, too." Over Prim's shoulder, Max caught Clint staring at Prim.

Max didn't like the guy. He hadn't had any use for him since he'd heard Clint had beaten a possum to death with a baseball bat in middle school.

"My mother-in-law is insisting I stay while the boys are there."

"That will be fun."

Prim rolled her eyes. "What did Hadley put in that coffee?"

Max laughed and opened his satchel. He pulled out his iPad. Last night he'd loaded the parade entries onto a spreadsheet. "Ready to get down to business?"

She smiled up at him with such warmth his heart stumbled. "I thought you'd never ask."

Chapter Fourteen

Your pie is ready for pickup.

Prim sent the text, then returned to the living room, where the boys sat playing Legos in their pajamas, their hair still slightly damp from the shower.

"Ten minutes," she told them. "Make sure you pick out the books that you want me to read."

"Okay," Connor said.

Callum nodded and carefully added the piece that linked the span of the curved bridge.

Prim lifted her glass of wine. "Anyone want to come and sit on the porch swing with me?"

Two identical red heads shook at the same time.

"I'll be right outside on the porch." Prim glanced down at Boris, who lay sprawled out on the floor beside the boys, chewing on a raw-hide. "Boris, you're on duty."

Prim took the merlot to the porch and settled on the swing. Despite it being nearly eight o'clock, the air was warm. Though she still wore the sleeveless dress she'd had on that morning when she and Max had walked the parade route, she wasn't at all chilled.

Speaking of Max . . .

She lifted the phone. No response to her text.

"Where's my pie?"

She jumped, the wine sloshing in her glass. Setting the phone down, she tried to hide her delight, but it rang in her voice. "You didn't have to come tonight."

"It's cherry pie. Of course I did." He sauntered to the swing, motioned her to scoot over, then dropped down beside her. "Are the boys already in bed?"

"They've got another ten minutes." She breathed in the scent of lilacs and pine. "It's such a nice night, I wanted to enjoy it a little."

He nodded as if he understood. But of course he did. He'd always understood.

"We got a lot accomplished today."

Prim sipped her wine. "Eliza is bound to be impressed."

"She's a tough audience."

"She won't be able to deny that the changes we made in the lineup will make the parade even better." Just the thought of Eliza having to give them a compliment brought a rush of pleasure.

"It's good we walked the route or we wouldn't have noticed that patch of road construction." Max glanced at her glass of wine. "That looks good. Do you have any more?"

"I'm not sure how well it will go with cherry pie."

"I like to live dangerously."

Prim snorted out a laugh. "Yeah, me too."

She saw his eyes darken, and he turned toward her, his hands rising up to grip her shoulders. "Prim."

He opened his mouth, but before he could say more, "Flight of the Bumblebee" filled the air.

"Sorry." Slipping the phone from her pocket, she silenced the alarm.

"What was that?"

"I set the alarm so I could know when ten minutes was up. After a day of fishing, they're exhausted." She dropped the phone back in her pocket. "Give me a few minutes to read a quick story and tuck them in."

"Would you let me?"

Prim dropped back down, not sure she'd heard correctly. "You want to tuck them in?"

"Sure. I didn't get a chance to see them today. And this way you can relax. Callum and Connor aren't the only ones who had a busy day." He leaned over, brushed the hair back from her face, and planted a kiss against her temple. "You need some pampering, too."

"I—I don't know what to say."

"Just say yes."

"Ah, sure, fine with me."

"Smart woman." He stood, shot her a wink. "I've got this."

Prim leaned back in the swing. Through the open screen door she heard Max's deep rumble and the boys' squeals of delight.

Slowly she swung back and forth, letting the light breeze ruffle her hair as she sipped her wine. She thought about what it would be like to be married to a man who was committed to his family, like her father had been.

The boys wouldn't just have her to care for them, to love them, to be there for them, they'd have a dad, too. And she would have a husband, a helpmate, a lover to be with her through the good times and bad, to share her joys and her sorrows.

Not all marriages were the kind she'd had with Rory. Not all relationships were equal. It could be different.

She could see Max . . .

Prim shook her head in an attempt to banish the image. It had been good at first with Rory. They'd enjoyed each other's company, had done activities together. All that had changed once the twins were born.

She knew she hadn't given Rory the attention he craved, but she'd been so tired. Between working full-time and two demanding babies, there had been nothing of herself left to give. Little by little, he'd become more focused on his life and less on her and their sons.

However much he'd loved her, however much she'd loved him, it hadn't been enough to keep him home. Closing her eyes, she forced herself to focus on only good memories.

"Don't tell me I'm going to have to put you to bed, too."

Prim's eyes flashed open.

Max chuckled. "I thought that would get your attention. Here."

She stared at the neatly cut piece of pie in his hand. "You brought me a piece of pie."

"I got one for myself, too." Max held up his other hand. When she took her plate, he sat beside her. "You were right about the twins being tired. I didn't even make it through the first book when they conked out."

He'd not only tucked them in, he'd read them a story. Tears filled her eyes. Turning her head, she blinked them back before he could see.

Max took a bite, closed his eyes for a second. "This pie is amazing."

Prim sampled the pie, the cherries tart against her tongue. "Not as good as Ami's, but pretty good."

Max lowered his fork. "You do that a lot."

"Do what?"

"Put yourself down."

She stiffened. "I'm simply stating a fact. It stands to reason Ami would be a better baker than me. It's what she does for a living. I—"

"Hey." His hand closed over hers.

"Ami's the baker in the family," she repeated.

"Okay, Ami's the baker." He forked off another piece, chewed. "Though, seriously, this pie is excellent."

She couldn't stop the rush of pleasure. "Thank you."

"What about Marigold?"

"What about her?"

"What is she?" He gestured with his fork. "Ami is the baker. Marigold is the . . ."

"She's the artist." Prim didn't hesitate. "A genius with hair."

"Fin?"

Prim thought for a second. "Fin is the social one. She's . . . charismatic."

"I agree." He watched her eat a bite of pie before speaking again. "What about you, Prim?"

"I'm just me." She gave a little laugh, lifted her shoulders, let them fall.

"C'mon, you can do better than that."

If his tone hadn't been so light and teasing, she might have taken offense. Instead, she stopped to consider.

"You're not going to like this answer. But truly there's really nothing all that special about me." She dropped her gaze to focus on her pie. "Sometimes you have to accept the truth even if it hurts."

Why, oh why, had she added that last little bit? She should have cleared her throat so it wouldn't have given the false impression she was all emotional about something that didn't really matter.

Max placed his pie plate on the porch rail with careful, deliberate movements, then took her plate from her hands.

"Hey, I wasn't finished with that yet."

"You can have it back." The smile on his lips didn't quite reach his eyes. "Just give me a minute."

She lifted a hand. "If you're going to yell at me—"

The look of horror that crossed his face had her stopping.

After setting the plate aside, he took her hands in his.

"It's often difficult to look at ourselves objectively. That's why I, Max Brody, neighbor and lifelong friend"—his eyes met hers and he waited until she nodded to continue—"am going to tell you everything that's special about Primrose Bloom."

Prim considered telling him not to bother but had to admit she was curious what he would say. As she stared into those now-serious blue eyes, her heart began to thump like a bass drum.

"The Primrose I've known since childhood is incredibly smart. When we were in eighth grade she scored at the college level in math. She's not just book smart. She knows how to make people feel good about themselves."

"Thank you—"

He put a finger to her lips. "I'm not done."

A look of tenderness crossed his face. "She's a person who values home and family. When her mother got sick, she quietly went about making sure things got done at home, then spent time reading to her mother when she was bedridden and too ill to read herself. She did all this quietly, without fanfare, not because she had to but because when she loves, she loves with her whole heart."

Tears stung the backs of Prim's eyes.

"You're a wonderful mother. Having one child is difficult, but two at one time is an extra challenge. You take care of the boys and the house, you make sure they have what they need, and you don't complain."

"I'm their mother. I love my sons."

"I know you do. It's only one of the many things I . . . admire about you." His gaze was soft as a caress. "You're also a true friend. You stepped up when Gladys was in trouble and took over her burdens even though you'd barely had a chance to get settled in your new home."

His hand closed around hers. "You're an amazing woman, Prim. You're incredibly special. Don't let anyone—even yourself—say differently."

Prim wasn't sure who made the first move. She wasn't sure it mattered. All she knew was his arms were around her and he was kissing her and she was kissing him back.

Inside, a tiny hope blossomed. Maybe Fin and her other sisters had been right. Twelve years was a long time to wait . . . when you'd found the right man.

⸻

"I wish you didn't have to go." Max stood beside her porch, hands in his pockets, the morning breeze cool against his face.

"Deb would hunt me down and skin me alive if I didn't show up with 'her boys.'" Prim's mouth curved in a soft smile. "I think the twins would be disappointed, too. They enjoy seeing their grandparents."

She'd put pink color on her lips and smelled like lemons.

"I would have watched Boris."

"Thank you for that." She leaned close, and for a second he thought they would kiss. Apparently remembering the two sets of eyes trained on her, at the last second she merely patted his cheek. "My dad loves Boris and he'd already offered."

Max wanted to kiss her. He wanted her to wrap her arms around his neck and cling to him. He wanted to take her up to his bedroom and—

"Well," she said, her face flushed even though the outside air was cool. "I should go."

She didn't move a muscle.

Neither did Max.

"Drive safe. If you run into any trouble on the road, call." His tone brooked no argument. "Let me know when you arrive in Appleton. I'll have my phone with me."

"You don't have to worry about me."

"Sorry. Goes with the territory." Then, before he could talk himself out of the gesture, Max leaned over and kissed her.

⁂

Rory's spirit lived in the Delaney house on a quiet street in Appleton. Freshly polished high school trophies with silver soccer balls and gold footballs gleamed on a wall of shelves in the living room. Pictures of him holding various medals were there, too. In the main hallway, there was a collage of photos: him as high school homecoming king, fraternity president, and mountain climber. There were numerous shots of him at the tops of soaring peaks, usually with a fist stretched high in triumph.

The joy on his face warmed Prim's heart. Though she hadn't always agreed with his priorities, Rory had fully lived every day of the years he'd been given. Not many people could say the same.

There were also a few wedding pictures mixed in and several of them holding babies wrapped in blue blankets, looking tired but happy. But mostly the shots were of Rory. In the meticulous arrangement, Prim saw love . . . and profound grief.

She couldn't imagine what it would be like to lose a child, and her heart ached for his parents' loss.

"Come join me in the kitchen." Deb's eyes settled on the photos for a split second before she averted her gaze.

They'd arrived just before noon, and although Prim had offered to take her in-laws out for lunch, Deb wouldn't hear of it. Which was why Prim followed her mother-in-law into the kitchen, where Deb predictably refused her offer of help.

There was no choice but to sit at the table while her mother-in-law tossed together a lunch of homemade mac 'n' cheese accompanied by a crisp green salad.

Connor and Callum dived into the mac 'n' cheese like Prim hadn't fed them in years. They might have ignored the salad except for the fact that Deb, recalling their penchant for dried cranberries, had mixed some in with the romaine. Prim had to hand it to her mother-in-law. The woman's mind was like a steel trap when it came to what "her boys" liked. She'd been that way with Rory, too.

Immediately after lunch, Mike took the twins outside to play catch. He listened attentively while they prattled on about their T-ball "team." Once again, Prim followed Deb, this time onto the front porch, where they sat in matching high-backed rockers with tall glasses of lemonade in hand.

While Prim believed her mother-in-law to be a fine woman and didn't hold it against her that she'd been opposed to their marriage, she'd never been able to warm up to her. Even when Rory had been alive, she'd felt like an outsider. She wished she knew how to bridge the gap between them.

Deb's eyes grew misty as she watched the twins play catch with their grandfather. Mike was in his early sixties and still very active, although Prim thought he might be favoring his right knee. Like his son, he'd been an athlete in his younger years.

"Mike has been looking forward to this visit." Deb's voice thickened with emotion. She cleared her throat before continuing. "I have, too. I realize we just saw the twins last month, but they already seem bigger to me."

On that point, she and Deb were in total agreement. "It feels like every day they grow up a little more. They're always learning something new."

The boys were keeping their eye on the ball, just like Max had taught them. Prim's heart swelled, a heavy, sweet mass in her chest.

"Are you all settled in your new home?"

"Pretty much." Prim leaned back in the rocker, took a sip of the tart liquid. "The boxes are unpacked. I don't have the place decorated the way I want just yet, but it's starting to feel like home."

Deb's eyes grew distant with memories. "I always loved Good Hope."

Prim remembered how involved the couple had been in the Good Hope social scene when they'd lived here. "I was surprised, shocked really, when you announced last year that you and Mike were moving away."

"Too many memories there." Deb's smile turned melancholy, and Prim had to bite her tongue from saying, *and yet you built a shrine to him here*. "Each time I'd drive by the soccer field, I'd see Rory in his knee pads and cleats. I'm surprised it isn't that way for you."

Prim gave a noncommittal smile. There was no point in telling Deb that she hadn't had that problem. For her, high school seemed like a lifetime ago. Most of her memories of Rory were in Milwaukee.

"I assume you'll be staying home with the boys." It was a statement, not a question, and Deb continued on as if no response was expected. "I never understood why you worked when you had babies at home who needed you. Not once did I regret my decision to put Rory first."

This was old ground that, for some reason, Deb seemed determined to walk down again. Prim took a deep breath. "As I've explained before, I didn't have a choice. We needed the health insurance through my job. Rory may have earned more as a contract employee, but health insurance wasn't part of his benefit package."

"Rory could have stayed under our coverage if he hadn't married. He settled down so young, too young." Distress filled her voice. "He was still a boy when he became a father. And while I am so very thankful for my grandsons, I don't think Rory was ready."

Prim merely sipped her lemonade. Once again, they were in total agreement. Getting pregnant on their honeymoon hadn't been planned, and Deb was right, Rory hadn't been ready. He'd loved his sons fiercely, but the bulk of meeting Callum's and Connor's needs had fallen on her shoulders.

"Kids will break your heart." Deb heaved a heartfelt sigh. "As a parent you have to let them make their own decisions and their own mistakes."

Prim's fingers clutched the cut-crystal tumbler so tightly her knuckles turned white.

"Oh, my, look at that throw." Deb clapped her hands, her face alight with pride. "Wonderful job, Callum."

"Grandpa threw me a ball that went way high," Connor called out, obviously not wanting to be left out. "I kept my eye on the ball and I catched it."

Caught it, Prim corrected silently.

"I saw that, sweetheart. You're both doing so well." Deb lowered her voice and turned back to Prim. "I'm happy to see that you're getting them involved in the community, but I'm not sure T-ball is the best choice. Their father found the game slow and tedious. I'm certain in time they will, as well. Have you looked into getting them into a soccer league?"

"That experience will have to wait until spring." Prim kept her tone casual. "I missed the sign-up for the fall league."

"You'll just have to put that on your calendar so you don't miss it again. It's not fair for children to suffer because of our negligence."

Prim forced herself to breathe, in and out, as she counted slowly to ten.

Deb tapped her finger against the side of her glass. "On second thought, I'll go online and look up those dates for spring. That way I can text you when it's time to sign up."

"You don't have to go to all that trouble."

"It's no trouble at all. I'm happy to do it. Some of my favorite memories were sitting in those soccer stands and watching my son play." Deb's brow furrowed. "But after a while, just driving past those nets and bleachers became too painful. That's when I knew we had to move."

The lines on Deb's face had deepened since the death of her only son, Prim realized, and her anger melted away in a flood of sympathy.

Prim touched Deb's hand. "Rory was a star."

It was all the encouragement her mother-in-law needed. Prim had heard the stories many times, had even been present during some of the highlights, but out of respect she would listen again.

Prim sipped her lemonade and watched her boys play catch with their grandpa while Deb took a familiar trip down memory lane, recounting all of Rory's athletic and social triumphs.

By the time the game of catch ended and Deb paused to take a breath, Prim was exhausted. When the boys tumbled through the front door, eager for the promised piece of chocolate cake—their daddy's favorite—Prim didn't even protest.

Over the course of the evening, Prim lost count of the number of times Rory's name was mentioned. She only knew if she'd been doing shots each time she heard it, she'd be passed out drunk on the floor by now.

It wasn't Deb's or Mike's fault. She understood their need to keep their son's memory alive. Yet even when Rory had been alive, it had been this way. It had all been about him. It was still all about him.

She'd never liked feeling invisible, never liked being the one who'd tied Rory down when he should have been out there living life to the fullest, never liked being the one who'd gotten pregnant when they'd decided—actually when Rory had decided and she'd agreed—not to have children.

That, too, was old ground. Prim still recalled the horrified look on Deb's face the day she'd reached her limit and snapped that it took two to make a baby. She was nearing that point now but knew losing control would serve no purpose.

"Well." Prim rose from the living room sofa when the last video of Rory's exploits on the soccer field ended. "I think it's time I hit the road."

"You're leaving?" Mike's kind eyes, so blue and so like his son's, were astonished.

"I thought you were planning on staying," Deb said, already rising to walk Prim to the door. "Though I certainly understand if you need to get home for the dog."

"My other grandpa is watching Boris." Callum looked up from the floor where he'd been building a Lego bridge while watching the "movie."

"Yeah," Connor added. "We dropped Boris off before we left."

"I didn't want him to spend all day and evening alone." Prim had rehearsed what to say if she decided not to stay. It was the reason she'd left her bag in the trunk of the car, rather than bringing it in when she'd arrived. "Boris can be a bit of a mischief maker."

"One time he got into the garbage and dragged it all over the house." Callum gestured wide with his arms.

"He barfed on the couch once." Connor held his nose. "It smelled really bad."

Deb looked properly horrified. "That would never be tolerated in my home."

"It's what dogs do," Callum said solemnly. "Sometimes he—"

"I'm sure Grandma has heard enough stories." Prim shot both boys a warning look.

"I'm thankful Rory never wanted a dog." Deb waved a dismissive hand. "He was too busy with his activities to have time for one anyway."

Prim saw no need to mention that shortly before Rory died, he'd brought up the possibility of them getting a puppy. She'd put her foot down. Working full-time, caring for twin toddlers, and having a husband who seemed to be gone more than he was home had stretched her to the breaking point.

She wished he'd have gotten the chance to have a dog, but it hadn't been the right time. Now it was too late.

Prim kissed the boys good-bye, hugged her in-laws. She promised to drive safely and not go over the speed limit on the trip home.

Before she reached the highway, she stopped at a convenience store to grab a cola and wash down a couple of ibuprofen. By the time she hit Green Bay, her headache, like Appleton, had been left in the dust.

Chapter Fifteen

It was after five by the time Prim reached Good Hope. Though she had the time, Prim decided to let Boris spend the night and get him in the morning.

Anita would likely be with her father, and Prim had no desire to see her headache return. When she turned onto her block she noticed that while most of the houses in the neighborhood showed signs of life, Max's house looked empty and dark.

She wondered where he was tonight.

None of your business, she told herself as she pulled into the attached garage and let the door glide shut behind her. After bringing her suitcase inside, she went out to the porch to get the mail.

Still no signs of life next door.

Once inside, Prim tossed the mail onto the kitchen table, then took a moment to respond to a rather abrupt-sounding text from Eliza. She added a smiley face to the return message that assured the executive director she and Max had the parade under control.

Once she'd hit Send, Prim realized that while her headache might be gone, she still felt jittery and on edge, as if something momentous was about to happen, which was totally crazy.

The only thing momentous in her night was likely a glass of wine or a bowl of ice cream. She smiled. Considered. Why not both?

First she set about getting comfortable. In the bedroom, she stripped off her clothes and pulled on a pair of loose cotton pants and a tank. She slipped her feet into atomic-orange flip-flops before returning to the kitchen.

After plopping a large dip of rocky road in a bowl, Prim poured herself a glass of Brachetto d'Acqui, a dessert wine Fin had recommended. Known for its floral notes and hints of red berries, it was supposed to be great accompaniment to anything chocolate.

As the night was beautiful with a light breeze to keep the bugs away, Prim took the food and drink to the patio and flipped on the outdoor lights.

She started to sit down, then realized she'd left her phone on the counter. While inside, Prim discovered the book Deb had specifically asked her to bring with her to Appleton sitting on the counter.

In her rush to get on the road, she'd left Rory's high school annual behind. Impulsively, she scooped it up along with the mail, a handful of napkins, and her phone.

She ate a spoonful of the deliciously decadent ice cream while flipping through the mail. Most were bills forwarded from her Milwaukee address.

The official-looking envelope with a prominent Milwaukee law firm's name had her tossing the other pieces of mail aside and slitting open the vellum with her finger.

The settlement check dropped into her lap as she read the letter.

Closing her eyes, Prim leaned back in her chair. She'd wanted the closure, had *needed* the closure. But as she opened her eyes and stared at all the zeroes, a healthy dose of pain laced her relief. Was this all a man's life was worth?

Fighting a surge of anger, Prim stuffed the letter and the check into the envelope. The money would provide her and her boys with financial security for the rest of their lives. But a good man had died because of a company's careless disregard, and that was nothing to celebrate. In fact, the thought made her slightly sick.

She took a fortifying drink of wine, then opened the yearbook, deliberately avoiding the back section with all the sporting pictures. There'd been enough talking, enough thinking, of Rory in the past twenty-four hours. Keeping to the middle of the book, she let it fall open. To her surprise, Prim found herself gazing at her own smiling face.

A much younger version of herself, to be sure. She looked happy, as if she didn't have a care in the world.

The photo was of her and Max. He looked happy, too, with his arm looped around her shoulders. Her heart gave a little ping. They were holding up their mathlete medals and grinning like idiots.

As she studied the photo, something rustled in the bushes. She looked up and saw a figure in the shadows. She surged to her feet, her heart racing.

Close. So close. No time to call for help. No time to run. He'd catch her before she made it to the door.

"You better get out of here," she called out with a show of false bravado. "I've called the sheriff. He and his deputies will be here any second."

Heart thumping, she tightened her grip on the book, the scream turning to a whimper when Max stepped into the light.

He lowered the fireplace poker he held like a fencing foil and gestured to the glass of red wine. "Got any more of that?"

———————

"What the heck, Max?" The book slipped from Prim's fingers and fell to the chair. "You scared me to death. And what's with the poker?"

Her hair, the color of the sky at sunset, was a billowing cloud around a too-pale face.

"I'm sorry," he said with genuine regret. "I thought you were in Appleton. I saw the light out back and I wanted to be prepared."

Her eyes went round as quarters. "You thought my house was being robbed."

"As you'd told me only this morning you planned to be out of town for several days, it seemed a good possibility."

She cocked her head as if listening. "Should I expect police sirens?"

It had been his first impulse, and he'd had the number keyed in, just in case. "I didn't call Swarts. I thought I'd check things out myself first."

Her brow furrowed. "If there was a burglar, you could have been hurt. They might have had a gun."

"Worried about me?"

"Of course," she said immediately. "You—you matter to me. You're my friend."

Max glanced at the bowl of ice cream and the nearly empty glass of wine and strove to inject a little levity into the situation, which still felt tense.

"I believe it's customary when friends stop over to offer refreshments."

She expelled a breath, gave a quick nod. "What can I get you? Ice cream? A glass of wine?"

"I'll start with the wine." He motioned to the chair. "You sit. I can get it."

"The bottle is on the counter. You can find a glass in the cupboard to the right of the sink." She collapsed into the chair and brushed back a strand of hair with a hand that trembled slightly. "The, ah, wine is perfect with chocolate ice cream, so if you change your mind . . ."

He glanced at her dish. "If I decide I want some, I'll whine until you offer me some of yours."

She chuckled and he was pleased to see color returning to her cheeks.

Max returned moments later with the bottle and a glass. When he set down the bottle, he noticed the mail. "Don't tell me you're being audited, too."

"What?"

He took a sip of the wine and savored the unusual taste. The hint of raspberries teased his tongue, and he decided it probably would be excellent with chocolate.

"The envelope." He gestured with his head when he saw she was waiting for a response. "Looks official."

The light in Prim's eyes disappeared.

"It's the settlement check." At his apparently blank look, she continued. "The lawsuit over the defective climbing harness."

He hesitated. "That must be a relief."

"Financially, it's a godsend. The severance from my job back in Milwaukee was set to run out next month. I plan to look for work once the boys are back in school, but I might have had to look sooner if this hadn't come through." She paused as if realizing she'd been babbling.

"Then receiving the check is a good thing." He took a sip of wine, giving her time to steady. "Why the long face?"

"It feels like blood money." She waved a hand when he started to protest. "I know it's not, but it *feels* that way, like I'm capitalizing on Rory's death."

Feelings weren't always rational, Max knew, and she certainly had a right to feel any way she wanted.

Impulsively, he reached over and took a big spoonful of what turned out to be rocky road into his mouth. "Ummm, this is delicious. Really good."

Her mew of displeasure had his lips wanting to twitch, but Max suppressed the impulse. The light was back in her eyes and he felt a surge of fierce satisfaction.

"You've got chocolate on your mouth." She leaned close, dabbed at the edge of his mouth with a napkin, and made a *tsk*ing sound. "I can't take you anywhere."

Her face was inches away. When she looked up and he gazed into those beautiful hazel eyes, Max realized that while he might regret kissing her, he'd regret *not* kissing her more.

Without taking his eyes from hers, he set aside his glass and the bowl, then closed his mouth over hers.

Prim's pulse was a swift, tripping beat. Max was going to kiss her. And she had a pretty good idea where that kiss would lead. Logic told her to take a step back.

She didn't move a muscle. Just for tonight she would be that young woman with that happy smile and her entire life—and endless possibilities—stretched out before her.

Just for tonight, she'd follow her heart.

Before she had time to reconsider, Max's lips were on hers, exquisitely gentle and achingly tender.

If he noticed the momentary hesitation before she began kissing him back, he gave no indication. He continued to kiss her with a slow thoroughness that left her weak, trembling, and longing for more.

"I want you, Prim." His voice was soft, reaching inside her to a raw, tender place.

Blue eyes had darkened to black in the dimness, but she didn't need light to read his expression. This was it, the moment of truth. Did she have the strength to reach out and grab what she wanted . . . just for one night? Something told Prim if she turned him away now, he wouldn't ask again.

Leaning over, he nuzzled the base of her jaw, then took the fingers of her hand and kissed them, feather light. "How far we go is up to you."

Where she went with her life had never been fully up to her.

She and Rory had dated for so long, it had been simply understood they'd one day marry. Like it had been understood she'd become an actuary, even though tax work was what really interested her. Even now she understood—and accepted—that her needs were subjugated by her children's needs.

But tonight was hers, and oh, how she wanted him.

As she gazed into Max's eyes, the contact became a tangible connection between them.

"Max." She spoke his name, then paused, not sure what to say next.

He waited, his steady gaze shooting tingles down her spine.

Time seemed to stretch and extend.

Gently, he stroked her back, cradled her head. "Tell me what you want, Primrose."

What *she* wanted. Her heartbeat hitched. The thought was empowering; heady. Anticipation fluttered through her.

After the tiniest hesitation, she smiled.

"I want you." Her voice came out as a husky caress.

A look of tenderness crossed his face. "I'll make it good for you. I promise."

She gazed into his eyes. Could he hear her heart pounding? Running her hands up his chest, Prim kissed him. "I'll make it good for you, too."

The grin he flashed was lopsided, his fingers not quite steady as they touched the curve of her cheek, trailed along the line of her jaw.

She wound her arms around his neck and he folded her more fully into his arms, anchoring her against his chest as his mouth covered hers in a deep, compelling kiss.

Prim stepped back from his embrace, her entire body quivering with need . . . and yes, excitement, too.

"Race you to the bedroom. But first, one for the road." She gave him a ferocious kiss, then took off running, her breaths laced with laugher as he surged to his feet in pursuit.

When they reached the bedroom, she spun around to face him, her pulse rioting. She swallowed her nerves. Tonight, she would be herself. Or how she'd always longed to be. "Bet my clothes hit the floor before yours."

He chuckled, a low, pleasant rumbling sound. "I like your style, Primrose."

Seconds later his clothes landed in a heap beside hers.

Then, before she even had a second to breathe—or to worry if this might be a mistake—his lips were on hers. The taste of him was new, yet somehow familiar. Like raspberries and chocolate, it was a combination Prim found wildly erotic.

"I won," she murmured against his mouth and felt any remnants of her nervousness fade at his quick laughter.

"No." He scattered kisses along her jawline. "I'm definitely the winner here."

He shifted, gathered her close against him, and kissed her temple. "Before we get too crazy, I need to ask if you're protected."

"No worries." Prim tipped her head back to gaze into his eyes. "I was having trouble with my periods. I went on the pill last year."

"I always used a condom." His expression turned serious. "I've never had sex without one. But I never expected tonight . . ."

Prim felt like a balloon that had been popped just as it was ready to soar.

"That's okay." Somehow she managed a smile that hovered briefly on her lips. "I understand."

"I, ah, don't want you to get the idea I'm some guy on the make, but things have been so hot between us, I just happen to have one with me and a whole box at home. I wanted to make sure if we ever got to this point you'd be fully protected." The words were like a caress as he twined strands of her hair loosely around his fingers.

Relief surged and Prim's heart tripped at the desire in his eyes. "Well, then, what are we waiting for? Let's get this party started."

He made a sound low in his throat, his mouth suddenly voracious on hers.

Her body responded with breathtaking speed. Though she sensed Max would move slowly if that's what she wanted, a desperate need fueled her actions.

She wanted to run her hands over his body, to feel the coiled strength of skin and muscle sliding under her fingers. She wanted him to touch her in the same way, wanted to feel the weight of his body on hers. Longed to feel him inside her.

The warmth in her lower belly turned fiery hot as they continued to kiss. His hand closed over one breast, cupping it high in his palm, circling the peak.

Desire became a pulsing need. She slipped her hand between them, smiling when she encountered a hard bulge.

His shaft jumped. Max rested his forehead against hers and laughed softly. "You're not going to want to do that again."

Her heart performed a series of flutters. When she offered him a sly smile, he kissed her nose. "We don't want this party to be over before it has even begun."

No, Prim definitely didn't want that. Though she did want to devour him, one greedy little bite at a time. She nipped his shoulder just to get a taste.

She didn't recall moving to the bed. All she knew was she was beside him, her mouth plastered to his, the kisses urgent and fevered. It was as if they both feared this was a dream and they might wake at any moment.

Her fingers trembled as she caressed his face, his silky hair. Her senses spun like an out-of-control Tilt-A-Whirl. Prim was glad she was lying down or she'd have lost her footing.

Then his hands were back on her, his fingers lifting and supporting her yielding flesh as his thumbs brushed across the tight points of her nipples. The stroking fingers sent shock waves of feeling through her body.

Her nipples stiffened, straining toward the delight of his touch. Before long, his mouth replaced his fingers. He couldn't seem to get enough of her breasts, kissing and licking each pink peak thoroughly, dragging his teeth across the sensitive skin.

Prim bowed up, surging against the pleasure that swelled like the tide inside her. She squirmed, whimpering in frustration. She pushed her hips against him, rubbing his erection.

She wanted, no, she *needed* . . . "Inside me."

"Not yet." His hands stroked, brushed, lingered until every nerve ending in her body was on fire.

It took only a second for him to roll on the condom; then, reaching up, he grasped her arms and pulled her to him for an openmouthed, intimate kiss. Desire, hot and demanding, flooded her.

Just when Prim thought she would break apart—or go mad with longing—he plunged into her with a hard thrust.

She wrapped her legs around his hips, holding him to her. Reveling in the fullness, the feel of him inside her, she met him thrust for thrust.

Fire scorched her veins as her pulse throbbed hard and thick. The orgasm hit with breathtaking speed. Her entire body clenched and released in spasms of pure pleasure.

Seconds later, with a low, savage sound, Max climaxed deep inside her.

After they were spent, he rolled off her. She tried to sit up, but he wrapped his arm around her, not confining but comfortable. They lay that way for a long time, just listening to each other breathing.

"How was it?" His breath was warm as he spoke softly into her ear.

With a start, Prim realized she was stroking the back of his neck, twining her fingers in his thick, soft hair. "Passable."

She giggled, honest-to-goodness giggled, when he gave her shoulder a little nip.

"Hey, what was that for?"

"Passable?"

"Okay, okay. It was terrific. Just don't let it go to your head."

"You go to my head. You're lovely."

His husky voice, the way he looked at her, as if she were the most beautiful woman he'd ever seen, gave her a pleasurable jolt.

She drew air slowly into her lungs. Had this been a mistake? It didn't feel like one.

With his gaze still fixed on hers, Max bent his head and kissed her softly on the mouth.

"What was that for?"

"For being you."

Definitely not a mistake.

He propped himself up on an elbow.

"Spend the weekend with me." Shadows played in his eyes, making them unreadable, but his voice was soft, persuasive. "We'll hang at my place. Just you and me."

A smoldering heat flared through her. She hesitated, fearful of the intimacy yet at the same time thrilled at the thought.

"All weekend?" The nonchalant tone was worthy of an Academy Award.

"Two long days." His finger trailed up her arm. "Two long nights."

"Why?"

"I want to spend time with you. Carpe diem and all that."

The music that had been playing in the background took on a seductive beat. *Say yes, say yes,* the pulsating rhythm urged.

Max caught her hand in his, brought it to his mouth, and pressed an openmouthed kiss into her palm. "Say yes."

Prim let her eyelids flutter shut for just an instant and imagined having Max to herself for the whole weekend.

She'd learned long ago that regret over something you wished you'd said or done but no longer had the chance to do could be its own kind of hell.

He kissed her fingers, trailed kisses up her arm. "Say yes."

Carpe diem. *Seize the day.*

This was what she wanted. *He* was what she wanted.

Right now she couldn't think of a single reason to say no. The rightness of the decision washed over her.

"Yes." Prim flung her arms around his neck. "Yes. I'll stay with you."

Chapter Sixteen

Max waited while Prim retrieved the suitcase she'd packed for Appleton. Spending the weekend together was a good start. But it wasn't enough, wouldn't be enough. The way he was feeling right now, a lifetime didn't seem long enough.

When she emerged from the door leading from the garage, Max hurried to her side and lifted the suitcase from her hands. He ignored her protests. Prim deserved to be pampered, and this weekend he would have that privilege.

She shut off the living room lights, but he placed a hand on her arm when she reached for the doorknob. "We probably should go around the back."

He gestured with his head. "Avoid the neighborhood watch."

"I didn't even think . . ." Worry suddenly furrowed her brow as if a thought had struck her. "My dad agreed to watch Boris while I was out of town. Now that I'm back, the responsible thing would be to pick him up, bring him home."

Max kept his face expressionless. Three would definitely be a crowd, especially if one of the three was a hundred-pound dog that didn't know the meaning of personal space.

"Your dad loves animals." Max kept his tone even. "In fact, I'd venture to say he considers Boris a third grandson."

A hint of a smile lifted those luscious lips he hadn't kissed nearly enough. "He and Boris are buddies."

"I bet Steve would like you to have a relaxing weekend with no responsibilities." The tension gripping Max's shoulders eased when she nodded.

She cocked her head. "How'd you get so smart?"

"Smart?" He made a scoffing sound. "Brilliant would be more accurate."

She rolled her eyes.

He took her hand as they crossed the yard, releasing it only to open the gate between her place and his. As he'd left the French doors unlocked, there was no need for him to pull out his keys.

Once they were inside, Max locked and bolted the door. "Can I get you something to drink?"

Prim shook her head, and all that wild, glorious hair tumbled around her shoulders. "I've had more than enough this evening, thank you."

He'd also had more than enough wine, but not nearly enough of her. "If you change your mind—"

"I'll let you know." Her gaze met his. "If you recall, I don't have any trouble letting you know what I like."

The impish gleam in her eyes had him shaking his head. "What am I going to do with you?"

She moistened her lips. "I have several ideas for later."

Later.

He didn't want to wait. He wanted her again. Now.

Even as he yearned to persuade, this was *her* weekend to indulge. He would let her take the lead.

"If you'd like to watch a movie, I have some DVDs, or we can see what's on cable." Max imagined sitting beside her on the sofa, his arm settled around her shoulders. He already knew it would be impossible for him to sit close and not touch.

Instead of listening, Prim was blatantly checking out his digs.

He watched her gaze linger on the granite countertops he'd had installed last year and the distressed gray cupboards before her attention shifted to the living room. Like her house, his home had an open floor plan.

An overstuffed burgundy leather sofa and matching chair were arranged in front of a large stone fireplace.

"I love your fireplace." Prim moved to the mantel and ran her fingers along the smooth rock.

His mouth went dry as he recalled those fingers trailing down . . .

She glanced back at him over her shoulder. "Your place is so clean."

Max cleared his throat. "No kids or dogs."

Prim smiled. "Makes a difference."

"There's a stack of DVDs, some games and cards in that cabinet." Max gestured to the two-door cabinet to the right of the fireplace. "Pick whatever movie you want and we'll watch it."

Prim's teeth caught her lower lip for a second while her eyes took on an impish gleam. "You're being very agreeable tonight, Mr. Brody."

"I'm feeling pretty agreeable," he told her.

"Good to know." She opened the cabinet and began scouring the contents.

Max stood back and watched. While the leprechaun pants and green tank weren't particularly sexy, on her they were as enticing as black silk and lace.

She bent over and his body sprang to life.

Prim abruptly whirled. "What are these?"

His heart sank as well as a certain other body part when he saw what was in her hand.

"Feel free to toss those to the back of the cabinet." Max waved a casual hand in the air even as his blood turned to ice. Why hadn't he dumped that blasted deck of cards in the garbage when he'd had the chance?

Even as Max asked the question, he knew the answer. They'd been a gift from his mother. While he thought the deck, each individual card containing a specific question, was ridiculous, Vanessa Eden was convinced they were a great relationship builder between her and her son. She often insisted on pulling out the deck and discussing a question or two when she stopped over.

Prim must not have heard him. She'd slipped several cards from the deck and was flipping through them. A broad smile lifted her lips as she looked up. "This looks like a lot more fun than a movie."

Max surrendered to the inevitable. If Prim wanted to play, they'd play. He took solace in the fact he'd make sure she was sitting next to him on the sofa while they bared their souls.

If he could convince her to take off an article of clothing or two during the course of the evening, all the pain of playing that ridiculous card game would be worth it.

Prim dropped down on the sofa and kicked off her flip-flops. As this was her first time in Max's home, it would be understandable if she felt a little awkward.

The funny thing was, the only thing she felt was relaxed.

It had to be the sex. It was as if all the stress and tension inside her had been pummeled out of her.

"What's that little smile about?" Max sat down beside her, rested an arm above her shoulders on the back of the sofa. "Plotting what deep, dark secrets you're going to get me to reveal?"

Prim arched a brow. "Do you have deep, dark secrets?"

"Nope." He grinned and she felt warm all over.

"Actually." She placed the cards in her lap. "I was thinking how comfortable I am with you."

His fingers toyed with her hair. "Same here."

When those blue eyes met hers, Prim experienced the connection all over again. She didn't want to think about what would happen after this weekend. For now she'd just go with the flow.

Prim dropped her gaze to the cards and flipped through the deck.

"Since the Fourth is coming up, we could watch *Independence Day*," Max suggested.

It was obvious this was a last-ditch effort on his part to avoid the cards. Which, after seeing several of the questions, she fully understood.

"We're doing the cards." Then, because that sounded so self-serving, Prim added, "If we're going to be good neighbors, we should know each other."

He trailed a finger up her arm. "I'd say we know each other pretty well."

The simple touch sent heat coursing up her arm. Impulsively she leaned over and kissed him, warm and long and sweet.

He smiled. "What was that for?"

"For being such a good host."

The look in his eyes said her comment had pleased him. Though being spontaneous usually came hard for her, she vowed to make an effort this weekend. She didn't think it was going to be a problem. With Max she felt safe, comfortable, and cherished.

"I can't believe you played this game with your mother. Listen to this one." She held up a card and read aloud, "What's your favorite body part of the opposite sex?"

"Your mouth."

Prim blinked. She lifted her fingers to her lips. "My mouth?"

"I love how you smile. The way you kiss." Max leaned forward, his lips warm against hers.

Fueled by desire, her blood began to thrum. She gazed up at him through lowered lashes. "Me? I like your ass."

He sat back, his eyes wide.

Prim continued. "Puh-leeze, like you aren't aware that you really rock a pair of jeans."

She resisted the urge to laugh when he flushed.

"I don't know what to say."

Even as the teasing words left her lips, Prim wondered what had gotten into her. She felt as young and carefree as a college girl. "Just say you'll show it to me later."

"That's an easy promise to keep." He glanced down. "My ass, huh?"

"It's stellar." Prim snuggled close. She was so happy she'd returned to Good Hope instead of staying in Appleton. "Ohmigoodness."

She straightened up so quickly she nearly clipped Max in the jaw. "I promised to call Deb and Mike as soon as I got home."

Without a word, Max rose. Crossing the room, he scooped up the phone she'd left on the kitchen table, then tossed it to her.

She glanced at him as he dropped back on the sofa beside her. "Sorry."

He waved a dismissive hand. "I'm still basking in the glow. *Max Brody* and *stellar ass* in the same sentence. Who'd have thunk it?"

Any woman who'd seen him, that's who. Prim immediately banished the disturbing thought of other women ogling him and located her in-laws' contact number.

"Hi, Deb." Prim infused her voice with a friendly warmth when the woman answered. "I'm sorry I forgot to call. I made it home safely. How are the boys?"

She listened as Deb relayed every minute detail of the twins' evening, including the fact that Mike and the boys were currently at the park.

"That's sounds like fun." Prim batted at Max's hand, which kept trying to snake under her shirt. "I'm surprised you didn't go with them."

"We've got a big day planned tomorrow. Which meant I had to get my chores done around the house this evening." Under all that sugary sweetness, Deb's tone held a decided bite. "If you'd have stayed, we could have gotten them done in half the time."

Prim didn't take the bait. "I know the boys will have loads of fun with you and Mike. Is there a good time for me to call this evening to say good night?"

She listened for what seemed an eternity.

"I understand," she said when Deb paused to take a breath. "Please let Callum and Connor know I called, and tell them I love them very much."

Less than a minute later, she placed the phone nearby on the coffee table just in case Deb changed her mind. Then she rested her head against Max's shoulder.

"Everything okay?" Gently, he stroked her hair, his voice as warm and soothing as the gesture.

"Mike took the boys to Memorial Park. I'm sure they're having a great time."

"Do you want to pick them up? Bring them home?"

"Why would I do that?"

"You're worried about them."

"I'm frustrated." She blew out a breath. "I wanted to say good night, but Deb claims they'll be too busy to talk on the phone once they get home."

"Call anyway."

"It'll be fine." Prim sighed. "I know they're safe. If there are any issues, Deb will be on the phone in seconds."

"This is nice."

She lifted her head from his warm shoulder. "What's nice?"

"Sitting here, like this, with you." He pointed to the card sitting on top of the deck. "*What's your idea of romance?* This is my idea: sitting on the sofa, relaxing after a busy day. Oh, and after having the best sex of my life."

She rolled her eyes. "You're easy to please."

His slow smile made her forget anything else except him. "Tell me your idea of romance."

She didn't immediately answer.

"I know what it isn't. It's not about candy or flowers or trips," she said after a long moment, thinking of Rory's way. "For me it's sitting around the dinner table sharing the events of the day. It's having my guy take my hand when we walk down the street. It's having him there at night to hold me when it's time to go to bed and being there when I wake up."

"That's what you deserve and so much more." He kissed her temple. "You can have all that. Just say the word. Whatever you want, it's yours."

A longing for what could never be rose like a tidal wave inside her. Fighting to retain control over her rioting emotions, Prim blinked rapidly and concentrated on the next card. "What one thing would you like to change about me?"

With careful deliberateness, Max took the card from her hand. He laid it and the deck aside, then pulled her tightly against him. For several seconds they simply sat there, the only sound the gentle whir of the ceiling fan.

"I don't know about you, but I'm starving," he said finally. "How about I order a pizza?"

"Green and black olives? Extra cheese?" On the trip to Milwaukee eons ago, all the other mathletes they'd hung around with had been into boring hamburger or equally boring pepperoni. Which meant they'd had a whole pie to themselves.

Max grinned. "Is there any other combination?"

Chapter Seventeen

It was nearly nine o'clock on Saturday morning before Prim and Max rolled out of bed. After a long shower, where Prim got an up-close-and-personal look at Max's ass as well as another favorite body part, he made breakfast.

She'd been prepared to cook. After all, it was something she'd done daily for the past ten years. But Max insisted she sit, enjoy her coffee, and admire his stellar ass.

The last part made her chuckle. With coffee cup in hand and clad only in one of his shirts, Prim called and spoke with her sons. After ending the call, she watched him expertly flip a pancake.

"You'll make a wonderful husband someday." The second the words left her mouth, Prim wished she could call them back.

Max simply smiled and flipped another cake.

Perhaps this wasn't a particularly sensitive subject, after all. "I'm surprised some pretty young thing hasn't snatched you up."

"My mother thinks I'm too particular." He chuckled. "Considering she's never found a man who comes close to her memories of my father, it's a strange thing for her to say."

Prim, as well as most of the other people in Good Hope, was aware of Vanessa Eden's history. She'd married Brian Brody at nineteen. Max had been born a year later when Brian, who'd enlisted in the military, was overseas. Max had been only four when his father was killed in Bosnia.

"Is that why you don't want children?"

Max paused, spatula in hand. "I want kids."

Prim frowned. "You said you didn't date women with children."

"The missing word is *casually* date." He returned his attention to the bacon. "I never wanted to be the guy who is in and out of a child's life. I know, from personal experience, how hard that can be on a kid."

Prim's admiration for him inched up another notch. She'd watched many of her divorced friends in Milwaukee deal with their heartbroken children as well as their own heartache when a relationship ended.

"That's one of the reasons I'd vowed not to date until the boys were grown," Prim told him.

Max turned off the griddle and the frying pan. He slipped the pancakes onto two plates, his gaze focused on the food. "A serious relationship between two people well suited would be different."

His tone was nonchalant as he placed the plate of eggs, bacon, and several pancakes in front of her.

Prim waited until he'd taken the seat across the table from her before she reached over and took his hand. "I agree with that, too."

When his fingers curved around hers and his thumb caressed her palm, Prim let out the breath she'd been holding.

As if he was finding as much comfort in the touch as she was, Max didn't immediately release her hand . . . and she didn't pull back. They'd made love this morning in the shower and late last night again before they'd fallen asleep in each other's arms. For some reason, this felt as intimate as when their bodies were fully joined.

Finally, he gave her hand a squeeze and released it. "We better eat before it gets cold."

"Talk to me, Max." Prim lifted a crisp slice of bacon to her mouth but kept her eyes on him. "Are you interested in dating me?"

He met her gaze. "Naw, I just want to have sex with you."

Her lids flew wide and her fork fell from her numb fingers into the syrup-drenched pancakes.

"Just kidding." Max grinned and rose to get her another fork. His smile had already faded by the time he held it out. "You've made it clear how you feel about dating before the boys are out of high school."

Prim took the fork from his hand with fingers that trembled slightly. Setting the utensil down, she laced her fingers tightly together. "That's how I felt when I moved here. I thought that was best for the twins and for me." She'd spoken in the past tense, and a slight flicker of his lashes told her he'd noticed.

With a sober expression, he leaned forward, his gaze firmly fixed on hers. "I guess the question is, what do you want now?"

Max had placed the decision regarding their future at her feet. Whatever she decided would not only reflect her intelligent assessment of the situation but her guts. Prim knew it took just as strong an intestinal fortitude to walk away from a situation as it did to stay.

She wondered briefly if Rory had ever gotten this feeling when he was ready to rappel off a high peak. A moment of terror mixed with heady anticipation.

Still, she wasn't impulsive. When she'd initially decided not to date, it was so she could give her full attention to her sons. The question was, would the boys suffer if she had a relationship with Max? They liked him, wanted to be around him, and all indications were those positive feeling went both ways.

For Prim, being around Deb recently had brought the woman's overinvolvement in her son's life front and center. That kind of helicopter parenting hadn't been healthy for Deb or for Rory. Such a relationship wouldn't be healthy for Callum and Connor, either.

Watching her intently, Max took a long sip of coffee.

"I'd like to date you," Prim blurted out as if she'd just decided to throw caution to the winds instead of making a logical, rational decision. "I'd like to give it, give us, a chance."

"What about the boys?" The smile that had begun to slowly spread didn't hide the worry in his eyes.

"Callum and Connor like you. You're their neighbor, their coach, their grandfather's friend. For now, it doesn't have to be more complicated for them than that."

He reached across the table to cover her hand with his. "I won't let them be hurt."

"*We* won't let them be hurt," Prim said firmly. "We'll take this dating thing slow and easy."

"Slow and easy can be fun." There was a devilish twinkle in his eyes.

Prim only rolled her eyes.

Max shoveled in some eggs, chewed thoughtfully, then chuckled. "Do you realize we just made a major decision without utilizing a spreadsheet and reviewing all the data?"

Stabbing a bite of pancake, Prim couldn't stop a grin. "We didn't even negotiate terms."

His expression turned serious. "Do you have any nonnegotiables?"

Prim chewed, considered. "Ah, no sleeping together when the boys are in the house."

He waited several heartbeats.

"Let me make sure I have this straight." He took a sip of coffee. "We'll keep having sex but we'll refrain from tearing off each other's clothing when there are children in the house?"

"That's the nonnegotiable."

"Makes sense." He paused. "Ah, I'm not sure if you noticed, but they're not in the house now."

When a hungry look filled his eyes that had nothing to do with food, Prim knew once again they were on the same wavelength.

"I was thinking of starting the day with a card game."

Max groaned. "I'm going to kill my mother."

"No. No. No." Prim waved an airy hand in the air. "This game is one I know you'll like."

He lifted a brow.

"Poker."

His eyes lit up. "I like—"

"Strip poker."

His grin was broad and wide. "Now you're talking."

Max rose.

She motioned him down. "After breakfast."

He dropped into his chair with a disappointed thunk. Picking up his fork, he gazed across the table at her. "Do you even know how to play?"

"You'll soon find out." This time it was her turn to grin. "Now I have a question for you."

"Fire away."

She pointed with her fork. "Do you want that last piece of bacon?"

Over the next hour, Max saw a different side of Primrose Bloom. This crazy, fun-loving side was one he'd caught only brief glimpses of in the past.

The first time had been when she was ten and someone—he couldn't even remember who—had brought a bag of chocolate-covered crickets to school. None of the girls would try them . . . except for Prim. She'd eaten one, pronounced it delicious, then eaten several more. When she'd caught him staring, she'd given him a saucy smile and eaten another.

At that moment he'd fallen hopelessly in love. Hopeless because, even back then, she'd been Rory's girl.

"Your play, Brody."

Max glanced at the cards in his hand. He was down to his boxer shorts. She still wore all her clothes, including one of his jackets, zipped up to her chin.

Max had been confident that jacket would be off by now and he'd be working hard on getting her to take off whatever was underneath.

"Four of a kind." He spread the cards on the table, showing four kings.

Her lips quirked up in a half smile.

Darn. She'd beaten him again.

She showed him her hand, tilted her head. "Remind me. Does that"—she pointed to his cards, then to her own—"beat this?"

"Thank you, God."

Prim's brows drew together. "What did you say?"

"I said, four of a kind beats a full house."

"Oh." She smiled brightly. "Does that mean it's time for me to take something off?"

"That's exactly what it means. Take off the jacket," Max suggested. "You have to be warm."

"Good suggestion." As she fumbled with the zipper, Max wondered how many layers would be revealed underneath.

Two or three, he decided. At least two.

Though the fastener didn't appear to be stuck, she raised her hands and looked beseechingly at him. "Can you help me?"

Pushing back his chair, Max rose and rounded the table. By the time he reached her, she was on her feet and waiting for him. "Thank you, Max."

"My pleasure."

She smelled like his shampoo and he found himself wanting her again. But first he had to win enough hands to rid her of all her clothes.

The zipper slid down easily, and when the jacket gaped open he realized that she wasn't wearing a shirt—or anything else—beneath it.

"You-you're naked." His gaze lingered on her breasts, on those erect nipples surrounded by a dusky peach color.

"Not yet." She shrugged and the jacket fell and pooled at her feet. "I hope to be soon."

"Let's play another hand."

"I'm tired of cards." Prim gazed up at him through lowered lashes. "I can think of a better way to spend our time together."

No, this was not the Primrose he thought he knew. As he scooped her into his arms to carry her to bed and she shrieked with laughter, he wondered just what other secrets he would discover this weekend.

By Sunday night, Max was a goner.

Despite his earlier agreement, he realized he didn't want to take things slow. He wanted to walk down the street holding Prim's hand. He wanted to wake up, like he had the past two mornings, with her beside him in bed. He wanted to sit across the dinner table from her and talk. Not only about sudoku and magic squares but about her thoughts and feelings.

He liked that family mattered to her. That had been evident last night. Marigold had unexpectedly called and Prim had taken an hour to console her baby sister.

Prim stood at the counter now, tossing a salad, humming while she worked. Love washed over him in a tidal wave of emotion.

Marigold called again just as he finished seasoning the steaks for the grill. He'd lingered on the patio longer than necessary, wanting to give them some privacy.

Prim was off the phone and adding slivered almonds and mandarin oranges to the romaine when he stuck his head in the door. Opening the door fully, he stepped inside.

Prim glanced over her shoulder. "Steaks on the grill?"

"Yep. They're sizzling away." He slipped behind her and wrapped his arms around her. Just touching her, just being close settled him. "How's your baby sister?"

"Better." She rested her head back against his chest. "Marigold heard through the grapevine that Steffan and his boyfriend are fighting and that's why he's been so owly. Though it doesn't excuse him taking out his frustrations on his employees, she feels better now that she understands the Jekyll-Hyde act."

"I hope whatever personal issues he has clear up soon, for her sake." Max tightened his hold, liking the way her soft curves fit against him. "Is she going to be able to come home for a visit?"

"If the stars align and Steffan doesn't go bat shit in the interim, she hopes to still be here for the Fourth. We conferenced Ami in on the call." Prim smiled. "She wanted Marigold to stay with her, but she'll stay with me. Ami and Beck are newlyweds. I reminded Ami that she's still at the stage where you love walking around naked just to get a rise out of your husband. In that scenario, three would definitely be a crowd."

"You get a rise out of me when you walk around naked."

"I like the way you rise to the occasion." Prim wiggled her eyebrows and made him laugh, just as the doorbell sounded.

Max lifted a brow.

"Don't look at me," she said. "This is your house. Whoever is at the door came to see you."

It was Beck and Ami.

After greeting Max with a bright smile, Ami shoved a covered dish into his hands. "It's scalloped potatoes. I wasn't sure what you were having for dinner, but these go good with just about everything."

Max shot a glance at his friend, who just shrugged good-naturedly. "I took them out of the oven, so you can thank me, too."

"Thanks to both of you." Max stepped aside and gestured them through the doorway.

Ami stepped to Prim and gave her a hug. "Are we interrupting?"

"Actually, you're just in time for dinner." Prim looped her arm through her sister's. "We have two huge steaks on the grill, easily enough for four."

Prim slanted a glance in his direction, passing the ball to him.

"If you haven't eaten, stay," he urged. "We'd love to have you join us."

He saw Beck and Ami exchange a glance. The way he figured, they might as well know it all. "Prim and I are dating. We're a couple."

Ami glanced at him. "You know, Max, I always thought you were a smart guy. Now—"

She paused and Max waited for the punch line.

Ami winked. "Now, I know it."

"Do you have plans for tomorrow?" Max toyed with a lock of Prim's hair and tried to keep his tone casual, as if her answer didn't matter.

Her sister and Beck had just left. Now, he and Prim were enjoying some alone time on the sofa. While Max had enjoyed their company, he was happy to have Prim all to himself for the rest of the evening.

"Lots of exciting stuff on tap. I'll pick up Boris in the morning, do some laundry, and clean the house." She lifted her head and looked up at him. "What about you?"

"My mother and I are meeting in the morning at the garden center. I want to make sure she has everything together for our appointment Tuesday with the IRS in Green Bay."

Prim's eyes widened. "Is she being audited?"

"Not her, personally, but the business. I do the taxes for the Garden of Eden, so I'll be attending as her representative."

Worry filled her eyes. "I hope everything goes okay."

"It should. As long as she gave me the right figures and has the receipts for those figures."

"It's been a busy day." Two bright spots of pink dotted Prim's cheeks. "I want you to know that when I mentioned to my sister that I was staying over here for the weekend, I never expected her and Beck to just show up."

"I like Beck. And I like your sister." He brushed a kiss across her cheek. "Having dinner with them was enjoyable. We'll have to do it again."

"Yes." She slid her hand down, linked her fingers with his. "This has been nice. Other than Eliza's three texts, that is. Does she really think we're so incompetent she has to check up on everything we've done?"

"Forget about her." His voice was a husky caress. "Let's talk about what you'd like to do with the rest of the evening."

"Hmmm." She tapped her fingers against her lips, her gaze thoughtful. When her eyes settled on the cabinet, Max froze.

Not the cards. Not the cards. Not the cards.

"Naked."

He paused. Had she really said the word *naked*, or had he said that because getting her naked was on his mind?

"Pardon?"

"Let's get naked, walk around the house."

Like newlyweds. His words. Supplied by his mind. Not hers.

"Sounds . . . interesting. Then what?"

As she stared up at him through lowered lashes, her lips tipped in a saucy grin as infectious as it had been in fifth grade. "We see what comes next."

Chapter Eighteen

Max parked his car down the street from his destination and began walking toward the water. A group of what looked like college students strolled just ahead of him. The willowy woman with blond hair and a throaty laugh made him think of his mother.

He'd spent the morning with her at the Garden of Eden going over receipts for deductions. Vanessa Eden was an intelligent, vibrant woman. Yet for over twenty years, every attempt she'd made to move on in her personal life had failed dismally.

He was surprised she hadn't figured out the problem before now. How could she expect to have a successful relationship in the present with her feet so firmly planted in the past?

For nearly twenty-five years she'd put his father on a pedestal. The young soldier had become larger in death than he'd been in life. Pictures of him filled her home and office. None of the men who'd come after his dad had stood a chance. You couldn't compete with a ghost.

Was it the same for Prim? Did Rory still have her heart? At the thought, a pain so sharp it stole his breath lanced his own.

No, Max told himself, Prim had definitely moved on. There was no way she could be so giving and loving with him and still be in love with someone else.

Music spilled from the open windows of the Flying Crane, a popular bar located on the waterfront. Tonight the place hosted a Milwaukee rock band as part of a weeklong Uncle Sam Jam fundraiser. Every penny of the nightly ten-dollar cover went toward the Giving Tree.

The Giving Tree had started back when Max had been a kid as a Christmas gift project sponsored by the rotary. Over the years it had morphed into a way for Good Hope citizens to help neighbors who'd fallen on hard times.

Neighbors helping neighbors.

That attitude was what made Good Hope such a wonderful place to live at any time of year. Though Max hadn't felt like partying at a bar, last night Beck had urged him to stop by even if it was just for a few minutes.

The band had apparently decided loud made up for any number of deficiencies. Still, as Max pulled open the battered wooden door and handed over his ten-dollar bill, he had to admit the beat was infectious. The Flying Crane was more crowded than he'd have expected for a Monday.

A fair number of tourists filled the tables, and that was always good for business. The bar's placement on the waterfront was a big draw. The inside held some ambience. A glossy curved mahogany bar took up an entire wall. Behind it a long mirror made the average-size bar appear huge.

Unfortunately, the high tin ceiling—while decorative—did nothing to improve the band's sound. Max let his gaze sweep the main bar area but came up empty. No Beck in sight.

"Can I help you find someone?" Part-time artist, part-time waitress Izzie Deshler stopped beside Max. The petite brunette's long, wavy hair had been pulled back into some kind of coiled tail. "Or get you something to drink?"

"A beer." Max flashed a friendly smile. "Whatever you have on tap. How've you been?"

"Keeping busy. Beck and Ami are having me paint a mural on their parlor wall." Izzie returned his smile. "I'll be starting it next week."

"I'm sure you'll do a great job." Max had seen evidence of her work and had been impressed. "If it's anything like your work at Muddy Boots, it will be amazing."

Thanks to Izzie, the hideous wallpaper in a coffee pot pattern of harvest gold and mud brown was now just a not-so-pleasant memory.

"Speaking of Beck, have you seen him?"

"He's out on the deck." She winced as the lead singer's guitar went sharp. "The noise in here can be a bit overwhelming."

For the first time he noticed the small earplugs nestled in her ears. He tapped his ears. "Smart woman."

She flashed a smile. "Self-preservation."

Max wove his way through the tables and out the door onto a large deck protected from the elements by a high-pitched roof sporting ceiling fans. The night was clear with a nice breeze off the water.

All of the tables were full. There were a good number of people milling around talking. *Undoubtedly enjoying a respite from the noise, er, music*, Max thought.

He found Beck at a table for four next to the railing.

Max pulled out a wooden chair opposite his friend and plopped down. "The band sounds better the further away you get."

"First sign of getting older, Brody, is when you start complaining about loud music." Beck grinned. "Next thing, you'll be eating dinner at four thirty."

"As if you have room to talk, Cross. I noticed you got a table far from the music instead of taking a stool at the bar and flirting with the female bartender."

Beck chuckled and tipped the bottle of Corona to his lips. "Aren't you drinking tonight?"

"Izzie is bringing me a beer." Max gestured with his head toward the doorway. "Unless she didn't hear me clearly because of the noise. Then it's anyone's guess what will be on her tray."

It wasn't until Max reached to take a handful of pretzels from the basket in the center of the table that he noticed the margaritas. "Who's joining us?"

Not to be sexist, but Max didn't know a single guy who drank margaritas. That was usually a woman's drink. Which meant . . .

"Is Ami with you?" Max should have known Beck wouldn't leave his new bride at home.

"You know how she feels about the Giving Tree. She came to show her support. Ah, there they are." Beck rose and held out his arms. "The lovely Bloom sisters."

"Not Bloom." Ami brushed a kiss across her husband's cheek. "It's Cross now. You *are* the one I married earlier this month?"

Prim held out her hands to Max as if she hadn't seen him in weeks rather than been naked in his bed twelve hours ago. "Beck told me he thought you might stop by. This is such a great cause."

He was shocked. And delighted.

Max glanced at his friend, who simply gave him a benign smile and turned back to listen to something his wife was saying.

He squeezed Prim's hands. "Good to see you, neighbor."

She flashed that impish smile that made his blood stir.

"Release the woman, Brody, and sit down."

"Shut up, Beck." Reluctantly, Max released Prim's hands.

He pulled out her chair.

She smiled her thanks.

Ami smiled so benevolently at them, Max half expected her to offer a benediction.

He felt like giving thanks himself. Tonight was an unexpected gift. He and Prim. Out together. Taking their relationship public.

Tomorrow, he'd be in Green Bay. By the time he returned, Callum and Connor would be back from Appleton. In a matter of hours, everything would go back to how it had been before the weekend.

Other than he and Prim were dating. The thought made him smile.

"How's the parade planning coming?" Ami asked.

Max exchanged a glance with Prim.

"Fairly well, I think," Prim told her sister. "We made a few changes to the lineup to make it more efficient. Those who it affects have been notified."

"Prim and I also walked the parade route." Max glanced at Beck. "We found a construction area that we thought might be an issue, but I checked with Jeremy. He assured me all construction in the parade route will wrap up this week." Max rubbed his chin. "I'll keep checking on it myself, just to be sure."

"Smart." Beck nodded approval.

Izzie brought his drink and added more pretzels to the bowl. The music from the band spilled out onto the deck and became a pulsing beat in his blood.

Max shifted to Prim. God, she looked pretty tonight in her sleeveless cotton dress of pale yellow. For a moment he felt sixteen again, about to ask a girl out for the first time. Only back then, the only girl he'd wanted to ask out had been already taken.

He pushed back his chair and stood, held out a hand.

Prim cocked her head.

"What are you up to now?" Beck took a long drink of beer, straight from the bottle.

"Prim and I are going to dance."

Warmth flooded Prim's eyes even as she lifted a brow. "Is that right?"

Ami pushed back her chair with a clatter. "I want to dance, too."

"Ahh, sweetheart."

But his wife was already on her feet, so Beck set down his bottle and slowly rose. He shot Max a glance. "You owe me."

Because he agreed, Max didn't argue. If Beck hadn't asked him to come down to the bar, he wouldn't be about to dance with the woman he loved.

Max enjoyed the energy of the crowd during the fast songs, but he inwardly cheered when the tempo slowed and gave him an excuse to embrace Prim. She remained cosseted in his arms as the band launched into its second slow song of the set.

Ami leaned close, her arms still looped around Beck's neck. "Why don't you and Max stop by the house for coffee and dessert? I realize it's a weekday, but I've got this new card game I'm dying to try out."

Max grimaced. "I'm not into card games."

"I'm sure it's a lot of fun." Prim chuckled. "What's it called?"

"Snap. Kids or adults can play it. I picked it up for the boys, but I thought we should check it out first."

Though he hid it well, the slightly pained expression on Beck's face said he wasn't any more eager than Max to play the game.

The music stopped. Everyone around them poured from the dance floor as the band took a break.

"It sounds like fun." Prim's enthusiasm garnered a bright smile from her sister. "I'm up for it, but I can't speak for Max."

"I'm with you." Max's gaze never left hers. "Count me in."

Max decided there was something special about being out with Prim as part of a couple. Being with her made an ordinary evening fun.

Even though he and Beck had groaned at the thought of playing Snap, a *children's* card game, they had competitive natures, as did the two women. From a quick read of the rules, Max learned the game had been around since the 1800s and was promoted as a game of skill requiring accurate observation and quick reactions.

Was it any wonder Prim was winning?

Three sets of eyes were on Max as he flipped over a queen of hearts and placed it on the pile in front of him.

"Snap." Prim's voice rang out an instant before Beck's.

"She did it again," Beck grumbled.

"One of these days you'll say it first." Ami brushed a kiss across her husband's cheek.

Max slanted a sideways glance at Prim.

She grinned at his thumbs-up, then added both Ami's and his own cards to the bottom of her growing facedown pile.

"You're a sharp one, Primrose Bloom," Beck told her.

Prim offered a smug smile. "Children's card games are a particular specialty of mine."

"Watch out, Vegas." Max's droll comment made them all laugh.

Ten minutes later, Prim jumped to her feet. "Snap for the win."

With her arms raised high, she did a circular happy dance, complete with hip bumps.

"My cards are gone," Beck admitted.

"All our cards are gone," Ami confirmed. "Little sister has won it all."

"We'll have to do this again." Beck's comment earned him a sunny smile from his wife.

"Get the four of us together," he quickly clarified. "Not play the game."

"I'd think you'd want to try again." Max plastered an innocent expression on his face. "Make up for that earlier Snap error."

"I swear Ami turned over a king," Beck insisted.

His wife patted his hand. "A ten looks a lot like a king."

Max snorted.

Prim elbowed him in the ribs. "Be nice."

Max just grinned and looped an arm around Prim's shoulders. He agreed with Beck. They definitely had to do this again.

"Time for coffee and dessert," Ami announced.

Though it wasn't particularly cold outside, Beck turned on the gas log—without the heat—in the parlor. With Prim's assistance, Ami brought out the tray of apple crisp, topped with real whipped cream, and coffee.

Beck and Ami confiscated the love seat while Max sat beside Prim on the ornate long sofa in a muted gold-silk-and-burgundy pattern.

Taking a sip of the strong chicory blend, Max relaxed against the soft fabric.

Beck set down his cup and leaned forward. Resting his forearms on his thighs, he leveled a gaze at Max. "What are your intentions toward Prim?"

Prim inhaled sharply.

Thankfully, Max had just swallowed his coffee or he might have spat it out all over the elegant cocktail table with the ornately carved legs and feet.

"Beck." Ami's tone held a low warning her husband ignored.

"I was just practicing for when we have little girls." Beck picked up the dessert plate, not even trying to hide his grin. "Gets quite a reaction." Ami rolled her eyes.

Max thought he saw a look of longing on Prim's face, but it was gone so quickly he might have imagined it. But he could visualize their baby girl quite easily. She'd be as pretty as her mother, with strawberry-blond hair and Prim's beautiful hazel eyes.

"Got quite the reaction out of this guy." Beck jerked a thumb in Max's direction.

The devilish gleam in Beck's eyes had Max trying to recall just what he might have said or done that might be the cause of this unexpected bout of torture.

"You and Prim have been friends for a long time. Ami and I started out as friends, too." Beck linked his fingers with his wife's, then brought their joined hands to his lips and kissed her fingers. "Look how that ended up."

"Anyone want more coffee?" Ami shot her sister an apologetic smile. She obviously hadn't fully regained her equilibrium, as she'd just poured them full cups only moments before.

"Thank you, Ami." Prim took a long sip out of her cup, emptying half. "I'd love more."

"I'm excited for the twins to be back," Ami chattered, shooting her husband a cautioning look. "That's tomorrow, right?"

"Unless Deb and Mike decide to keep them longer."

Max shot Prim a look. "Would they do that?"

"They'd call and ask, of course. But with them . . ." She scooped up a bite of apple crisp. "You just never know."

"Did she bring up the urn when you were there?" Ami turned to the guys. "Deb always brings up the urn."

Prim shifted uncomfortably. "Not this time."

Beck cocked his head. "The urn with Rory's ashes?"

"That's the one." Ami appeared oblivious to her sister's discomfort. "Not this Christmas, but the one before that, she gave Prim this attractive marble cube. We couldn't figure out what it was for until Deb told us."

Ami took a sip of coffee and shook her head.

"What was it for?" Beck asked the question poised on the tip of Max's tongue.

"She wanted some of Rory's ashes." Prim's tone was as flat as her eyes.

"She's determined to put him in their family burial plot." Ami stopped, appearing for the first time to notice her sister's expression. "I'm sorry, sweetie. I didn't mean to make you sad."

"You didn't." Prim smiled. "Were you able to find out when Fin would be back in the States?"

Max set down his cup and pushed to his feet. "If you ladies will excuse us, Beck wanted to show me what he has planned for one of the upstairs bedrooms."

Obviously puzzled, Ami turned to her husband. "Which bedroom?"

"Ah, the green one." Beck stood, bent over, and kissed his wife softly on the lips.

"I don't know of any plans," Ami said, still looking confused.

"I thought I'd run them by Max, see what he thought."

Ami's gaze shifted between her husband and Max. A look of understanding filled her eyes. She turned back to her sister as Beck led the way upstairs.

"What's this about?" Beck asked.

At least the guy was smart enough to wait until they were out of earshot to speak, Max thought. If only he'd shown the same common restraint downstairs.

"I thought Ami and Prim needed some time alone." Max climbed the stairs. "Talking about Rory's ashes made Prim uncomfortable."

"I wonder if it was just talking about the ashes that bothered her." Beck stepped into the upstairs parlor but made no move to sit. "Or talking about them with you present?"

Max had wondered the same thing. He didn't like the idea that there might be some things Prim wouldn't feel comfortable discussing with him. Yet he had to admit, something about her clinging so tightly to Rory's ashes disturbed him.

"I'm in love with Prim," Max confided in a matter-of-fact tone.

Beck slapped him on the back. "'Bout time you admitted it."

Though he wanted to scowl, Max kept his expression even. "I believe we can go the distance. But—"

"But what?" Beck prompted.

"Rory." Max raked fingers through his hair. "You've heard the stories. He and Prim had this fairy-tale thing going. Childhood sweethearts, married right out of college."

A shadow passed over Beck's face.

Too late Max realized that particular scenario was all too familiar to Beckett Cross.

Beck had led that fairy-tale life until a car accident had claimed his pregnant wife's life and that of their unborn son. Yet Max found hope in the knowledge that his friend had been able to find happiness with Ami.

"Ami said something about Prim not being interested in marrying again until her boys were grown." Beck's tone was casual, his face expressionless.

"That's what she said." Max kept his tone equally casual. "She also said she wasn't interested in dating. She's changed her mind on that, she may change her mind on the other."

"It's hard." Beck shifted his gaze to the fireplace, where the hearth sat cold and dark. "There's a lot of guilt when you think about moving on with your life. It can feel like a betrayal, as if you didn't love them enough. It's not logical, but emotions aren't usually logical."

"Some people never get past that point." Max thought of his mother. "Or maybe there's only that one person for them and no one else will ever be enough."

"That's rare." Beck turned and rested his back against the stone. "More than likely the person won't——can't—let go of the past."

Max exhaled a ragged breath, scrubbed his face with his hands. "Love sucks."

Beck gave a little laugh. "The rewards of finding someone who makes your life complete is worth the pain of the journey."

"I'm not sure how the journey will end, but I can tell you one thing." Max met his friend's gaze. "I won't be the one getting off the bus first."

Chapter Nineteen

Max found himself humming along with the radio on the short drive to the Garden of Eden. The second he pulled up, his mother appeared, red heels clicking on the concrete.

Vanessa put her briefcase on the backseat next to his before sliding in the front. "I wondered when you'd get here."

Max glanced at the clock on the dash. Nine o'clock. "I recall saying I'd swing by to pick you up around nine."

She gave a laugh, smoothed her hair. "Sorry. I guess I'm a little nervous."

It showed, he thought, as it so rarely did. For today's visit to the Internal Revenue Service in Green Bay, his mother had pulled her blond hair back in a chignon and worn a suit. Still, no dark and conservative for his mom. The suit was fire engine red and cut in a way to enhance her figure.

Though she would turn fifty on her next birthday, Vanessa had the figure and face of a woman half her age. Her beauty and vivacious personality were two of the reasons she never lacked for male attention.

"I swung by the café and grabbed a couple of coffees to go." He pointed to the cup holders. "The one in the front is yours. Cream and sugar already added."

"Thanks, sweetie." She lifted the cup and took a sip, smiled. "How'd you know I'd need this?"

"A visit to the IRS office can make anyone a caffeine addict." Max smiled. "Just remember we have receipts for all the deductions they want to look at, so the interview should be brief."

"What if they want receipts for other deductions?"

"If they needed us to bring those, they'd have let us know." He slanted her an assessing glance as he pulled onto Highway 42. "The thing to do in these situations is to only give them what they ask for. Also, don't volunteer any information. If you're asked a question, answer it but don't overexplain. Does that make sense?"

"I understand." She gave a little laugh. "Look, just speaking of the appointment has my hands trembling. By the time we reach Green Bay, I'm going to be a real mess."

His mother always kept her cool. To see her stressed over an appointment when they had their bases covered didn't make sense.

"Then we won't talk about it." Max kept his tone calm and matter-of-fact, trying not to show his surprise. "Tell me what's new. Dating anyone?"

"That was going to be my next question for you."

Max smiled. "I asked first."

"As a matter of fact, I am seeing someone." There was an odd note in her voice he didn't recognize. "Actually, I've been seeing him for a while now."

"Is it serious?"

This time her laugh was full and robust. "Honey, with two failed marriages and too many bad relationships to count, *serious* is not a word in my vocabulary."

He waited for her to elaborate, but when she didn't Max was forced to come up with some questions. Either that or face having the tables turned and being interrogated by her. "Who is he? Do I know him?"

She didn't immediately respond and he noticed the heightened color in her cheeks.

Vanessa Eden never blushed.

This was getting more interesting by the moment.

"Mom?"

"His last name is Vogele."

The name rang a distant bell. "Organic farming? A place outside of Egg Harbor?"

Vanessa took a sip of coffee. "That's him."

Did the Adam Vogele he was thinking of have a father? It was possible. After all, everyone had a father. But Max seemed to recall this Adam moving to the area about ten years ago. Had his dad come with him? "Tall, rangy guy? Dark hair?"

"Sounds as if you know him."

She appeared dazed at the thought.

"I don't think so. The guy I'm thinking of is thirty-three, thirty-four, tops. Beck's age."

"Yes. That's him."

"Okay, ha-ha, great joke." He chuckled. "Now tell me who it is that you're really seeing."

"I'm still in my forties, Max." A testiness filled her voice. "Fifteen years isn't that much of a difference."

She was serious. He passed another mile marker before he found his voice. "Ah, how long have you and Adam been seeing each other?"

"Since Easter."

"Three months. Wow. For you that's long-term."

She shot him a withering look and punched him in the shoulder. "Mind your manners."

"I'm just giving you a hard time. If he makes you happy, I'm all for it."

Her fingers twisted together in her lap. "It's not going anywhere."

"Who knows?" Max kept his tone light. "Adam could be *the one*."

"No." His mother's tone was subdued. "Your father was *the one*. I've spent the past twenty years searching for that same special something with other men, but I've finally come to the realization that Brian and I were soul mates. There is no one else."

"There could be someone else out there. Maybe you just haven't found him yet." Max wasn't sure why he was pushing. He just knew it felt important she agree.

"You'll understand when you fall in love. When you give your heart to someone, fully and completely, it no longer belongs to you. It's no longer available to give to someone else."

"You told me you loved Richard. I don't think you ever loved Todd, but Richard was different."

Max had liked most of the men his mother had dated or married. But stepdad number two had been his favorite and the one he'd missed the most.

Richard's leaving was the reason for his vow not to casually date a woman with children. He thought of Callum and Connor. The closer he and Prim got, the more they'd be hurt if he walked away. But he wouldn't walk away. That was the difference.

"I loved all three of my husbands in my own way." She sighed heavily. "But my heart still belonged to Brian. It wasn't free to give. Adam and I have fun. We're enjoying the rocket ride. When the soaring stops, we'll part friends."

"If that works for you, I'm happy," Max said at last.

"I understand Primrose now lives next door to you."

Funny you should mention her. Did you know we're dating?

The words were on the tip of his tongue until he pulled them. Max's relationship with Prim wasn't something they planned to keep private, but he knew if he brought it up, he'd be peppered with questions—and motherly advice—the entire drive.

Sometimes, he thought, complete disclosure carried too high a price. "Prim moved right around the time of Ami and Beck's wedding. How do you know where Prim lives?"

"This is Good Hope. Actually, she stopped by the nursery to buy some perennials a week or so ago." Vanessa's voice warmed. "She's grown into such a beautiful young woman. Those boys of hers are adorable."

"They're good kids," Max agreed, since she seemed to be expecting some sort of response.

"I have such admiration for her." His mother's voice was steady now. "And I feel such an affinity with her."

"Because you both had sons at a young age?" That made sense to him. It also made Max feel good to know that his mother liked Prim.

"Not that, although I'm sure it's part of it." Vanessa expelled a breath. "No, Prim and I both met and married our soul mates at a young age. We understand what it's like to truly be a one-man woman."

"Mommy." The twins tumbled from the car and ran straight into Prim's waiting arms.

She hugged them tight as Boris barked his welcome. They hadn't been gone all that long but it felt like years. Planting a kiss on the top of each red head, she stepped back and studied the two. "You look like you've grown a couple of inches since I last saw you."

"Grandpa Mike took us to the park and Grandma Deb gave us ice cream with a cherry on top," Connor announced.

Callum tugged at Prim's arm. "I kicked the ball into the net three times."

"Wow." Prim grinned. "Sounds like you had fun."

"We missed you." Connor had dropped down to his knees and slung an arm around the dog's neck. "And Boris, too."

"Connor." Deb stepped forward then, looking cool and put together in oatmeal-colored linen pants and a white silk blouse. "You're going to get grass stains on your jeans."

"There's Mr. Brody." Callum waved his hands wildly. "Hi, Mr. Brody. We're back."

Max, who'd been watering a patch of flowers with a hose, waved back. "Good to have you back, boys."

"He's our coach," Connor told his grandparents.

"And he lives next door," Callum added.

After spending the night with Max, Prim had gotten up extra early. She wanted to be dressed and ready whenever her in-laws and children arrived.

Deb's gaze sharpened but she said nothing.

"Always good to have a coach next door." Mike stepped forward and gave Prim a hug. "We enjoyed having the boys at our house. Thank you."

"You're very welcome. Thanks for taking such good care of them." She stepped back, studied a face that was still remarkably unlined despite the years and the sorrow. "You know, Mike, whenever I look at you, I see Rory. And now, as they grow older, I see his sons in you."

Tears welled in Deb's eyes.

"That's kind of you to say." Mike cleared his throat. "Deb and I were just commenting this weekend how much the boys are starting to look like Rory. Except for the red hair, of course."

"I had to contribute something." Prim touched his arm and offered a teasing smile. "Come inside. Have some coffee. I've got scones, too. Baked fresh this morning."

"I don't know if we have time. We're meeting friends in Ephraim." Deb hesitated. "It's their fortieth wedding anniversary and—"

"We have time for coffee with our daughter-in-law," Mike told her. "The party isn't until this evening."

Deb nodded. "Coffee and a scone would be nice."

Prim waved to Max as she ushered her in-laws inside. The boys and dog made a beeline through the house straight to the backyard.

Instead of Deb moving immediately to the kitchen, she paused in the living area, her gaze settling on the urn.

Mike gave Prim's arm a squeeze. "I'm going to see what the boys are up to out back."

"I remember when Rory was six." Deb spoke without taking her eyes off the urn. "He could be so stubborn. One more game of H-O-R-S-E, he'd tell his dad when it was time to come inside for a breathing treatment. Just one more game."

Prim wondered if Deb was even aware of the tears slipping down her face.

"He wanted so much to be like other kids, to do the things that they did." Deb turned to Prim. "I know I was angry when I found out you were pregnant. I'm sorry for everything I said back then. I'm glad now that Rory got to be a father. I only wish he could have lived longer to show you what a good dad he could be."

This was the apology Prim had never thought she'd receive from Rory's mother. Deb had taken a risk and opened herself to Prim by letting her emotions—all the pain over her son's lost hopes and dreams—show.

Prim wasn't sure how it happened, but her arms were suddenly around Deb. When the woman hugged her back, the anger and resentment Prim had worn like a too-heavy coat for all these years slipped from her shoulders to pool at her feet.

Deb and Mike stayed for two cups of coffee, then left to check in at their favorite B and B in Ephraim. Prim offered them the use of her extra bedroom for the night, but they refused.

Counting her blessings, Prim waved as her in-laws drove off. Their car had barely disappeared from sight when Ami drove up.

It amazed Prim that, after years of walking or biking everywhere—even in the winter—her older sister had finally conquered her fears and was able to drive again.

She stepped from the vintage red truck, looking as cool as strawberry shortcake in her pink-and-white-patterned dress. "Please tell me I missed them."

"Deb and Mike just left."

"Thank God." Ami gave Prim a hug, but when Prim would have stepped back from the embrace, Ami held on, giving her an extra squeeze. "I'm so sorry about last night. I shouldn't have brought up the urn with Max there. I'm normally not so insensitive."

Giving her sister's back a hard thump, Prim pulled away and held her at arm's length. "You did nothing wrong."

The boys chose that moment to tumble out the front door, a tail-wagging wolfhound at their heels.

"Aunt Ami," Connor yelled, then flung himself into her arms. "I missed you."

Ami hugged him tight. "I missed you, too, little man."

"I can use a slingshot." Callum squirmed when his aunt snaked out a hand and pulled him close.

Prim could see Callum was touched by Ami's display of affection, and that warmed her heart. But it didn't take her focus from his boast.

"Slingshot?" Prim's voice rose. "Who let you use a slingshot?"

"Grandpa Steve."

Prim made a mental note to speak with her dad about this matter the next time she saw him.

"We slingshotted rocks into the water when we went fishing," Connor offered.

"Did you catch any fish that day?" Ami asked innocently.

Both boys shook their heads.

"What a surprise." Ami grinned. "I hear you spent time with your other grandma and grandpa."

"Grandma Deb put a cherry on top of the ice cream," Connor began, ready to revisit the hands-down high point of his weekend.

The sound of an engine had Prim turning. Her heart tripled in speed when she saw Max pull out of his garage.

He stopped when he spotted her and rolled down the window. With one hand he motioned her over.

"I'll be right back," she told her sister and loped across the yard to his driveway.

His eyes met hers. "How'd it go with the in-laws?"

"Fairly painless."

"You sound surprised."

"I am . . . a little." She waved a hand. "They couldn't stay long because they have that anniversary dinner in Ephraim tonight."

"Will they stop back before heading to Appleton?"

"It didn't sound like it." Prim lifted one shoulder, let it fall. "But with them, it's hard to say. Where are you headed?"

"I got a text from Jeremy. He claims the road construction is completed."

Prim thought of the big hole in the concrete. "Are you serious? It's done?"

"That's what he said, but I'm checking it out just to be sure."

"Need help?"

"Looks like you've got a lot on your plate right now." He smiled, shifted the car into reverse. "Tell Ami and the boys hello."

Prim wanted to kiss him, wanted to hop into the passenger seat and check out the roadway with him. But she wasn't single and fancy-free, so she stepped back, gave a little wave, and watched him drive off.

Chapter Twenty

The sound of scratching woke her.

Pulled from a restless slumber, Prim lay perfectly still, ears straining. Had she left Boris outside? But if the wolfhound was in the backyard, wouldn't he be barking his head off by now instead of simply scratching at the door?

Still . . .

Prim slid out of bed. She slipped on a robe and cinched the belt tightly around her waist. Feet bare, she padded down the hall and eased open the door to the room where her sons slept. Boris lifted his head from the foot of Connor's bed, his dark eyes glowing in the dim light.

Tapping her fingers to her lips in a shushing gesture, she stepped backward. She left the door partially ajar so Boris could get out if he decided he wanted to sleep in his own bed.

In the hall, Prim stood very still and listened. The house remained silent. She'd almost convinced herself she'd imagined the sound when she heard the scratching again.

Even as she assured herself that the scratching noise was probably just a branch brushing the siding, her heart slammed against her rib cage.

Knowing she wouldn't be able to sleep if she didn't check it out, Prim turned toward the kitchen, her bare feet silent against the hardwood. For reasons she couldn't explain, she paused just short of the juncture where the hall opened into the living area.

Like a spy in a grade-B movie, she peered around the corner.

Her breath froze in her throat.

A dark-hooded figure with a flashlight stood jimmying her lock. He was pretty good at it, too. While she watched, the door slid open.

Prim whirled and sprinted down the hall. Scooping her phone up from the nightstand, she burst into the boys' bedroom.

After locking the door with shaking fingers, she spoke in an urgent, hushed whisper. "Callum. Connor. Get up. Help me shove this dresser in front of the door."

Callum sat up in bed, his eyes sleepy. "Mom?"

"Quiet. There's someone in the house." Prim didn't wait for help. Bracing her feet, she started pushing the heavy dresser toward the door. The lock might hold, but if it didn't, this would buy them some time until the sheriff arrived. "I need superhero help."

The twins were at her side in an instant. The moment the dresser was in place, she pointed to a corner spot out of range of the door. "Sit."

They exchanged wide-eyed glances but obeyed as she dialed 911. The operator answered immediately.

"9-1-1, what's your emergency?"

"This is Prim Delaney. I live at 522 Coral with my two little boys." Her voice cracked but she quickly brought it under control. "A man has broken into my home. He's here now. I don't know if he has a weapon."

"I've dispatched officers to your location." The woman's ca[l] was the opposite of Prim's breathless one. "Where are you?"

"My children and I are in a bedroom in the southeast c[ ] the house." Prim kept her voice soft. "We've locked and barric[ ] door."

"Officers are on the way. They should be there any minu[ ] woman's reassuring manner eased some of Prim's fears. "I'll sta[ ] line with you until the deputies get there."

Prim's fingers grew numb from clutching the phone s[ ] Finally, in the distance, she heard the sound of approaching si[ ]

"This is Sheriff Swarts," the deep voice boomed. "It's safe to com[e] now."

"How do I know it's you?" came the shaky reply through the do[ ]

"Prim, it's me, Max. I'm standing right here with Len." Max's co[ ]trol on his emotions hung by a thread. He desperately needed to se[e] her and the boys.

"Just a minute."

Max heard the sound of furniture being moved. After what felt like an eternity, the door eased open and Prim stepped out.

Her face was ghostly pale, her hazel eyes big. He opened his arms but she shook her head. By the look in her eyes, he wasn't the only one holding on to control by a thread.

The boys, appearing more excited than fearful, raced out and grabbed his hands, eager for his attention. Boris lumbered after them and yawned hugely.

"A man was in the house," Connor told Max.

"Did he have a gun?" Callum asked the sheriff. "Or a knife?"

"Maybe he had a bow and arrow," Connor suggested.

"Boys." Prim's voice held a sharp edge. "Enough."

"Grab some Legos from your room," Max told the boys. "You can id a jail and pretend to put the guy inside it."

The twins exchanged a glance, then hurried back into the room.

Prim watched them go.

"I've got some questions for you," Len told her.

"It was horrible." Prim closed her eyes. When her lips began to emble, Max realized her control was close to breaking. "I was so rightened."

Max went with instinct and pulled her to him. The quivering, which could have been hers or his, stopped after a few seconds. For several heartbeats she rested her head against his shoulder.

Then she gave a shuddering breath and pushed back.

Max cleared his throat. "You're probably wondering what I'm doing here."

She smiled wanly. "The thought did cross my mind."

"Max fought with the perpetrator," Len informed her.

Prim's startled gaze shifted to him.

"I stepped outside when I heard the sirens. I saw a man dressed in black running across my yard." Max's voice hardened. When he'd seen the guy coming out of Prim's house he'd gone wild with fury . . . and fear.

"Did you ninja punch him?" Connor asked.

It wasn't until the boy spoke that Max realized the twins had returned.

"Ninjas don't punch." Callum rolled his eyes. "They kick and karate chop."

"I tackled him." Max kept his tone matter-of-fact.

"That's cool, too." Callum gave a grudging nod.

"Yeah, that's cool," Connor agreed. "Ninjas tackle."

Max couldn't help but smile. "I gave a flying leap and we grappled. His face mask came off, then he took off running."

Callum and Connor looked at each other, grinned, then held out their clenched hands for a fist bump.

As Max obligingly tapped his fist against theirs, he swore he saw a fleeting smile touch Prim's lips.

"We've got officers searching for the guy," the sheriff told Prim.

"Do you have any idea who he is?" Prim asked. "I only caught a glimpse of him. And he was wearing a mask."

"Clint Gourley." Max wished he'd gotten in more than one good punch. "I saw his face."

Prim's quick indrawn breath told him she was as startled as he'd been to discover it was someone familiar behind the string of recent burglaries.

"Let's sit down." Len motioned for them to follow him down the hall.

The crime scene techs were hard at work in the living room sorting through the mess Clint had made in his search for valuables, so the sheriff directed them into the kitchen.

The twins lingered behind to watch the activity.

"Callum and Connor." Prim spoke sharply. "Come sit at the table, please."

"We want to see the police work," Callum protested.

"You may watch from the table," Prim said in an equitable tone.

"We can build the jail while we watch, Cal." Connor held up the bag of Legos.

Once they were all seated, Len gestured to the man who'd stepped in from outside. "This is Cade Rallis. I'll be retiring at the end of the month. Cade will be the interim sheriff until the spring election. He has spent a number of years on Detroit PD and brings a lot of solid police experience with him to our community."

Though Max knew Len had been considering retirement, this was the first he'd heard that an interim sheriff had already been appointed.

Max hoped retiring was Len's idea and that Anita and her kind hadn't pushed him out.

The sheriff's replacement was about his age, Max guessed, with dark hair and cool gray eyes. As he hadn't yet taken over the top spot, he appeared comfortable letting Len take the lead.

When Len introduced Primrose, Cade's serious expression eased into a smile. "Flower names must run in this community."

Prim inclined her head, her gaze puzzled. "Just in my family."

"Are you any relation to Marigold Bloom?"

If this was an attempt to relax Prim, it worked. The tight, pinched look to her face eased.

"She's my sister." Prim even managed a smile. "Do you know Marigold?"

"We met at Shannon Tracy's wedding at Christmas." Cade's expression warmed. "Is she still in—"

"Primrose," Len interrupted without apology. "Are you able to identify the man who broke into your home?"

She shook her head. "All I saw was his approximate size. He was wearing all black and had a ski mask over his face."

"He was a bad guy." Callum's brows furrowed. "Mr. Brody tackled him."

"I bet that made him sorry he broke into our house," Connor added.

Len cleared his throat. "Yes, well . . ."

"Max." Len shifted his gaze. "You're certain it was Clint Gourley?"

"I got a good look at his face when I pulled off his mask." Max looked at Prim and wished he could punch Gourley again for causing her—and the boys—a single moment of distress.

"I'm surprised he hit the house when someone was home." Cade rubbed his jaw. "That hasn't been his MO."

"I saw—" Prim stopped and shook her head. "No, I'm sure that had nothing to do with this."

Cade offered her an encouraging smile. "Every bit of information you can give us is helpful."

"Max and I were in my sister's bake shop recently when Clint was there. I happened to mention the boys and I were going to visit family in Appleton. I got the impression Clint was eavesdropping." Prim stopped, flushed. "See, I told you it was nothing."

"That's solid information." Cade glanced at the sheriff.

Len nodded agreement.

"What about your dog?" Len glanced at the wolfhound, who currently chowing down dog food as if he hadn't been fed in a week. "The barking should have alerted Clint someone was home."

"Boris slept through the break-in," Prim admitted with a rueful smile. "He has allergies."

"Mommy gives him drugs," Connor informed the sheriff. "It makes him tired."

"Benadryl," Prim clarified. "The vet recommended we try it."

Len shook his head. "Bad luck all around."

"Actually, we were very lucky."

Max saw Prim's words surprised the officers.

Cade studied her face. "How do you figure?"

"For whatever reason, I heard Clint before he got inside. He didn't see me when I peeked around the corner." Prim looked at her sons. "I had two brave little ninjas to help me push the dresser in front of the door."

She smiled at Max. "And someone close by who willingly came to our assistance."

Max let his gaze linger on the boys, who seemed to be bearing up quite admirably considering all that had happened.

What had Prim called them? Ah, yes, *brave little ninjas.*

Max rose to his feet. "I need to run next door for a second. I'll be right back."

"I think we have all the information—"

Max didn't wait for the sheriff to finish.

Prim was walking through the living room with Len and Cade, looking to see if anything was missing, when he returned.

Max knew nothing was taken. Clint had run out of the house empty-handed. When the man had staggered up from the ground, blood spurting from a nose Max was pretty sure he'd broken, the only thing left behind was a ski mask.

The boys remained at the kitchen table with their Legos, looking young and vulnerable in Spider-Man pj's.

How many times, Max wondered, had he played the brave little soldier role so his mother wouldn't worry?

"I brought something for you." Max dropped into a chair across from the boys.

"What is it?" Callum asked.

Connor leaned forward. "What did you bring us?"

Max pulled two action figures from a sack. They were favorites from his childhood collection of Teenage Mutant Ninja Turtles.

"This is Donatello." Max handed Connor the four-inch-tall figure with the purple mask. "He's the brains of the bunch."

Connor stared at Donatello, then up at Max. "Mommy says I'm smart."

"Donatello is also brave and someone others can count on." As Max's gaze settled on the boy, his heart swelled with emotion. "You were very brave tonight."

"What about me?" Callum demanded.

Max placed Raphael into the child's outstretched hand. "This is Raphael. He's funny and clever and very strong."

"I make Mommy laugh all the time." Callum lifted his arm, flexed a skinny bicep. "I'm very strong."

"You kept your cool and stayed strong for your mother tonight." Max paused to clear his throat. He widened his gaze to include both boys. "I've very proud of both of you."

Sensing a presence behind him, Max turned and found Prim standing there, hands clasped together. She offered him a wobbly smile before turning to her sons.

"Time for all good ninjas to get to bed."

"Aw, Mom," Callum began, but Max simply looked at him and he grew silent.

"Okay." Callum jumped to his feet. Without warning, the boy sprinted the few short feet to Prim, wrapping his arms tightly around her. "You were brave, too."

"You're smart, too," Connor added, joining the group hug.

To Max's utter astonishment, the boys released the hold on their mother and flung their arms around *him.*

Max was hit with a surge of love so strong it nearly toppled him. "Good night, boys."

They raced down the hall, turtles held high.

"Thank you, Mr. Brody," they called over their shoulders in unison.

"I'll see you get those back," Prim told him.

"What? No." Max shook his head. "They belong to them now. They earned them tonight."

Prim took a step forward. "Max. I—"

Len stepped into the room. "Primrose, I've placed a deputy out front. He'll remain there until we have Gourley in custody."

Prim inhaled sharply. "You think Clint will come back?"

Len shook his head. "The chances of that happening are minimal. Unless he wants to even the score with your neighbor, I don't believe you'll see him again."

"I'm staying over tonight." Max's gaze remained steady on Prim's face.

Prim lifted her chin, the gesture more weary than stubborn. "I appreciate the offer, Max, but it isn't necessary. The officer will be outside and you've already done so much."

"I'm not going anywhere."

An odd look filled her eyes.

"We'll let you two work that out." Len motioned to Cade.

Max stood silent while Prim showed the men out. The crime scene techs soon followed. Prim locked and bolted the door behind them.

"The boys and I will be perfectly safe." She ran a hand through her hair, and he remembered how soft those silky strands of red and gold had felt between his fingers. "Really, there's no need for you to stay."

"If Clint does come back, it's because he's looking for me." Max gestured toward the sofa. "I slept on plenty of those in my college days."

"I hate to make you sleep on the couch."

"With the boys in the house, it's my only choice." He grinned, let his tone turn teasing in an attempt to lighten the atmosphere. "You've got that big bed, but we both know that isn't an option. You'd be all over me in a heartbeat."

The tenseness in her shoulders eased as she swatted him with the back of her hand. "Stop it."

"Just telling it like it is." He pointed to himself, settled into a cocky stance. "You see me, you want me."

Max didn't know what to think when she stepped close and wrapped her arms around his neck.

"And you don't want me?" she asked.

God, yes, he wanted her. He wanted to kiss her, make love to her, and protect her from any and all harm.

"When I saw Clint come out of your house . . ." Max's voice sounded rough, choked, and foreign to his ears.

"We're all fine."

Max linked his arms around her waist and pulled her tight. No one, especially not some creep like Clint Gourley, was going to hurt her.

With a start Max realized she was stroking the back of his neck, twining her fingers in his hair.

Leaning over, he kissed the base of her jaw, then stepped back and cleared his throat. He glanced toward the bedrooms. "Nonnegotiable?"

After the tiniest hesitation, she sighed. "Nonnegotiable."

"Then I need some, ah, distance." Max pulled her hands down. Giving them a squeeze, he stepped back. "Good night, Prim."

Without a word, Prim disappeared down the hall. She returned moments later and shoved a blanket and a pillow into his arms. "Thank you, Max. For everything."

"No thanks necessary." He touched her lips with his, a brief contact that he knew would keep him awake for hours. "Just remember I'm here for you. Always."

Chapter Twenty-One

"Hey, Prim," an all-too-familiar feminine voice called out. "Who's this handsome hunk on your couch?"

Prim lifted her head up from the French toast mixture, a smile already on her lips. Her baby sister stood next to the sofa where Max slept. Or, rather, where he'd been sleeping.

Max had bolted upright. His hair was a rumpled mass that brushed the collar of his shirt. "Marigold?"

The petite pixie with the mane of golden curls leaned over and brushed her lips against his cheek. "Morning, sleeping beauty."

Tamping down a surge of jealousy, Prim set aside the bowl and hurried to greet her baby sister.

The twins had come running, skidding to a stop beside the sofa. They giggled.

"That's not Sleeping Beauty," Connor told his aunt, his freckled face serious. "That's Mr. Brody."

Max swung his legs to the side of the couch, then stood. He turned to Prim. "How long have you been up?"

"Long enough to make coffee and start the French toast." Prim shifted her attention to her sister and stepped forward to give her a hug. "I didn't expect you until the night before the Fourth."

"Change of plans." Marigold's tone was light, but Prim knew her sister and heard the edge.

"Well, after I get you some coffee and food, you can tell me all about it."

"I'm going to head home and grab a shower." Max rubbed his jaw, his cheeks covered in golden stubble. His gaze settled on Marigold. His brows pulled together. "How did you get inside?"

Marigold looked at him as if he'd spoken a language she didn't understand. "I, ah, opened the door and walked inside."

Max glanced at Prim.

Prim felt her face warm. "I must have left the door unlocked when I got the newspaper off the porch."

A muscle in Max's jaw jumped. "The doors have to be kept locked until he's caught."

"You're right," Prim agreed. "My error."

Marigold's suspicious gaze shifted from Max to Prim. "What's going on here?"

"Someone broke into our house last night," Connor said eagerly. Before he could say more, his brother pushed him aside.

"I'll tell her." Callum waved his brother silent. "A bad man broke into the house and Boris didn't bark, but Mommy heard him and she locked us in our bedroom. Mr. Brody tackled the man and pulled off his mask and the sheriff came and Mr. Brody gave us ninjas because we were brave."

Marigold's dazed expression made Prim grin.

"I'll show you my ninja." Connor raced from the room.

"She wants to see mine, too." Callum whirled and took off after his brother.

Obviously intrigued, Marigold angled her head. "I'm not sure I caught all that, but did someone really break into your house?"

"Let's get the boys some breakfast first. Then we'll eat and I'll tell you all about it." Though her sons didn't appear traumatized, Prim preferred not to recount the night's incident in front of them.

The twins returned, ninjas in hand, just as a knock sounded.

"I'll get it," Callum called out and turned toward the door.

"Stop," Max ordered. "I'll get it."

To Prim's surprise, both of her sons came to an abrupt halt.

Prim would have a talk with her sons after breakfast. She'd make it very clear that, until Clint was caught, the doors would remain locked. Not only that, only an adult would open the door.

"Be right back." Curious who'd come calling at this early hour, Prim gave Marigold's arm a squeeze and hurried after Max.

Sheriff Swarts and Cade—Prim had already forgotten his last name—stood on the porch.

Len smiled warmly. "Do you have a few minutes?"

"Of course." Prim motioned them inside. "May I get you some coffee?"

"We're fine," Len replied smoothly. "Thank you."

"Have a seat." Prim gestured to the living room, then turned to her sons. "Mommy needs to speak with the sheriff for a few minutes. I'd like you boys to play in your room while we're talking."

For a second Prim thought they were going to argue, but they clomped down the hall with their ninjas in hand, the dog trailing after them.

Marigold's gaze was fixed on Cade. That's when Prim recalled that the two had met.

"Sheriff, you remember Marigold." Prim then turned to Cade. "I believe you are also acquainted with my sister."

"Cade." Mischief, along with an unmistakable flash of interest, glittered in Marigold's eyes. "What a nice surprise. I thought you'd be in Detroit."

He chuckled, a low, rumbling sound. "I thought you'd be in Chicago."

"I'm just visiting over the Fourth." Marigold tilted her head.

There was a beat of silence.

"I'm the new interim sheriff in Good Hope."

Marigold arched a brow. "Is that so?"

"It's true." There was a lazy awareness in the lawman's eyes when his gaze settled on Marigold that told Prim her sister and this man were even more intimately acquainted than she'd first suspected.

"If we could get down to business." Len's tone was brisk.

Once Marigold and Prim were seated on the sofa, Len and Cade took their places in the two chairs. Max stood behind Prim and she felt his silent support.

"We caught him," Len announced without preamble. "Clint Gourley is in custody."

Relief flooded her. Prim closed her eyes and exhaled a ragged breath.

Marigold reached over and took her sister's hand, giving it a squeeze. "I take it Clint is the bad man who broke into the house last night."

"Yes," Len confirmed. "He broke into not only this house, but a lot of other homes as well."

"We wanted you to know." Cade may have spoken to Prim but his intense gaze remained on Marigold. After a moment, his mouth relaxed into a slight smile.

"I appreciate both of you taking the time to come by." Prim's voice shook with emotion. "It's a huge relief to know Clint is in jail."

After a few more minutes, Prim walked them to the door.

Once the door closed behind them, she wearily massaged her brow. "Appears the crisis is over."

Max's comforting hand settled on her shoulder. "Would you like me to tell the boys?"

"I'll tell them." Prim reached up and covered his hand with hers. "Thanks for everything, Max."

"My pleasure," he murmured, twining strands of her hair loosely around his fingers.

"It probably would have been more of a pleasure if he'd slept in your bed rather than on the sofa," Marigold pointed out, clearly enjoying herself.

Prim shot her sister a warning look.

Marigold lifted her hands. A tiny smile played at the corner of her lips. "Just making an observation."

"I should get going." Max hesitated, his gaze shifting from Prim to Marigold, then back again.

Marigold rolled her eyes. "Sheesh, if you want to kiss my sister, just kiss her."

Instead of a kiss, Max pulled Prim close. She squeezed her eyes closed briefly and released a long breath. When she was in his arms, she felt like she could handle anything.

He kissed her on the top of her head and was gone.

Prim sighed and watched him go.

"Stellar ass," Marigold commented and made her sister laugh.

Marigold and Prim had just finished cleaning up the kitchen when they heard a car pull into the driveway.

The sisters exchanged glances as Boris sounded the alert.

"Ami?" Marigold asked.

"I don't think so." Prim frowned. "She's at the bake shop. Or the café."

The boys were playing on the living room floor, happily slamming two big dump trucks together while making loud crashing noises. *All good there*, Prim thought as she passed them.

A sharp rap sounded against the front door a second before she pulled it open. Boris skidded to a stop. Prim's smile froze. "Deb. Mike. What a wonderful surprise."

She stepped back, motioned her in-laws inside.

"Who was at the door?" Marigold stepped into the room, drying her hands on a dish towel. "Did Ami—?"

Her sister halted, smiled. "Mr. and Mrs. Delaney. How nice to see you."

The boys jumped to their feet and ran straight into their grandparents' waiting arms.

The pleasure on Deb's and Mike's faces at such an exuberant welcome warred with Prim's sense of unease. "I thought you'd be on your way to Appleton by now. Come and sit down. Can I get you a cup of coffee? Or something to eat?"

With each grandparent now holding a boy's hand, Mike and Deb moved to the sofa.

Marigold started to back out of the room, but Prim wasn't about to let her sister get away. She pointed to a chair, and when Marigold chose the one farthest from the Delaneys, Prim took the other.

"We have wonderful news." Looking pretty and relaxed in blue capris and a white top with blue piping, Deb smiled brightly. "Or at least we think it's wonderful."

Deb cast a glance at her husband as if seeking his support. He offered an indulgent smile.

"We've decided to spend a few more days here in Door County. Catch up with a few old friends." Deb tightened her arms around Callum and Connor. "Spend time with our grandsons."

The boys cheered so loudly Prim had to lift a hand to silence them.

Marigold's smile remained fixed. Prim knew she'd get no help from her, nor could she expect it. This was her battle, *er, situation*, to handle.

"That *is* wonderful news." Prim tried to push some enthusiasm into her voice but wasn't sure she'd succeeded. "If you haven't already secured a place to stay, there are several nearby. But then, you probably know that yourself."

Prim realized she was rambling and clamped her lips tightly together.

When Mike shifted uncomfortably on the sofa, Prim felt a stab of unease.

"Actually, all the rooms on the entire peninsula—or all the ones we'd consider—are booked." Deb waved a dismissive hand. "We reserved the B and B in Ephraim months in advance. But we're not interested in staying in a motel. We'd much rather stay with you. That way, we can spend more time with these two cuties."

She gave the boys a tickle and they laughed.

"We won't be a bother," she added when Prim didn't immediately respond. "I'll help you." Deb glanced around the cluttered-with-toys living area. "Do some cleaning. Organizing a messy home is a specialty of mine."

"That's . . ." Prim took a deep breath, let it out slowly. "So kind, but I'm afraid my sister"—Prim gestured with her head toward Marigold— "will be staying with me for a while."

"Oh," Deb said.

Rory's parents, Prim told herself. *Be kind.*

"I could check with Ami. The furnished apartment over her bakery is open. It was Ami's home before she got married. It's a great location."

The fact that it wasn't within walking distance of her house was an extra bonus.

"That's so thoughtful," Mike began.

"It won't do." Deb shook her head. "Mike has been having issues with his knee. Stairs are a problem. He has an orthopedic consult scheduled for next week."

Prim wanted to ask how Mike had been able to manage the steps at the B and B last night but kept her mouth shut.

"I could stay at the apartment." Marigold's offer earned her a smile from Deb and a sharp glance from Prim.

"That is so sweet of you." Deb hugged each boy. "Grandpa and I are going to be right down the hall from you. Won't that be fun?"

Prim rubbed the back of her neck and tried not to scowl. To think, a second before she'd opened the door, her day had been bright and sunny.

Chapter Twenty-Two

Deb looked up from the book she was reading aloud and zeroed in on Prim. "Where are you going at this hour?"

Callum and Connor were nestled beside their grandmother on the sofa, with Mike reading the paper in a nearby chair.

"It's only seven." Prim waved a careless hand. "I'm just going next door to speak with Max. We need to iron out a couple of last-minute parade details."

The twins straightened, their attention instantly diverted from the book.

"Can I go with you?" Callum asked.

"I want to see Mr. Brody," Connor announced.

When the boys started to rise from the sofa, Deb pulled them back down.

"Not this time." Prim's tone brooked no argument. "Stay here with Grandma and Grandpa."

"Couldn't you simply call and ask your questions?" Deb called out when Prim turned to go. "Or text him?"

Prim turned back, resisting the urge to sigh. Of course she could call or text Max. But the fact was, she wanted to see him, and without her in-law chaperones present.

"I won't be long." Prim shifted her attention to the twins. "Be good."

Deb said nothing further but Prim clearly read her expression. Deb suspected this wasn't a business meeting and she didn't like it one bit.

Max answered after the first knock. His eyes lit when he saw her and a slow smile widened his mouth.

"My Christmas wish has come true," he announced, in a tone worthy of a showman.

Prim laughed. "As this is July, you've had to wait a—"

Before she could finish, Max enfolded her in his arms and began kissing her. She wrapped her arms around his neck and kissed him back with all the stored-up passion inside her.

When they came up for air, her knees felt like jelly.

"Oh, wow," she said, her heart hammering. "That was quite a welcome."

"You ain't seen nothing yet." Max lowered his head and scattered kisses along her jawline.

She arched her neck back and let him nibble, but when she was seized with an overwhelming urge to rip off his clothes, Prim forced herself to step back. "I can't stay. I need to get back."

He took her hand, lacing his fingers with hers. "So soon?"

"Deb is reading to the boys now, but it's almost their bedtime. I told her I needed to work out some parade details with you." Her lips twitched. "She didn't believe it, of course. But other than calling me a liar, what could she say?"

"Just in case she asks, everything is set with the parade. By the way, I just updated Eliza a few minutes ago, so we shouldn't be getting any more texts from her, at least not until tomorrow. I told her you and I will be in constant contact with several spotters along the route during the parade so we can make any last-minute adjustments."

"Good to know." Prim smiled. "This whole process wasn't as bad as I thought it would be."

He lifted their joined hands. "We make a good team."

"Yes, we do." Oh, how she wished she could stay. "How was Green Bay?"

He blinked.

"The IRS visit with your mom?"

"It feels as if that trip was a thousand years ago." Max shook his head. "It went well. The agent was satisfied with the documentation. I'm glad it's done and behind us."

"How is your mother?"

"She's dating again." Max tossed the words out there as if they were of no consequence, but something in his voice put Prim on alert.

"Is it serious?"

"He's Beck's age."

"Who is Beck's age?"

"The man my mother is dating."

Prim took a moment to clear her throat. "Have they been dating . . . long?"

"She says three months. In Vanessa Eden time, that's an eternity." A muscle in Max's jaw jumped. "She told me once it quits being fun, she'll end it. I've never understood that kind of mentality."

"What do you mean?"

Max gazed down at her. With great gentleness he moved a lock of hair behind her ear with one finger. "I can't see why anyone would invest the emotional energy in dating someone if they aren't a person you might consider marrying in the future."

"You picked a great week to spend time in Good Hope," Max said to Deb and Mike as they climbed the bleacher steps. "Next to the parade, the vintage baseball game is one of my favorite events of the Independence Day celebration."

Prim agreed. She'd been looking forward to attending the annual event with Max and her sons. Since Max had played last year, this was his year to sit out.

The game always drew large crowds. Everyone loved seeing the players in period reproduction uniforms using equipment common to the era while following rules from the nineteenth century.

The fact that Rory's parents had decided to tag along, while not unexpected, was disappointing. Prim consoled herself with the knowledge that her in-laws would soon return to Appleton. Life would then return to normal.

For now, the six of them sat at the top of the metal bleachers. Though they'd arrived early, the upper row was the only spot left with enough space for six.

She saw Max slant a sideways glance at Deb and Mike, their chaperones for the evening.

As long as Rory's parents were around, Prim knew there would be no personal conversation. In fact, it was difficult to have any kind of conversation at all, considering Deb seemed to be wired as tightly as the Energizer Bunny today.

When they'd reached the ball field, she'd tried to maneuver it so Max sat on the other side of Mike. Prim did her own maneuvering, making sure Max sat beside her.

As Deb rose from her seat to wave and call out to someone she knew, Max gave Prim a conspiratorial wink.

"You look extremely pretty this evening." His voice was low, for her ears only.

Prim's heart gave a skip and she suddenly felt quite breathless. Sensing Mike's curious gaze on them, she gave Max a smile, then focused on the field.

Just before Deb resumed her seat beside Prim, Connor slipped around his grandparents to sit on the other side of Max. When Max lowered his head to listen to what the boy was telling him, Deb's lips tightened.

"You know, Primrose," Deb said in an offhand tone that Prim guessed was anything but offhand, "you were fortunate to find a great love early in your lifetime."

Prim simply smiled, not sure where Deb was going with this.

"You need to honor that love and the commitment you made to my son." Deb gestured with her head toward Max. "Rory hasn't even been gone two years and it's obvious you're already looking to replace him."

"Yes, she is." Callum spoke loudly in response to his grandfather. "Aren't you, Mom?"

Startled, Prim turned toward her son.

"You are so going to play baseball next year. Grandpa Mike doesn't believe me." Callum's eyes—as blue as his father's had been—flashed. "Tell him. Tell him you're going to do it."

"It's true." Grateful for the distraction, Prim eagerly turned from Deb to Mike. "I may embarrass myself, but I've already agreed to play in the vintage ladies' game next year."

"Told you."

Callum's comment drew a censuring glance from Prim, but Connor fist-bumped his brother.

"Katie Ruth Crewes has been pushing to have a 'Bloomer Girls' team for several years." Prim wasn't about to let the topic end, not when it kept Deb at bay.

Deb frowned. "Bloomer Girls?"

"That's what the clubs that played back in the 1890s were called," Max answered before Prim could. "Ladies' baseball actually thrived until the—"

"Great Depression," Prim finished the sentence for him, and they both smiled.

Deb's gaze turned sharp and assessing. "I never realized, Primrose, that you were so interested in sporting events. I seem to recall my son had to practically beg you to attend his soccer matches."

Somehow, Prim kept a smile on her lips. When she spoke her tone was easy. "I've always been a baseball fan. When Katie Ruth called and said she was attempting to get enough women to field a couple of teams next year, Ami and I both volunteered."

Deb turned to Callum. "Your daddy never liked baseball."

"Really?" Callum tilted his head. A puzzled frown furrowed his brow. "Me 'n' Connor like it a lot. Mr. Brody is our coach."

The child grinned at Max, who returned the boy's smile.

"Is that so?" Deb glanced pointedly at her husband, but Mike was busy watching the game.

"Put on your glasses," Prim's father-in-law bellowed so loudly several people sitting nearby turned to stare. "That ump is blind. That was clearly a foul ball."

"Michael, you're making a scene," Deb hissed.

Prim only sighed. Mike was a nice guy, but he had been a sideline coach when Rory played, too. It had been only one of the reasons she'd shied away from Rory's events.

"They're playing by 1860 rules. Those rules say fair or foul batted balls caught on the fly or one bounce retire the batter," Max explained.

"Ridiculous," Mike muttered and refocused on the game.

Callum's gaze turned thoughtful. "They aren't wearing gloves. And Uncle Beck is throwing the ball funny."

"Gloves weren't worn until the mid-1880s," Max clarified when everyone remained silent. "Beck is throwing overhand, which is how they did it back then. Watch your uncle." Max gestured to his friend atop the pitching mound.

"I want to throw like that." Excitement filled Callum's voice. "Can I, Mr. Brody, please?"

Max ruffled his hair with obvious affection. "How about I give everyone a chance at our next practice?"

The boys cheered and high-fived each other.

Prim gave Max's arm a quick squeeze.

Deb cleared her throat. "Rory considered baseball too slow."

Knowing her mother-in-law was trying to steer the conversation back to Rory, Prim said nothing.

"I've got to go to the baffroom," Connor announced.

"Me too," Callum said.

Prim looked at her father-in-law, but he was busy speaking with an older man in front of him. She was about to ask Max if he'd take the boys when she felt Deb's tight grip on her arm.

"They're your responsibility. Not his," Deb chided, her voice barely above a whisper.

Heat flooded Prim's face. "Come on, boys."

As she slipped past Max on her way to the aisle, she briefly rested a hand on his shoulder. He looked up, and Prim felt herself steady at his warm look of reassurance.

Max settled back in his seat and watched her trim figure navigate the steps with her sons.

"Rory and Prim were so close, so in love."

He turned to Deb. "Pardon?"

"I said Prim and Rory were so in love. You were around back then. You must remember how she used to look at him, as if he was the only one in the world."

Max remembered.

"She won't find anyone like my son again and she's wise not to try. Prim has only to look at your mother's life to see how foolish that would be."

Though outwardly Max displayed no sign that her arrow had hit its mark, he felt the sting. He cleared his throat before speaking. "My mother?"

"Like Prim, Vanessa found her soul mate at a young age. Sadly, they both lost their spouses early on." Deb glanced over as if to make sure her husband's attention was still on the game. "But Prim is smarter than your mother."

Deb raised a hand to keep Max from interrupting.

"I adore Vanessa, so please don't think I'm speaking ill of her. In fact, I believe if you asked, she'd agree with me. It would have been better for her—and for you—if she'd have stayed single until you were grown."

Suddenly Max understood. "You're saying Prim should remain single."

"I'm saying it would be unwise for anyone, anyone who has the best interests of Prim and the boys at heart, to push for more." Deb's gaze met his and there was no mistaking the warning in those fierce blue depths. "Not to mention that person would only get his heart broken in the long run."

A hot dog vendor had finally made it to the top of the stands. Despite knowing he wouldn't be able to eat a bite, Max motioned the boy over and ordered six dogs.

He kept his expression bland as he handed foil-wrapped dogs to Deb and Mike.

When a crack of a bat signaled a home run, Mike grinned. "This has turned out to be a great day. I'm glad we came."

"Me too, honey." The smile Deb flashed rivaled the sun. "So very glad."

On the way to the car, Deb monopolized the conversation by chattering about how much Rory had disliked baseball. It took all of Prim's control to keep her mounting frustration under control.

Though she couldn't prove it, Prim knew Deb had to have said something to Max during the time she'd taken the boys to the restroom. Everything had been fine between her and Max—better than fine, actually—but when she'd returned he'd been cool as a stiff breeze off the bay. *Polite but distant.*

When the game was over, instead of going to the café as planned and meeting up with Ami and Beck, Max had made a lame excuse about needing to get some work done at home. Even the boys begging him to come hadn't made him waver.

Perhaps the hot-cold act should have annoyed her, but there had been a profound sadness in those placid blue depths. Oh, how she wished she could pull him close and kiss his sadness away.

Unfortunately, that had been impossible with Deb watching her with the intensity of a shark circling its next meal.

"Later, neighbor," she said to Max.

His gaze searched hers. "Good-bye, Prim."

As he walked away, she hadn't been able to stop herself from staring. She'd still been watching when he turned back, his expression somber, his eyes unreadable.

A cold shiver traveled down Prim's spine.

Something was desperately wrong.

She only wished she knew what it was so she could fix it.

Chapter Twenty-Three

"Retirement is wonderful." Deb forked off a piece of pancake and smiled at Prim. "If Mike and I had jobs, we wouldn't have been able to decide to stay in Good Hope at the last minute."

"Flexibility is nice." Prim kept her tone easy even as she shot Callum a warning glance when he reached for a piece of bacon on his brother's plate.

Boris moved to sit between Deb and Callum. Though feeding the wolfhound from the table was strictly forbidden, Prim suspected from the animal's position and hopeful expression that food occasionally made it off Callum's plate and into his mouth. Not always accidentally.

"Yes, I love being flexible. That's another reason I'd never have a dog." Deb made a shooing motion at Boris, who simply stared uncomprehendingly at her.

Prim cocked her head. Normally she could follow her mother-in-law's circuitous logic, but not this time. "I don't understand."

"You can't be spontaneous when you have a dog." Deb looked at her husband for confirmation but found him intently reading the stock reports on his phone. "You have to make arrangements to kennel them even if you're only going to be gone a day or two. If you decide to stay a week, well, that can add up to a lot of money in boarding fees."

Stay a week?

Was Deb actually considering remaining in Good Hope through the Fourth? Prim fought a surge of panic. She was holding on to control by her fingertips now. No way could she go that long without strangling the woman.

"Mommy."

Callum's solemn face looked up at her. "Me and Connor have something to tell you."

Were there any words spoken by a child that could bring more terror to a parent's heart? Prim tried to imagine what they'd done. It had to be big or her son wouldn't look so serious.

"Can it wait until after we eat?" Conscious of Deb's intense scrutiny, Prim kept her tone light.

The boys looked at each other and shook their heads.

"Okay." Prim smiled at Deb and Mike. "If you'll excuse us for a few minutes, the boys and I are going to sit on the porch swing and have a little talk."

"Why can't they tell you right here?" Deb demanded. "We aren't even through with breakfast."

Ignoring the question, Prim rose.

"We won't be long." Two small hands were clasped tightly in hers as they left the table.

Prim took a seat in the middle of the white-lacquered swing, a boy on each side of her. Even as her mind raced with all the dire possibilities, she offered an encouraging smile.

When they only exchanged glances, she prompted, "You know you can tell me anything."

Callum met her gaze. "We really like Mr. Brody."

Connor nodded vigorously. "We like him a lot."

"That's nice." Prim still hadn't a clue where this was headed. "Mr. Brody is a good neighbor and friend."

As well as an excellent lover, her mind supplied before she silenced the thought.

The boys sat silently for several seconds before Connor reached around her and punched his brother in the arm. Callum shot him a glinting glance before turning back to his mother.

"Me and Connor want Mr. Brody to be our daddy." The tension eased from the boy's face as if finally saying the words was a relief. "He's fun and he likes baseball and he—"

"We like him better than our real daddy." As he often did, Connor completed his brother's thought.

The smile that had begun to blossom on Prim's face ended in a sharp inhale of breath. She wanted the boys to like Max, she really and truly did, but hearing them say they liked him *more* than their own father was like a knife to her heart. *Oh, Rory, I'm so sorry.*

"Our real daddy didn't like baseball." A frown marred Callum's brow for a second before it smoothed. "We like baseball a lot. Mr. Brody likes it a lot, too."

"If he didn't, he wouldn't be a coach," Connor added, his blue eyes serious.

"If you married Mr. Brody, he could be our daddy *and* our coach." Callum smiled as if the mere thought brought him pleasure. "That would be so cool."

"So cool," Connor echoed. "What do you say?"

Without any prompting her sons had blessed her relationship with Max. Though her head spun that they'd already made the leap to marriage, she found comfort that when—or rather, *if*—she and Max got to that point, the twins would be all for it.

Callum pinned her with those clear blue eyes, so like Rory's. "Are you going to marry him or not?"

"She most certainly is not." Deb's voice slashed like a whip through the screen door.

Prim's heart stopped, simply stopped beating, when her mother-in-law shoved open the door and strode onto the porch like a bull entering the ring. The woman had obviously been eavesdropping and had built up quite a head of steam over what she'd heard.

"Callum. Connor. Please go into the backyard." Prim gave both boys a reassuring smile. "We'll talk more about this later."

The twins hesitated. Looking as formidable as the Incredible Hulk, their grandmother stood between them and the front door.

"You can go around the side of the house," Prim instructed. "Just make sure to latch the gate."

"Okay, Mom." Callum turned to his brother. "Race you."

Wanting to be on even footing, Prim stood as the twins disappeared around the corner of the house. She lifted her chin, met her mother-in-law's steely-eyed gaze with one of her own. "I don't appreciate you listening in on a private conversation."

Deb's hands were clenched into white-knuckled fists at her sides. "They told you they liked Max Brody more than their own father."

The pain in the woman's voice tempered some of Prim's anger. Prim couldn't begin to imagine how hard hearing that sentiment spoken with boyish fervor had been on Deb. "I know. Hearing that made me sad, too. But it's understandable. Rory passed away when they were four. Though I've done my best to keep his memory alive—"

"Do you call bringing another man into their lives keeping his memory alive?" The pain was gone, replaced by fury. "I'm beginning to believe you never really cared about Rory. Certainly not the way you should have cared. Maybe if he'd been more content at home, he wouldn't have felt the need to go on all those adventures. Perhaps he wouldn't have taken that last trip and he'd still be alive today."

Prim staggered back as if shot.

Deb paid her no mind as the venom continued to spew. "Despite knowing how much we loved him and he loved us, you refused to let me have a say in his burial. Okay, maybe he did want to be cremated," she said quickly when Prim opened her mouth. "But you only followed select parts of his wishes. You didn't scatter his ashes like he wanted. I told Mike you couldn't make him want to be with you in life, so you're punishing him by keeping him close in death."

Prim flinched as the words hit their mark, but she lifted her chin.

"Regardless of what you believe, I did love your son. And I tried to be a good wife to him. Maybe you're right, maybe I wasn't what he wanted, but that doesn't give you the right to speak to me in this manner." Prim kept all emotion from her voice. She refused to cry. She wouldn't give Deb the satisfaction. "I believe it's best for everyone if you pack your bags and leave my house."

"You're kicking us out?" A look of shock crossed Deb's face. "For what? For simply trying to have an honest dialogue?"

"I want you to leave." Prim edged around Deb and strode into the house. Only when she reached the bathroom did Prim let the tears fall.

In exactly twenty-five minutes, Mike backed the Buick out of the driveway and drove off.

Prim stood on the porch with a boy on each side of her. Her expression remained stony while the twins waved and smiled.

The second the Enclave disappeared from sight, Prim expelled her breath. She thought she'd feel better with Deb and Mike out of the house. But Deb's accusations lingered, and Prim's emotions remained as tangled as her hair on a windswept day.

"Can we go in the back and play ball?" Callum asked.

"Sure." Absently she tousled his hair. "Your gloves are in the hall closet."

"We don't need gloves." Gazing up at her, Connor's young face was earnest. "They didn't have gloves yesterday."

For a second she was confused. Until she realized he was referring to the vintage baseball game. Though it seemed as if gloves would provide some protection for little fingers, she wasn't going to push the point.

"Take the ball outside then, and—"

Prim's breath caught in her throat at the sight of Max on the other side of the sliding glass door. The boys rushed him as if they were linebackers and he was the quarterback with the ball.

"Yay, you came just in time."

His serious expression grew quizzical. "In time for what?"

Callum held up the baseball clutched between his fingers. "To play ball."

"We're not using gloves, neither," Connor assured him.

With his free hand, Callum tugged on Max's arm, his expression hopeful. "Throw us the ball. Please."

The look on Max's face seemed to indicate he was waging some kind of internal struggle. Was he concerned she'd be upset? She offered a reassuring smile. "I'd love to watch you play."

"Let's go, boys." His voice was deep and husky, as if he were fighting off a cold.

She let her gaze linger on him as she followed them out the door. Right now all she wanted to do was rest her head on his shoulder and feel his strong, comforting arms around her.

Max tossed the ball with the boys for nearly thirty minutes before calling it quits. Callum and Connor continued to play in the backyard when Max stepped inside.

"How about a glass of iced tea?" she asked, following him when he strode into the living room.

"I don't want anything."

Something was wrong. Prim sensed it. She hoped it wasn't anything serious, because her emotions were still raw and unsettled from her encounter with Deb.

Still, she wanted Max to know if he needed her, she was here for him. "Tell me what's wrong and what I can do to help."

The tight clench to his jaw and his rigid stance sent her stomach into somersaults. Ready or not, it appeared she was about to be thrust into her second serious conversation of the morning.

Max passed a palm across the sweaty surface of his forehead. He should have known better than to get involved with someone whose heart still belonged to another. He'd ignored the signs and now he was paying the price.

He'd known this moment would be hard. He just hadn't realized his heart would feel as if it was being torn from his chest before he'd even begun to speak.

The sight of the urn in the corner cabinet reinforced he was making the right decision. "I don't know if I told you, but I dated a woman last year. Her name was Lori."

"I don't recall you mentioning her." There was a hint of trepidation in Prim's voice. "Was it serious?"

Max continued as if she hadn't spoken. "Lori and her longtime boyfriend had broken up several months before she and I started dating. I knew she was on the rebound, but she assured me whatever feelings she'd had for her ex-boyfriend were gone."

"She still cared for him."

Had Prim said the words? Or had he? It scarcely mattered.

"We'd been together for six months when she told me they were getting back together." His lips lifted in a humorless smile. "She liked me a lot, cared about me. But she loved *him*."

"Oh, Max. That must have hurt." Prim moved to his side, as if ready to console.

Max stepped back, keeping some distance between them.

"Initially it hurt," he said, thinking back. "I've since realized that while I liked her and enjoyed her company, I didn't love her, either."

Prim remained silent, her hands folded together in a tight knot.

Max ran his fingers down the side of the urn, resisting the overpowering urge to smash it against the wall. "You loved Rory."

"Yes."

The single word struck like a punch to the gut. He didn't know why. Of course she'd loved Rory. Hadn't she married the man? Given him two sons?

Callum and Connor. God, he'd never wanted to hurt them.

"I love you, Prim. I think I've always loved you." His voice sounded flat and dull even to his own ears. "But I can't be with a woman whose heart isn't free."

"My heart *is* free." She closed the distance he'd placed between them, this time touching his arm. "Rory has been gone nearly two years."

"He may be gone, but you haven't let him go." Max dropped his hand from the urn as if the shiny black enamel had turned scalding hot. "You told me he wanted to be scattered to the winds, but yet you keep him here. It's as if you can't bear to let him go."

Two bright red patches of color dotted her pale cheeks. "Why is everyone all of a sudden so concerned about that damn urn?"

Less than an hour before, Max had watched the Delaneys throw their suitcases in the Buick and drive off. As far as he knew they'd had no prior plans to leave. It didn't take a math genius to connect the dots.

"So I'm not the only one who finds it odd you've kept his ashes."

"This conversation—or whatever it is we're having—is about you and me, Max. Not about Deb." The words burst from her mouth as the temper she usually kept under tight control flared. "If you don't want to be with me, just say it. Don't make up some silly story that me being in love with Rory is the reason we can't be together. He was my husband. Of course I loved him. A part of me will always love him. Is that what you want to hear?"

"Will Rory always be between us?" Though Max was convinced he knew the answer, he pressed again, harder this time.

"Rory was my husband. He's Callum and Connor's father." Instead of angry, she now sounded weary. "I don't know why you feel you had to come up with a reason for walking away. You could have just said it wasn't working for you."

Not working for him? Didn't she understand how much she meant to him? How hard this was for him? "I—"

"Frankly, I think a smart guy like you could have come up with a better excuse." Prim's lips twisted. She gave a humorless laugh. "If Deb were still around, she'd tell you to consider yourself lucky because I don't have what it takes to keep a man's attention. You know what? She's obviously right."

Before he could respond, her jaw jutted out and fire returned to those hazel eyes. "But I did the best I could during my marriage. I'm doing the best I can now. I didn't need this from her and I don't deserve this from you. Get out, Max. Get out of my house and don't come back."

"Prim." He reached out. He wouldn't leave her. Not now. Not like this.

Ignoring the outstretched hand, Prim went to the door and jerked it open. "Good-bye, Max."

Despite the approaching thunder of little feet, Max would have stayed, nearly did. But he'd been caught up in too much drama as a child to knowingly put Callum and Connor in that situation.

Without another word, Max brushed past Prim and walked out the door.

Chapter Twenty-Four

"Mo-om, what are you doing in there?" Connor called out.

Prim shut off the faucet she'd been running full bore.

"Can we have a snack?" Callum asked through the closed bathroom door.

"I'll be out in a second." After blowing her nose, Prim flooded her eyes with Visine, not wanting her sons to notice the redness.

Not that she blamed herself. What woman wouldn't cry when the man she loved walked out on her?

Love.

Yes, she loved Max Brody. She could admit that now. For all the good it did her.

Drawing a steadying breath, Prim opened the door.

She kept busy organizing closets and then playing with her sons. Each time Boris let out a woof, she wondered if she'd soon hear a knock and Max would be at the door.

Prim scolded herself for being so foolish. He'd made it clear he didn't want her. The fact that he'd also said he loved her didn't mean a thing. He'd left, and actions meant more than words.

The ringing of her phone shortly before supper had her tensing again. *Please, dear God, don't let it be Eliza wanting an update on the parade.* She relaxed when she saw the readout. *Ami.*

"You must be jumping for joy." Her sister's voice held a hint of amusement before she began to sing, "Happy days are here again."

"What are you talking about?"

"Hadley told me she saw the Delaneys heading out of town earlier today."

Prim closed her eyes and gripped the phone as the emotions she'd kept tucked deep all day welled. She was forced to clear her throat before speaking. "My life is a massive train wreck."

Within the hour Beck had picked up the boys and taken them back to his house for a sleepover, complete with a promise of ghost stories told in the spooky third-floor attic.

Ami and Marigold arrived shortly after the twins left, with bags of chocolate and bottles of wine.

Seeing her sisters started the tears flowing.

Now the sisters sat in Prim's living room, feet bare and up on the furniture in a way their mother would never have allowed in the family home. Wrapped chocolates of every variety had been scattered across the coffee table with a liberal hand. Additional bags were in sacks next to the chairs, just waiting to be sampled.

"Are you ready to tell us what happened?" Seated next to her on the sofa, Ami shifted to face Prim. Her warm green eyes invited confidences.

"Start at the beginning." Marigold popped a chocolate into her mouth. "Don't leave anything out."

Though her baby sister's tone was matter-of-fact, Prim saw the concern in Marigold's eyes.

"Deb saw that Max and I had grown . . . close." Prim took a sip of wine, then another. "Though we tried to be discreet, apparently the connection showed. I could tell it bothered her, but I never thought she'd—"

Prim's eyes filled with tears, recalling the look of almost *hatred* on her mother-in-law's face.

"Take another gulp of wine," Marigold urged. "Heck, chug the bottle."

"We want her relaxed," Ami told Marigold, "not drunk."

The sisterly banter brought a smile to Prim's lips. She took another sip of the pinot and pulled up the events of the morning. "It all started when Deb overheard the twins telling me they wanted Max to be their daddy. Not only that, they said they liked him better than their real daddy."

Marigold visibly winced. "Ouch."

"That had to hurt." Ami grimaced. "What did you say?"

"I told her I didn't appreciate her eavesdropping on a private conversation." Prim tightened her hold on the wineglass. "It was knee-jerk. I don't recall exactly what I said after that, except I know I told her that hearing the twins say that they preferred Max made me sad, too."

"I imagine Deb took it hard," Ami said softly.

Marigold snorted. "Ya think?"

Ami tipped her wineglass and pointed it at her youngest sibling. "Cool it."

"Deb accused me of not loving Rory." Prim closed her eyes against the pain. "She said if he'd been happier and more content at home, he might not have felt the need to go on all those adventures, that maybe he'd still be alive."

"That's a low blow." Ami's tone could have frosted glass.

"Bitch." Marigold spat the word.

"Maybe it's true." Prim raised a hand to stop her sisters' protests. "Seriously, I don't think I *was* enough for him."

Without warning, Prim surged to her feet, startling Marigold, who'd leaned forward to scoop up some chocolates.

Setting her wineglass on the coffee table, Prim began to pace, finally pausing by the corner cabinet. She trailed her fingers down the urn. "Deb suggested I'm keeping him close in death because I couldn't keep him close in life."

Out of the corner of her eye, Prim saw her sisters exchange a glance.

Ami moved to her side. "I never thought that, but I did wonder why you haven't scattered his ashes by now."

Marigold unwrapped a couple of chocolates, her gaze never leaving Prim's face.

"I—I don't know."

"I think you do." Ami gently stroked Prim's arm.

"It's true I hated having him gone so much. I missed him. The boys missed him. After he died, it did give me comfort to have him close. That probably doesn't make sense, but—"

"It makes perfect sense," Ami reassured her. "His death was unexpected. But it's been two years, Prim."

Prim suddenly stiffened. Her voice turned frigid. "Is two years the magic amount of time?"

The calm and unruffled way Ami looked at her reminded Prim of their mother. Nothing they ever did or said could make her lose her cool.

"There's no magic time. You and I both know it's different for everyone." Ami gazed into her eyes. "I was simply wondering if you still feel the same need to keep Rory's ashes now as you did back then."

"I wasn't ready to let him go then, but I am now." Simply saying the words had the weight lifting off Prim's heart. "I think I've been ready for a while."

"There's no rush." Ami touched her hand.

"We can go along, if you want," Marigold offered.

"Or if you feel there's someone who could benefit more from taking this step with you, that's okay, too." Ami's soft voice soothed and comforted.

"Max brought up the urn." Prim swallowed hard against the sudden lump in her throat. "He said he couldn't be with me because I was still hung up on Rory."

Prim thought of all the years she and Rory had spent together, all the memories they'd shared.

"I can't remember ever not being in love with Rory. From the moment we met, that was it. He never even really proposed, there wasn't any need. We both knew we were meant to be together." Her smile faded. "We were so young. We never even bothered to think it through. There's so much I would have done different. So many questions I would have asked. Who marries someone without asking the important questions?"

Ami only squeezed her arm.

Marigold tossed her a couple of pieces of candy. "Have some chocolate."

For several seconds the three refueled in silence on chocolate and wine.

Prim broke the silence first.

"I chose to walk down the aisle and marry Rory. I did have a choice, at least as much as he did." Prim glanced down at her hands, seeing in her head the diamond in the modern platinum setting she'd once worn. "I sometimes wonder if, given another chance, he'd have chosen me."

"You were happy together." Once again Ami's mellow tone soothed. "He loved you."

"We *were* happy," Prim agreed. "We were very different people who didn't always see things in the same way. But that can be a good thing."

"He loved you," Ami repeated. "You centered him. And he made you realize the importance of enjoying every day."

"Carpe diem," Prim murmured, sinking back down on the sofa.

Ami dropped down beside her on the overstuffed cushions. "Exactly."

"Max said he wouldn't pressure me, but that's what he did today. Then he walked away." The stabbing pain in Prim's chest returned, making breathing difficult.

"You made it clear you weren't going to marry anyone until the boys were grown," Ami reminded her.

Prim sighed. "That's what I said."

Ami and Marigold exchanged a look.

"You must have had a good reason for saying that." Marigold unwrapped a chocolate she'd been playing with, finally popping it into her mouth.

"The best interests of the twins have to be my priority."

Marigold looked puzzled. "Don't you want the boys to have a father?"

Prim lifted her hands, let them fall. "What if he got tired of me? What if I wasn't enough?"

"Hogwash." Marigold washed down the chocolate with a big gulp of wine. "You're everything Max ever wanted."

"He said he'd never leave me. Or the boys." Recalling the promise in his eyes had Prim tearing up all over again. "But he did. He walked out that door. Of course, I told him to leave, but still, he left."

Her lips turned down like an unhappy clown's, and try as she might, they refused to lift.

Ami patted her hand sympathetically.

Prim's eyes were drawn to the urn. "He thinks I chose Rory."

"You did choose Rory," Marigold reminded her. "You married the guy."

"No. Now. He thinks I'm still choosing Rory." While it likely wouldn't change anything with Max, it was time to let Rory rest in peace. Ami's fingers tightened protectively on Prim's hand. "It will be okay."

"It'll never be okay. I've lost Max." Then she rested her head on Ami's shoulder and cried like a baby, or like a woman who'd just lost the man she loved.

It was at times like these that Max wished he had a father. Someone to bounce ideas off of, someone to tell him that he'd made an ass of himself. He suspected if his dad were alive, that's just what he'd tell him now.

Why had he let his mother's comments and Deb's barbs get to him? Things had been going so well between him and Prim until he'd gotten himself riled up and made a big deal about a jar of ashes. So what if they sat in her living room cabinet? So what.

He knew Prim cared for him. She wouldn't have slept with him otherwise. Maybe she didn't *love* him, not yet anyway, but he and Prim were a helluva lot closer than she and Rory had ever been.

She would love him. It was just a matter of time. Which meant he needed to be patient and not do stupid-ass things like going over to her house and insisting she choose between him and her dead husband.

If he and Prim were to be together, he needed to understand—and accept—that Rory would always be a part of her life. And when he came to her, hat in hand, he needed to make her see that he wasn't just spouting words of apology, he meant them.

The drive to Sturgeon Bay took less than thirty minutes. He pushed open the door to the jewelry store on Third Avenue and felt the blast of cold air. His shopping list today was short and sweet. Two items of jewelry.

One, a nod to the past.

The other, a promise for the future.

"I was surprised to get your phone call." Deb stood beside Prim at the edge of the Good Hope soccer fields.

"Thanks for driving all the way back from Appleton." Prim shifted from one foot to the other. "I'm sorry Mike couldn't join us."

"His orthopedist had a cancellation and Mike grabbed it." The shadows under Deb's eyes were more pronounced in the sunlight. "Besides, he thought you and I had some things to discuss that were best done one-on-one."

Prim took a deep breath, let it out slowly. This was going to be even more difficult than she'd imagined.

"I'm sorry about yesterday," Deb blurted. Two bright spots of red dotted her cheeks. "I said some pretty horrid things to you. Things I didn't even mean."

Prim opened her mouth to speak but Deb bulldozed ahead.

"My son loved you. He made that very clear. He was always telling us he'd won the jackpot in the wife department."

Tears stung the backs of Prim's eyes. "He said that?"

"He did." Deb glanced at the field. "I know that you were a better wife to him than he was a husband to you."

"That's not—"

"We both know it's true. I'm sorry for what I said. But it still breaks my heart to think of his sons forgetting about him." Deb pressed her lips together and her eyes shimmered with tears.

Prim placed a hand on the woman's arm. "You have my word. I won't let them forget about Rory. He's their father, and I'll do everything I can to keep his memory alive."

"So will Mike and I. If . . ." Deb paused. "You let us see them."

"Of course you can see them." Prim didn't hesitate. "You're family. You love them and they love you."

"I thought, after how I acted you might not want—"

"That's behind us," Prim assured her. "Although I can't promise you that I'll be single forever, or that there won't be another man who'll fill the role of father in the twins' lives."

"Mike and I both like Max Brody," Deb said, surprising her.

"I wasn't specifically speaking about Max, but I'm glad you like him. He's been a good friend and neighbor to me."

"Callum and Connor certainly think a lot of him."

"Yes, they do." Knowing she'd postponed the inevitable for as long as she could, Prim reached down and carefully extracted the urn from the bag at her feet. "I was wondering if you'd like to help me scatter Rory's ashes at a few of his favorite spots around town. I've written down a few locations, but I know you can probably add to the list. I thought we could end at Eagle Tower at Peninsula State Park. Rory always said he felt invincible at the top, looking out over Green Bay."

Tears slipped down Deb's cheeks, but gratitude filled her swimming eyes. "Thank you. I'd like that very much."

They made eight stops in all before climbing the steps leading to the observation tower. Prim had worried the deck might be packed with tourists, but a group of ten were on their way down when she and Deb reached the top.

It was a clear day, giving them a perfect view of not only the park and nearby islands, but the Michigan shoreline as well.

"Before we empty the jar, I want to give you this." Prim pulled the marble cube that Deb had given her last year from her jacket pocket and pressed it into her mother-in-law's hands. "I put some of Rory's ashes in here. If you want to bury it in the family plot, I'm sure he'd be okay with it. He loved you both so much."

Deb hugged Prim tight for several long moments.

Finally, with arms locked and united in their love for a man who'd enriched both their lives, they offered up his remaining ashes to the wind.

Chapter Twenty-Five

After dropping Deb off at her car, Prim headed to the town square. Though it had been an emotional morning, a sense of peace wrapped around her shoulders like a favorite sweater.

The center of town buzzed with activity. Prim felt as if she'd stepped into an alternate universe. Bicycles, Big Wheels, trikes, and wagons filled the square. Many were already decorated for the children's parade that would start in an hour.

Some kids had brought their bikes and trikes down to the square to decorate. Wanting to inhale the atmosphere and excitement while supervising the twins' efforts, Ami and Marigold had staked out a prime spot next to the gazebo.

Prim spotted her sons immediately. They wore identical T-shirts with exploding rockets on the front.

"Hey, boys," Prim said as she walked up.

"Hi, Mom." Connor looked up from where he and his brother were diligently putting red, white, and blue plastic straws around the spokes of their bikes.

"We're almost done," Callum told her without looking up.

"This is the last step," Marigold confided.

"Thanks for helping out."

"My pleasure." Marigold's eyes softened as she watched her nephews. "I'd forgotten how much fun this kind of thing can be."

"We went all out," Ami said.

"I can see that."

They'd already taken care of the handlebars, using toilet paper tubes, paint, stickers, and curlicued ribbons to make streamers. The bike helmets looked like something from Mars. The twins had gone crazy with festive pipe cleaners topped with cutout stars.

Crepe streamers had already been woven around the frames of the bikes.

"Do you have the vests?" Prim asked.

"You bet we do." Marigold pulled a bright red vest that held dozens of blue jingle bells from a bag at her feet.

Both boys looked up.

"Not until just before the parade starts," Marigold told them in a tone that said this wasn't the first time she'd said the words.

"How did it go?" Ami asked in a low voice.

"Good." Prim thought of the way Deb had clutched the tiny marble box to her chest. "It felt good, too."

"Have you seen Max?"

"I stopped by the house after dropping off Deb but he didn't appear to be at home." Though Prim wanted to speak with Max, she told herself it was for the best he hadn't been there. "We wouldn't have had time to talk anyway."

"Can we put on the vests now, Aunt Marigold?" Callum asked.

"Please, can we?" Connor added his pleas.

There was something about those blue eyes that made her think of Rory and how much he'd always loved the Fourth. And as she thought of her husband, she remembered her promise to Deb.

"Before you put them on, let me tell you a story about the time your father decided to walk the entire parade route on stilts dressed as Uncle Sam."

"I wanna walk on stilts like my dad," Callum said immediately, looking around as if a pair might be lying on the ground nearby.

"Did he make it the whole way?" Connor asked. "Or did he fall?"

Prim exchanged smiles with her sisters and rested a hand on each boy's shoulder. "This is what happened that day—"

Max's trip into Sturgeon Bay ended up taking longer than he'd planned when his car developed mechanical problems just as he was leaving the nearby town. It was late by the time he returned home, and the house next door was dark.

The next morning he fielded a couple of calls about the parade, then headed downtown to look for Prim and celebrate Independence Day in Good Hope. Flags hung from nearly every house he passed. When he drove through the downtown area, each ornate light pole boasted Old Glory.

Booths offering everything from fresh fruits and vegetables to jewelry filled the town square. He drove slowly to avoid hitting the pedestrians cutting across the street from the shops to the square.

Though Max knew there were a few who wished their beautiful surroundings could remain only for them, he loved seeing people flood into Door County, bringing their energy and their wallets.

He stopped at a light, noticing Izzie Deshler had set up an easel and was doing caricatures. If the number of people milling around her stand was any indication, she was doing a booming business.

A few feet away he spotted Ami and Gladys at a face-painting booth. He recalled Prim mentioning how much she was looking forward to working the booth in the morning with her sister.

Prim was likely busy. He should wait.

But for how long? They'd be together on the dais for the big parade at noon but would be surrounded by people. What he had to say to her required privacy.

Max slowed his vehicle to a creep, searching for an empty parking space. After driving nearly a mile, he had seen plenty of children walking around with rockets and variations of the stars and stripes painted on their faces, but not a single parking spot.

He circled back and pulled into Beck's driveway, parking in front of the carriage house. Max assumed his friend was at Muddy Boots, but when he started toward the sidewalk, Beck stepped out his front door.

"That'll be twenty dollars."

Max turned. "For what?"

Beck gestured to Max's car. "Since it doesn't appear you came to see me, I can only assume that my driveway has been turned into a parking lot."

Max rolled his eyes. "I looked for a spot on the street for thirty minutes."

"You snooze, you lose, Brody." Beck's gaze searched his face. "I was at Muddy Boots earlier. I thought you might come by."

Max waved a dismissive hand. "I've been busy answering last-minute parade questions."

"Ami and Prim are face painting in the town square."

"Thinking about getting your face painted, Beck?"

Beck snorted and began walking. Max fell into step beside him. Despite the crowd, they reached the booth in a matter of minutes.

When they arrived Ami was taking money from three middle-school-aged girls. One sported swirled lines of red, white, and blue that went over one eye and under the other, with several sparkling stars tossed into the mix. A blonde wearing braces had opted for red and white stripes down one cheek topped by blue with white stars. The smallest girl had gone simple with red, white, and blue stars on each of her thin cheeks.

"I haven't had a chance to work on a handsome man this morning." Gladys cackled and rubbed her hands together. "Now I've got two to pick from. Oh, my, which to choose? This is a difficult decision."

Beck held up both hands. "I just came by to kiss my wife."

As if to further illustrate, he tugged Ami close and kissed her softly. "Happy Independence Day."

Max glanced around. "Is Prim here?"

"She was out looking for—" Ami stopped and waved a hand in a vague gesture. "Let me text her."

Max shifted. He was tempted to take off and do his own searching when bony fingers surrounded his wrist. He looked over.

"I've always believed waiting is a sign of true love." Gladys's pale blue eyes met his. "Wait for her."

"I can't do anything else," he confided.

"Splendid." Gladys tugged him in the direction of a black folding chair. "Since you're not busy, I have a new design I've been dying to try out."

———

Prim's cell hadn't stopped buzzing all morning. She'd given up dropping it into her purse and decided it was just easier for everyone if she never put it down. As if on cue, the phone vibrated in her palm.

`Where R U? Max is at booth.`

God bless Ami. Prim barely paused to respond to her sister before taking off toward the center of town. She was out of breath by the time she reached the town square.

Her heart skipped a beat when she spotted Max. The rightness of her decision washed over her. She skidded to a stop in front of him and widened her eyes. "Is that a dragon on your neck?"

Red rose up Max's neck.

"He got himself a patriotic dragon." Beck didn't bother to hide his grin. "Complete with a red-and-white-striped body and blue stars on the neck and head."

"I think it turned out extremely well," Gladys said proudly.

"It's very . . . nice." Prim gazed into Max's eyes. Could he hear her heart pounding? "I've been looking for you."

He studied her for several seconds, his steady gaze shooting tingles down her spine. "I've been looking for you, too."

"We always were on the same wavelength." She tried for flippant but instead sounded breathless.

"The parade starts in an hour." He touched her bare arm with the tips of his fingers. "May I show you to our station?"

"Of course you may." Gladys gave Prim a not-so-little shove in Max's direction.

Ami looked up from the rocket she was painting on a little boy's cheek and made a shooing motion.

"Sorry I wasn't much help this morning." Prim hadn't realized how many little fires needed to be put out before a major parade.

"We understand you have important . . . duties." Gladys gave a sly wink, then turned to Beck. "While you and Max are dealing with the parade, I'm going to give this guy his own dragon. Bigger and better than anything I've yet done today."

Beck's look of alarm had Prim chuckling as Max maneuvered her through the square, sidestepping a group of tourists, each holding an ice cream cone in imminent danger of toppling.

When he placed his palm against her back, Prim felt a surge of hope.

The raised platform where they were to oversee the parade stood six feet off the ground. A blue fabric background with patriotic bunting decorated the front of the structure. The stage where city officials and dignitaries would sit was sheltered from the elements by a red awning.

At the moment they had the dais to themselves, but Prim knew it wouldn't be long before the mayor and town board members arrived, along with several other prominent citizens.

There were chairs but Prim was too agitated to sit. Her future rested on the outcome of this conversation. "The other day, when you said you loved me, did you mean it?"

"Yes." A look of tenderness crossed his face. "There is no one else for me, Prim. There never has been. Not since you ate those crickets in fifth grade. When you asked for seconds, I was hooked."

"Crickets?"

His mouth relaxed in a slight smile. "Not important."

When he took her hands, Prim realized his were trembling as much as hers. Her heart rose to her throat. Once again she tried to speak, but he pressed a finger against her lips.

"You don't have to worry about me leaving and the boys being hurt. I'm not going anywhere. The other night I left because I didn't want Callum and Connor to be caught in the middle of a discussion they wouldn't understand. But when I told you that you'll always be able to count on me, I meant it. I won't let you go unless you make it clear that's what you want."

Tears filled her eyes as love surged. When a couple of salty drops spilled over, he wiped them away with his thumbs.

"I was wrong to say what I did about Rory's ashes. He was your husband. He'll always be Callum and Connor's father." Max reached into his pocket. "Hold out your hand."

When she did, he dropped a silver heart necklace in her hand. The locket was engraved *always in my heart*. "Max. This is—"

"It's for Rory's ashes. I know he'll always have a place in your heart. I'm okay with that." He expelled a ragged breath. "You loved him a lot. Maybe you'll never be able to love me that much. But if one day you love me even half as much as I love you, it will be enough."

Her heart pounded in her head. Was this really happening?

"I can promise to always be there for you." He stepped forward, as if he simply had to touch her. With one hand, he smoothed her hair back. "I will love you forever."

"You said you couldn't be with someone who still loved her husband, even if he had passed away."

"I was a fool," he said simply. "I can't imagine my life without you in it. I love you, Prim. And I love Callum and Connor."

He pulled her down to sit, then took a seat beside her on a folding chair.

"Rory isn't between us. He was my husband. I loved him." Prim cupped his cheek with her hand. "He's my past. You're my future."

"Prim." Just her name, spoken in that low, sexy tone she loved, made her shiver.

"I don't need this, though I appreciate the gesture more than you'll ever know." She pressed the locket into his hand. "Deb and I scattered Rory's ashes yesterday."

Clearly startled, Max blinked. "All of them?"

She nodded. "Other than what I gave to Deb to bury."

Deciding to give those ashes to Deb had been a difficult decision. Rory had made his wishes very clear. Yet it seemed to Prim there was a duty to those left behind that must be considered. Rory was a good son who'd loved his parents dearly. Prim firmly believed if Rory could have seen the comfort having those ashes gave his mother, he'd have agreed with the decision.

"That was nice of you." He pulled her into his arms, holding her tight, stroking the back of her head.

"Sometimes I wish I could go back in time and fight for you. I'd make it clear how much you meant to me." His gaze shifted to the water. "But then I think, if you hadn't married Rory, then the boys wouldn't be here. I can't imagine life without Callum and Connor in it."

"I can't either," she said softly.

"When we were playing that card game you asked what one thing about you I'd change." He took her hands in his. "I'm telling you now, there is nothing I would change. You're perfect just the way you are. You and me, we add up. The only thing I want to change, that I *will* change, is to make you see that we are meant for each other."

Her stomach felt as if it had dropped three feet straight down, but she held his gaze.

"I already see that, Max." She touched her lips to his. "I love you."

"I want it all, Prim." He gripped her hands tightly and his voice took on desperate urgency. "I don't just want to date you. I want to spend the rest of my life with you. I want us to be a family. I want to sit on the sofa and relax with you after a busy day. I want to walk down the streets of Good Hope holding your hand. I want to hold you when it's time to go to bed and be there when you wake up."

Love swirled inside her, filling her to bursting. Being with him was what she wanted. It was what her sons wanted. Prim knew in her heart—and her head concurred—that being with Max, making a life with him, was the best thing for her and her boys. She couldn't imagine anything more wonderful. "That—that sounds heavenly."

Without warning, Max released her hands, reached into his pocket, and dropped to one knee, flipping open a small box. "Primrose Bloom Delaney, I want all that with you and more. I promise that I will love, honor, and cherish you and your boys for the rest of my life. I want to be a husband to you and a father to them. Will you do me the honor of becoming my wife?"

The old-fashioned filigreed ring with its emerald-cut diamond glittered in the sunlight.

For a second Prim had trouble catching her breath.

"Yes, oh, yes." The words tumbled out as Prim took the ring from his shaking hand. She slipped it on her finger just as a loud boom rent the air, followed by a flash of red and a shower of glittery stars against the pale blue sky.

As Max closed his lips over hers, Prim knew this was only the start of what would be a star-spangled and dazzling life together.

$\mathcal{E}$pilogue

Fin hefted a box marked "toys" and grunted. "You have rocks in here?"

Prim grinned. All morning her family—and what seemed like half the population of Good Hope—had been moving her household items into Max's home. The duplicate furniture had been donated to a needy family.

"I'm actually not sure what's in there. It could be rocks." Prim rested her hands on her hips, amazed at how good her sister looked despite lugging boxes next door all morning.

For today's move Prim had pulled her hair back into a tail and tugged on her oldest jeans and a faded tee. Fin's layered hair looked as if she'd just stepped out of a salon, and she wore heels with trim black pants.

"Let me help with that." Jeremy Rakes lifted the box out of Fin's hands and was gone before either of them could respond.

Fin whirled, but the mayor was already out the door. She turned back to Prim, an unreadable expression on her face. "I didn't know he was here."

"There are so many people here, I'm not sure if I noticed Jeremy before or not." Since her sister's hands were now temporarily free, after glancing down to make sure her own were clean, Prim stepped in and gave Fin a hug. "Thank you for coming for the wedding and staying to help us move. I know it was short notice."

Once Max had proposed and Prim had accepted, they'd decided there was no reason to wait to get married. Within four weeks they'd recited their vows in an outdoor ceremony, then celebrated into the early morning hours at a reception hosted by Ami and Beck.

"I'd never miss my little sister's wedding." Fin's green eyes met Prim's. "I always thought you and Max were a perfect fit. I'm happy you two finally got the memo and proved me right."

Prim had always thought Fin and Jeremy were a perfect match, too, but that was one thought she didn't dare voice. In terms of her and Max, Prim totally agreed.

"Mom." Callum burst into the room, trailed closely by his brother. "Grandma and Grandpa want to take Connor and me to the ball field. Can we go?"

Only seconds after the boys appeared, Deb and Mike stepped into the boys' bedroom.

"The twins were getting a little antsy and we thought it might be fun for them to have an outing." Deb placed a hand on Callum's shoulder.

Prim wondered if "antsy" was another word for "underfoot."

"If it's okay with you," Mike added.

"Can we, Mom, can we please?" Callum begged.

"Sure, that's fine." Prim crossed to her in-laws as the boys cheered and raced out of the room to find their gloves.

She took Deb's hand, gave it a squeeze. "Thanks."

A look of surprise crossed Deb's face. "For what?"

"For coming to the wedding, for helping with the move." The outpouring of support she and Max had received humbled Prim.

"You and the boys are family. And now, so is Max." Deb smiled tremulously. "We were happy to be invited."

"It meant a lot." Mike's voice came out unnaturally raspy.

Prim was saved from responding when the twins returned, gloves in hand.

"We even found a ball." Connor held it up.

"I can hit it almost every time now," Callum boasted.

"An athlete." Mike tousled Callum's hair. "Just like your daddy."

"You know, I'm actually developing an affinity for baseball." Deb gave a little laugh. "We'll have them back by five. Just in case you need help with dinner."

Fin waited until Deb was out of earshot before she turned to Prim. "Her being that nice is downright spooky. Next thing you know we'll be linking arms with Anita Fishback and singing 'Kumbaya' around the campfire."

Prim chuckled at the image. "I'm counting my blessings that Anita hasn't yet deigned to make an appearance."

"Probably because she knows there is work to do." Fin's droll comment had them both giggling.

"You gals are having way too much fun." Marigold flashed a cheeky smile as she awkwardly maneuvered several suitcases down the hall.

"Let me help with those." Cade Rallis's smile showed a mouthful of perfect white teeth.

Before Marigold could react, he'd lifted the luggage and disappeared down the hall.

Fin cocked her head. "Yummy."

"Hands off, Fin." Marigold's tone may have been light, but Prim heard the warning.

Apparently so did Fin. She raised her hands. "Just appreciating the view."

Prim laughed. It felt good to have all of her sisters together. She bent over to pick up another box and felt strong arms wrap around her from behind.

"I appreciate the view, too." Max pressed a kiss against her neck.

"Now I see why the boxes are slow in coming." Ami's cheery tone sounded from the doorway.

Prim turned in her husband's arms. "What can I say?" A warmth flowed through her veins, as thick and sweet as honey. "He can't keep his hands off me."

"She speaks the truth." Max tightened his hold on her.

"If it were any other couple I'd be gagging by now, but that's actually very sweet." Marigold's gaze lingered on Prim and Max. "It reminds me of what Mom used to say about us finding our prince."

Fin rolled her eyes and received a short jab to the ribs from Marigold.

"I found mine." Ami's eyes softened the way they always did when she thought of Beck.

"Me too." Prim tilted her head and looked deep into the brilliant blue eyes of the man she loved, the man who was now her husband, the man she would love for all of eternity. "And you were definitely worth the wait."

Acknowledgments

A heartfelt thanks to Sharon Tubach, accountant extraordinaire. Any accurate portrayals of life in the accounting world must be attributed to her. Any mistakes are my own.

Thanks to my Facebook buddies Kym Maltman Collar and Sue Chilson for suggesting "Boris" as the name for Prim's beloved Russian wolfhound.

To editors Chris Werner and Lauren Plude—working with you on this book was an absolute pleasure!

About the Author

Photo © 2013 Marri Corn Photography

Cindy Kirk started writing after taking a class at a local community college. But her interest in the written word began years earlier, when she was in her teens. At sixteen, she wrote in her diary: "I don't know what I would do if I couldn't be a writer." After her daughter went to college, she turned to her first love and jumped straight into book-length fiction. She loves reading and writing romance novels because she believes in happily ever after. An incurable romantic and an eternal optimist, Kirk loves seeing her characters grow and learn from their mistakes and, in the process, achieve a happy ending through the power of love. She and her high-school-sweetheart husband live in Nebraska with their two dogs.